THE ILLUSION OF INNOCENCE

Also by Jacqueline Jacques
and available from Honno

Archie Price Novels
The Colours of Corruption

THE ILLUSION OF INNOCENCE

by

Jacqueline Jacques

HONNO MODERN FICTION

First published by Honno Press in 2015
'Ailsa Craig', Heol y Cawl, Dinas Powys, South Glamorgan,
Wales, CF64 4AH

1 2 3 4 5 6 7 8 9 10

The Author would like to stress that this is a work of fiction and no
resemblance to any actual individual or institution is intended or implied.

A catalogue record for this book is available from the British Library.

Published with the financial support of the Welsh Books Council.

ISBN 978-1-909983-37-3 paperback
ISBN 978-1-909983-40-3 ebook
Cover design: Sharon Shaw
Text design: Elaine Sharples

This book is dedicated to Peter, my long-suffering husband, without whose patience, humour and common sense it would never have been finished.

One

1897

The moon was up, bright enough to see the dirt in his fingernails: brick dust and soot scraped off the wall with the frost. This close, he could see the crystals growing on the ivy leaves. The holds showed up as clear as day, but it didn't make the climb any easier. His feet were in danger of slipping; it was so cold he could scarcely feel them. Just had to trust that they'd remember what to do, feet following where his hands led, to the safe holds on the edges of bricks, on the sills, on the drainpipes.

There was a dark gap up and to the right, between two bricks – he might be able to pinch a finger and thumb in there, but they looked old. There was a risk of dislodging loose mortar, and if that rained down on frozen ivy leaves, pitter-patter, it would have them all at their windows. *'Sound carries on a still night,'* Tuddy always said. The next brick along looked a better bet, if he could stretch that far… He leaned up, careful not to let his face touch the brickwork. Take your skin off, frost could. Lucky his fingers and toes were tough, callused. They didn't stick. Steady though, take it easy, Freddy, he told himself. No rush. You know the drill: *'Always check the next 'old before you leave go the last one.'* He could hear Tuddy's cracked old voice in his ear. *'Got a firm grip, 'ave ya? Sure? On'y when you're sure o' your grip do you move yer leg up. And make love to the wall, hug her, keep her close, and she'll be good to you. Don't know what I'm talking about, do you, son, but you will.*

1

Now find the place where yer fingers was and tuck yer little tootsies in there. Got an 'old, 'ave ya? So now you can move the other 'and… Tha's it, boy. Reach up far as you can and push off. Feel for the corner o' the brick wiv yer fingers and latch on 'ard. Check. Check, *you little bleeder! Right then, next foot… And shut it wiv the grunting and moaning. Sound carries on a still night. Tha's it, tha's the ticket. An' up you go, Freddy boy!'*

Tuddy had been a chimney boy in the old days, but he'd had to stop when his sweep broke his neck falling off a roof. *'Dollop o'dead meat. Had to scrape 'im off the cobbles. Oo was gonna look out for me then, eh? On'y yours truly. Same as wiv you, Freddy. On'y not up chimleys, eh? Bleeding dirty work and no dosh, neither. Whereas climbing up the other side of the brickwork has great possibilities. Burglarising, that's the ticket.'*

'Great possibilities' was right. You never knew what your pickings were going to be. It was a risk. A gamble and a thrill. Never mind scraping holes in your britches, tearing your toenails, never mind the knocks and scrapes and bruises. That buzzing in your ears, in your chest, in your blood, warming you on a cold night – nothing like it. Photography, his other trade, didn't come close.

Thank God for Tuddy, putting him on to this. Nearest thing to family was Tudd. *She* didn't count. Would *she* have been outside the clink, waiting for him with a fag, a job and a horse? No. *'Tuddy looks after his own,'* the old bugger liked to say. He might slap you around but he saw you got your share of the takings.

Where was he heading? Not that window with the light in, for sure. Two along, though, that looked more promising. It had to be the lavvy with the window ajar to let out the foul air and let Freddy boy in. Very obliging.

He took a moment to get his puff back. *'You sound like a fucking steam train, Freddy boy,'* went Tuddy's wheezy old voice in his head. Well, he was out of practice. Six years in chokey never did much for your lungs, though he'd kept his fingers strong, picking oakum, and his toes, kicking the walls.

Recovered, he hooked a leg over the windowsill and heaved himself on to it. He stood up, took a moment to get his balance, then sli-i-id the bottom window up. *Ssshhh...* In he went, pouring over the sill and into the unlit room like water, without the splash. Oh yes, this was it. Like he'd never been away.

Still on all fours, muscles tense, he strained to listen. Anyone stirring? Nope. All safely in the land of nod.

Gently he pushed the door and it opened with nary a squeak. Not the next room along but the one after. That had to be the master bedroom, the one he wanted. That was where a crazy old collector might likely stash the good stuff. Tuddy had said, '*Trust me, mate, I cased the gaff good. I swear there ain't no dogs and they'll all be akip, the servants, upstairs. It's a piece of cake, Freddy. I'd do it meself on'y the legs ain't what they was.*'

There's a door framed in light, tight shut. That'll be the one. Bleeding key in the keyhole on the other side. Can't see a thing. Is it locked? The old geezer ought to be asleep, this time of night. But you never can tell.

He tried the handle.

It wasn't a bedroom after all, but an office. Shelves of books and files, a desk — and an old geezer sitting there in the candlelight, in nightshirt and cap, his back towards the door!

He didn't seem to have heard him. Freddy crept forward...

Gotcha! His iron grip covered the toothless old mouth, digging into soft cheeks, while his other hand whipped off the nightcap. The geezer was twisting and gurgling, trying to bite, trying to pull away the obstruction, but his shocked eyes rolled back when Freddy grabbed a thick glass ashtray and smashed it down on the scabby old pate. The eyes closed, the head lolled, and blood trickled down a large hairy ear.

Serves you right, you old buzzard.

He prised the old gums apart, balled the nightcap, which stank of old men's sweat, and stuffed it over the yellow tongue. Now then, how was he going to keep it there? A gag? Aha! Nice long

3

bedsocks on a cold winter's night. They'll do the trick, grandad, thank'ee kindly.

One of the pair took care of his mouth, knotted tightly at the back of his head, and the other... He tied the old, blue-veined wrists together behind the chair, leaving the long papery fingers to dangle, and turned his attention to the desk.

Was this the box Tuddy was on about? A tin box, he said, about eighteen by twelve. Not for himself, he had hastened to add. A client. Right.

A box of dirty postcards, no less. Hundreds of them. What were they worth, he wondered? They looked old. Printed with sepia ink and the cardboard edges furred with fingering. But these were more than dirty, these were nasty. Not fun, not by any means. And Tuddy's client wanted these? He'd have a look around in a mo, see what else was going begging. Tuddy mentioned jewellery and ancient coins, Spanish doubloons and pearls, said he should help himself. But the box was the main thing. He was most particular about the box. His client must be sick in the head.

He picked up the postcard the old man had been so engrossed in and examined it in the candlelight. What was so special, apart from it being more twisted and weird than most? He turned it over. *Studio Hans Voss*. Hmm, the name rang a bell. A Dutchman? Dead, long since. Quite famous. Pa – the man he called Pa – used to rave about the man. Wasn't he one of the first photographers or something? Daguerreotypes came to mind, or something of the sort, printed on metal. *Hans Voss...* He mulled over the name. Had he ever heard it mentioned in connection with porn? Good God, he smiled, the term would never sully Pa's sanctimonious lips.

But these were printed on cardboard. What was the date? *1839!* Blimey, that *was* early! Perhaps this was the first – *the first* – photographic pornography ever. In which case, they were worth their weight in gold. Carefully, he gathered up the loose cards that grandad had been mulling over and slid them back, was putting the lid back on when a hand shot out and grabbed his wrist,

4

making him jump three feet in the air. Jesus! The old geezer had managed to get his hands free somehow and was clawing at the box, squealing at him behind the gag.

'Let go, you mucky old bastard!' he snarled. But the old geezer hung on, squeaking obscenely. There came a wooden, rasping sound. The old geezer was pulling open a drawer, reaching inside.

Oh no you don't, matey! Quick as a wink, Freddy pulled out his knife and flung it. There was an instant's pause, when neither could quite believe what was happening, and blood began a slow trickle from the blade's entry spot, down from the wrinkled brow over one hooded eye. The old man flopped forward.

Shit. You stupid old geezer! What did you wanna do that for? Shit. He'd spoiled things properly, put the kibosh on the whole operation. Let. Bloody. Go. Freddy gritted his teeth and dragged the box from its owner's dying grasp, across the desk into his sack, smearing blood everywhere. No time to look for Spanish doubloons and precious gems. He had to get out of there, double quick.

Shit, the knife, the knife! He couldn't leave that for the filth to find. Pulling it from the bony skull was hard, he had to hold the old man's head with one hand to brace it. He was still swallowing bile as he pushed the window up and went skidaddling down the wall.

He darted down the garden and tossed the sack over the back wall, then climbed up and over, sitting upright to summon the horse up close. But, just as he was about to hit the saddle, a voice rang out in the night.

'Stop, thief!'

For God's sake! It was only the filth! The policeman must have seen the bloody horse and been lying in wait, truncheon at the ready.

Freddy's mind was whirling. He couldn't think. He had to get away and, having killed one man, what did he have to lose? His blade was in his hand, still sticky with grandad's brains. He flung it at the copper, and followed it with another. The first buried itself in the uniformed chest, the second in his back as he fell. But the bugger carried on moving, turning his head this way and that, feeling around for his lost whistle. Quickly, Freddy slid down and untied the horse. He had to finish the job, one way or another.

Two

The poor devil was lying in a hospital bed, broken and bandaged to the gills. They'd left openings for his lips and eyes, but he was either in a coma or already dead. 'Heavily sedated,' the nurse informed his visitor, 'to dull the pain.'

Archie tiptoed around, conscious of his size elevens and every sound he made: the scrape of the easel as he stood it by the bed, the bump of the drawing board against its supports, the rattle of thumbtacks in their tin. He extracted them singly, as delicately as a pinch of snuff, and pushed them into the board, ready to pin up the witness's selection of eyes, nose, mouth, chin, forehead and hair. Even the drawing paper was too loud as he turned the cover sheet to the back. He looked up, but the patient hadn't stirred. Nearly there now: four thicknesses of paper, pencils and a putty rubber, and fitful sunlight from the long casement window falling between him and his work. No shadows to interfere with accuracy – though he guessed accuracy was a vain hope. The police were snatching at straws. Perfectly understandable, of course: James Tomkins was one of their own.

The fire in the corner sparked and flared. A coal shifted. Archie flexed his fingers and took a deep breath. Lord, the smell of ether was delicious, but it was probably not wise to inhale too enthusiastically. He needed to be as relaxed as the witness but not unconscious.

'Jim…' he whispered into the cloth bulge that was probably the injured man's right ear.

The mummy turned its head towards him.

'Jim, old friend, it's Archie. I'm here to see if you remember the bastard who did this to you. Tyrell told you, did he?'

The lips moved. 'For pity's sake, Arch…'

'Sorry, old man, have to do this now while it's fresh in your mind.'

'Waste…' he managed to say before swallowing, his speech slurred and unclear. On the bedside cabinet was a glass of water. Archie slipped the straw between the parched lips. 'Waste a time, Arch,' he croaked through broken teeth. 'Didn't see his face – too dark.'

'Well, you never know.' Archie tried to sound cheerful and optimistic but he too had his doubts.

As Detective Inspector Tyrell had described it, two nights before, while on his beat, Constable Tomkins had happened upon a horse, saddled and patiently awaiting her owner's return, at twenty past two in the morning, in the dark lane behind the mansions in affluent Upper Walthamstow. The horse, her eyes yellow in the light of Tomkins' lamplight, was an elderly, underfed nag, breathing steam into the frosty air. She'd been loosely tethered to the ring-handles of massive coach-house doors set in a perimeter wall. The doors, when he tried them, were bolted from the inside. The wall was ten feet high, at least, and topped off with broken glass, but something had been thrown over that. He found something strange tied to the pommel of the saddle by their laces – a worn pair of men's boots, still warm. Who, he wondered, goes about on an icy night in his bare feet? A burglar? From the waiting horse, it was clear that whoever it was intended to return that way.

The officer snuffed his lantern and settled down to wait, breathing on his fingers for warmth. He knew he should blow his whistle to summon help, but if the villain inside heard that at the back of the house he would just escape from the front. Tomkins' feet and fingers were numb and his jaw beginning to judder when he heard someone on the roof, loose tiles shifting. A horse whickered in the stable. There was a pause, a grunt and then a sack sailed over the wall, landing with a thud at Tomkins' feet. Not jewels, then, nor the family silver. No tinkle or clatter of loose objects. Now a pale hand came creeping over the wall, now a bare foot, and now the rest of him lying prone along the ridge, protected by whatever he had thrown over the shards.

(Had Tomkins somehow managed to remove this protection, had he moved the horse on, had he run round to the front of the house, where the street lamp meant you could at least see a hand in front of your face, the outcome might have been very different, in DI Tyrell's opinion. The intruder would have been trapped and Tomkins could have roused the sleeping household and summoned back-up. 'But there you are,' the Inspector had sighed, shaking his head at Archie across the table, 'that's Jim for you – thinks he's God's gift to law enforcement, bloody young fool.')

Tomkins had to try and deal with an armed villain on his own, and had been well out-classed. The man had stabbed him twice and forced his horse to trample him, not once but a few times – an act of violence entirely at variance with the creature's mild nature. At some point the villain must have been satisfied that his victim was dead and had ridden off.

Thankfully, the night-soil man had found what he took to be a corpse in a pool of fast-freezing blood and summoned help. The next the young constable knew, he was in a hospital bed, numbed now with ether and his inspector sitting beside him.

Uniformed officers called at the house and found the door opened by a distraught housekeeper, her skin 'very pasty', wringing her hands and crying into her apron. 'Oh sirs, oh my stars, oh who would do such a terrible thing? Come in, come in. He's upstairs in his study…' Standing back to admit the sergeant and his constable, she must have seen their confusion. 'The boy *did* tell you?'

'Boy?'

'Stable lad – I sent him to fetch you – only a minute ago. Oh.' She bit her lip, realising that it was too soon, that they were on some errand of their own.

'See, it's the master. He's – he's dead, he is.' Her voice squeaked. She collected herself. 'His bed hadn't been slept in when I took his tea up. I – I found him in the end, not ten minutes since. Oh dear, oh dear, I was that flustered, I didn't know what to do for the best. So I sent the boy – I'm surprised you didn't pass him. But here you are, as luck would have it, so you'd best come and see for yourselves.'

The room she showed them into was an office of sorts. In the middle was a table heaped with files and papers. Dark blood had pooled on the leather-topped desk and dripped into a second puddle on the floor. Though stabbed in the forehead, the large old gentleman had flung himself forwards, his arms and fingers outstretched, as if trying to catch something, some large, flat-bottomed square object judging from the blood streaks left behind.

The sergeant informed the housekeeper that this was a murder scene and was off-limits to everyone, servants or family, until the police had finished their investigations.

Shaking her head and mopping her eyes, she said, 'There was only him here, sir. Jeremiah Fitzell.' He had been a gentleman of independent means, a seasoned traveller and collector of souvenirs. And, realising that her master would travel no more, bring nothing new home to dust, the woman again pinched her nose with her handkerchief.

'You must understand,' she said, sniffing, gesturing at the room's disarray, 'he wouldn't let us touch anything in here. He wanted it left just so, and the missus, God rest her soul, had no say in it either when she was alive. The son, Walter, ain't lived here in donkey's ages. He lives in Walthamstow, but he never visits. Something in the city, he is. They never got on, him and his pa, not from day one.' She hugged her shawl tighter around her quivering frame. 'Shall I shut the window, sir?'

'I'll do it,' the sergeant insisted. It was bloody parky. He hoped that closing the window wouldn't be tampering with the crime scene. It was perfectly clear to everyone the murderer had used it either to enter the premises or to leave, or both. Down the outside wall he'd gone with the sack that Tomkins had described slung over his shoulder, to make his getaway over the back wall, there to encounter poor old Jim. He was one of those wretched portico thieves, a cat burglar, that the Met had been having so much trouble with.

The housekeeper went to rustle up some tea, leaving the policemen to rummage among the books and magazines, some of them of a 'specialist nature'. When the coroner asked them to be more explicit, both men fumbled for words. 'What the Butler Saw' was the only way they could describe it.

Even more than twenty-four hours later Jimmy Tomkins was in a poor state to help Archie. He was adamant he hadn't seen his aggressor's face.

'You're a lucky so-and-so, you know, Jim,' Archie said, patting his hand lightly.

'Call this lucky?'

'Two stabbings and a trampling and you're here to tell the tale? Lord, I should say so. Your blood froze on your skin and stopped you bleeding to death. Better off than old Jeremiah Fitzell, poor bloke. Dead as a dodo and for what? There was something in the sack, but the servants can't think what's missing.'

Archie murmured soothing words, congratulating his friend on living through the ordeal, expressing his hopes for a speedy recovery, and promising to look in on Winifred and little Albert from time to time, to make sure they wanted for nothing.

Tomkins gave him an exhausted smile, his eyelids drooping. Archie fingered his lower lip. Was Jim sufficiently off his guard?

'Did he seem afraid at all, your attacker, worried or angry?' he said.

Tomkins replied, 'No expression, Arch. A right cold fish – looked like he didn't give a tinker's damn about anything at all.'

Aha! They were in business.

Tomkins' eyes blinked wide as this sunk in. He must have seen the man's face, after all, in the moonlight. A shudder passed through his body, making him wince.

'Someone walk over your grave, Jim?'

The response was a rueful shrug.

Gently, Archie asked him to look at some of his examples of faces. 'Just tell me if anything strikes you as similar in any way to the man you saw.' He held his sheaf of drawings horizontally above Tomkins' eyes, removing each front page when the invalid shook his head. By answering yes and no, Tomkins was able to tell him that his assailant was in his late twenties to early thirties, of average height and build, and that his forehead was broad with longish, wavy hair brushed straight back. He couldn't describe the colour but guessed it was grey or fair.

'Well done, Jim. We're on our way.' Archie sketched the chosen face shape and lightly outlined the hair. 'Now what about the eyes?'

'No,' he said to the first set that Archie showed him, and, 'No,' to the second. The third time he said, 'Yes.'

Archie frowned. It was unusual for a witness to decide so quickly. 'I've a lot more to show you,' he insisted, 'small, large, piggy, close-set…'

'No.' Tomkins was certain. 'Those are they. Brown. And the eyebrows.'

Was Tomkins too exhausted to bother? Was he simply trying to get the sketch over and done with?

Archie sketched and coloured in the widely spaced brown eyes and lightly defined eyebrows and held up the drawing for Jim's approval.

'Yes.'

Perhaps he'd think more carefully about the nose. Archie had nine pages for him to look at. But again, the response was almost immediate. The nose Tomkins chose was in the top row of the very first page, a very ordinary, straight specimen.

'You sure?'

'Yep.' He yawned and promptly fell asleep.

'Any progress, Mr Price?' A nurse popped her head around the door as Archie was sketching in this nose.

He made a face. 'Yes and no.'

She came over, with a swish of long skirts, and examined his handiwork. 'Mmm, nice, but he doesn't look much like a villain to me.'

'Nor me…' Should he call it a day? He'd never abandoned a witness sketch in all the years he'd been a police artist and hated to do so now.

Gently, he shook the long-suffering policeman awake.

'You still here, you bloody Welsh git? What do you *want*?'

I want to catch the bastard who did this to you. I want to catch Fitzell's murderer, to see him brought to justice. I cannot bear that evil people can steal and kill and get away with it. I want to do my bit to see justice is done.

'How about a moustache?'

The bandaged head slowly rolled from side to side. 'No,' he managed to whisper, and then continued to move his lips.

'What is it, old man?' Archie put his head closer. 'Sorry, can't hear. Have a drop more water.'

'Mutton chops,' he heard eventually. 'Side whiskers.'

Archie's spirits rose at this but dipped again when, after scanning a few pages of lips, the injured man chose, almost out of desperation it seemed to Archie, a very average thin-lipped mouth and insisted that the chin and neck belonging to those lips were also like his aggressor's. In other words, *leave me alone.*

But they hadn't finished. 'What was he wearing, Jim?'

'Dark…'

'Jim-my,' pleaded Archie.

'Dark jacket, britches, neckerchief. All dark.'

'Hat? Gloves?'

'Nope. Oh, and Archie…'

'Yes?'

'Bare feet.'

Archie frowned. Yes, Tyrell had mentioned them. On a freezing cold night, he thought, surely the villain would have needed some sort of protection against the icy puddles, the frost striking up through the ground? Archie's own right boot was lined with cardboard and his chilblains were tingling in the hospital's warmth. But then this was a burglar, a 'portico thief', who had swarmed up to the second floor like a kitten up a curtain. No, shoes wouldn't have done.

Archie finished off the sketch while the patient dozed. When it was done and Tomkins awake again, he held it horizontally above his gaze.

'Do I need to change anything?'

There was a long pause while the victim viewed his aggressor's image: not a villainous face at all, handsome if anything. The man could have been a pre-Raphaelite Saint George, Archie thought, or a stained-glass window angel Gabriel. Jim's eyes filled with tears. Archie said, 'Please, Jim. Try. Does that look anything like him? Anything at all?'

Tomkins blinked and wagged a forefinger. What did that dumb show indicate?

'Jim,' Archie asked again, feeling brutal, 'does anything need changing?'

His eyes closed as he whispered, 'Nothing – you've got him,' and tears seeped into the bandage around his face.

It was over. Archie shifted his gear to the matron's office, where he intensified the darks and lights in the drawing without changing any of the features. Then he clipped a cover over it before placing the precious evidence in a box file to protect it from smudging. Battling the bitter wind, hat rammed onto his head, scarf and coat-tails flying, he set off down the hill to the printers in the high street. They thawed him out with a hot toddy and cake and sat him before the fire where he answered all their questions about the state of the young policeman. The printers' oaths were heartfelt. When feeling returned to his fingers, Archie took his usual seat by the window and set to work etching the image onto copperplate. The police had their posters by teatime the next day.

Three

Polly ducked under the cloth. Dark. Secret. Private. She breathed fast as she viewed her target: the premises of Chas. Packer Esq., Family Butcher. Today, he'd made a special effort with his display especially for the camera. There were white carcases of mutton hanging out front, like Pop's combinations ballooning on the clothes line, great fat sides of pork, legs of beef, chickens and rabbits strung like macabre Christmas decorations across the window. A pig's head stared blindly out. If she could just move the tripod a fraction forward to minimise the front picket fence … there. And here came the master butcher, cleaver in hand, to pose proudly before his chopping block.

'That's lovely, Mr Packer. Now if you'll look this way, please, still as you can.'

There were customers in the way, peering around the door, grinning inanely. She flapped her hand and they slid out of view, taking their silly smiles with them. Smiles spoiled photographs, devaluing a work of art. The boy took his place at her side, ready with his tray of flash powder. She felt for the dials, dear, familiar and smooth with wear, twisted one, then the other, until the butcher was in focus, sharp and clear. She removed the shutter, snapped her fingers, counted one, two — the boy struck his match — five, six seconds, then snapped her fingers again and the boy held the match to the tray of chemicals, magnesium mixed with nitrate for daytime studies.

A blinding flash painted everything with a skin of silver-white light, carving every knob and knuckle, every layer of fat, every succulent morsel of red meat, from sooty-black shadows. The proprietor tried not to blink. The light vanished, leaving a cloud of stinking chemicals. Polly replaced the shutter and removed the plate.

'Good,' she said. 'Come to the shop on Friday and I'll have it ready for you, Mr Packer.'

Her preferred photographs were more candid, informal: shoppers examining stalls, sorting through second-hand clothes in the baskets and boxes out on the cobbles, shrewd eyes considering a buy, frowning, unaware of the camera's presence. She liked children playing in the street, buskers and beggars, the man with the weighing machine, the workmen digging up the road. People caught off guard were far more interesting than the posing and knowing. There was nothing remotely inspiring about shopfronts, but if they helped to pay the rent... So far, a half-dozen shopkeepers had been swayed by the nice young woman offering to make images of their premises for nothing: a print for the owner to put behind his counter, and one to put in her own shop window. She hoped that when the other hundred-and-thirty-odd shopkeepers in the high street saw their neighbours' establishments recorded for posterity, they would pay to have their own shopfront made into a picture. And the neighbouring businesses in Hoe Street. Her appointment book was filling up nicely and she hadn't lived there five minutes. She explained to her new customers that her father had been Jonas Porter of Hackney, a photographer of renown, and she had been his assistant from as soon as she was old enough to hold the 'flash-pan' until the day he died. She had taken over his studio (their front parlour), building up her own portfolio, until her mother also passed away. Then she had come here, as Hackney held too many bloody awful memories.

This last she kept to herself, and if she shed a tear or two in the privacy of her darkroom, or sat bold upright from night terrors night after night, fingers clawing at the sheets, it was nobody's business but her own.

Four

As he passed by the section house on his way down the high street, Archie saw the 'Wanted' poster on the police noticeboard. But he took no pride in his handiwork. Such a bland face. Would anyone recognise the villain and come forward? He doubted it. Detective Inspector Tyrell and his team were going from door to door with the picture, the length and breadth of Walthamstow; they'd scoured the gaming houses and brothels, the billiard halls and gypsy encampments; all neighbouring police forces were alerted, and even the Met had copies of the poster. But so far, nothing. The police were stumped. Jeremiah Fitzell had had no enemies that anyone knew of, he owed nobody money, and his murderer had left no clues: not a hair, not a button, not a footprint. All they had to go on were claw marks on the windowsill that had melted with the frost, and Jim Tomkins' witness statement. It looked as if this would have to be written off as an unsolved mystery.

Winter sunshine and empty pockets prompted Archie to take his sketchpad outside for a spot of 'busking'. Wearing his warmest clothes, his much-loved slouch hat for shade, Lizzie's hand-knitted muffler snug around his neck, and fingerless gloves, he set up his easel outside the framer's shop and dashed off the portrait of any high street shopper who could bear to sit still for five minutes. It was one of his favourite Saturday-morning pastimes since moving back – painting among the stalls, breathing in the familiar smells of root vegetables fresh from the clamps, spring greens, overwintered onions, home-made cough candy, sarsaparilla and newly baked buns, not to mention the savoury hum of horse manure. It was an opportunity to pass the time of day with old friends and it was the best way he knew of honing his sketching skills. He and the framer had an arrangement: George would keep the tea and biscuits coming, and Archie would send his patrons into the shop with any masterpiece they wanted mounting. As he worked, passers-by would peer over his shoulder and they, too, might then drift into the shop, to browse the paintings, his among them.

It was incidental work like this, drawing for the police, making posters, and illustrating journals, books and newspapers, that put bread on the table, while commissions – such as they were – provided the jam.

He'd continued to rent the studio over the greengrocer's after marrying Lizzie. There was no space in her cottage or the adjoining pottery large or light enough for painting, plus clay dust and wet oil paint didn't mix. He was glad now he had. It was comforting to have friends close by. Out there, in Woodford, you could die of loneliness and grief, when even the sound of a teaspoon stirring a cup reminded you of your terrible loss and your wife's dear dirty fingernails. After the funeral – a double one, Lizzie and the baby sharing a grave – Clara, Lizzie's child from her first marriage, had been packed off to live with her grandparents in Camden. They'd felt, and he'd had to agree, that if he wasn't prepared to run the pottery in Lizzie's stead, he'd have to make a living from painting, and a jobbing artist could not look after a spirited child.

But the terrible silence, following the little girl's departure, proved more than his sanity could bear. When he found himself talking to Lizzie's ghost, he knew he'd have to move on. So he'd sold the pottery, lock, stock and stewpot, and put the money into trust for his stepdaughter. Then he'd driven the mule cart to Walthamstow with never a look backwards.

But he couldn't lift a paintbrush without depicting her dear face. On every wall of his studio, every vertical surface, pinned, propped and nailed, there was his darling, sleeping, sitting, bathing, cooking, making her distinctive art nouveau tiles: Lizzie, Lizzie…

The day he ran out of canvas, last year, he'd sat for a long time counting his loose change and tossing up whether to buy more painting materials or food for himself and the mule. As he'd glanced up from the small pile of coins, he realised that his reproductions of her dear face were no more alive, no more warm and breathing, than miserable old Queen Vic on her near-black penny. He couldn't recapture Lizzie's warmth, her voice, her touch, the way she turned her head, the way she smelled on bath night or wash day or baking day, no matter how bright he made her eyes, how many tender smiles he painted. Only in his head, in his memory, could he have her back. It hit him like a blow – his heart may even have stopped for a second – that she was quite, quite gone.

Straight away, he put on his coat and hat and went down the road to the police station to ask for his old job back. With money in his pocket again, he bought fresh pigment and, from his window, painted the beggar, a one-legged Boer War veteran about his age, who sat every day on the pavement outside the public house, with an old tin mug containing a few desultory coins. As he'd brushed on the dun colours he'd whispered, 'That was a close one, Lizzie. There but for the grace of God…'

The high street market was a scrum, despite being off limits to traffic on a Saturday once the stalls were set up and the wares delivered. Shoppers, eager for a bargain and the Sunday dinner, swarmed over road and pavements, queued at every stall, every butcher shop, baker's and fishmonger's; perambulators ran over toes, bustles and shopping bags took up too much room, children rode on their fathers' shoulders or ran the risk of being trampled underfoot or lost. Among the hubbub of crying babies, distraught mothers, hawkers crying their wares and shoppers arguing and haggling, Archie's easel was an island of tranquillity. Or it was until Bertha Reeves, the publican's wife, plumped herself down on his orange box. Sitting still was beyond her.

'What I want to know,' she muttered, through clenched teeth, like a ventriloquist, 'is when Percy's Palace is gonna make me a rich woman. It's been an 'ole in the ground for nigh on three years.'

As he shaded around the woman's double chin, Archie asked himself the same question. Percy Reeves, her husband, landlord of the Horse and Groom, ran a successful theatre beyond the saloon bar doors, but he had set his heart on a proper music hall further down the road. He had bought the land years back, but there had been no progress to speak of. The Walthamstow Palace would have set the town on the map and Archie's pockets jingling. The enormous mural that Percy had asked Archie to paint in the foyer, featuring every singer, comedian, actor or acrobat on the London stage, would have netted him a cool fifty guineas.

Whenever Archie asked about progress, Percy would fob him off. 'Plans are afoot, Arch, plans are afoot,' he'd say, drawing another pint and avoiding the tall customer's eyes. 'Not to worry, my son, I ain't forgot what I promised you.' And Archie would frown into his glass and try to swallow his impatience.

His pencil hovered over the jet beads that ringed the landlady's plump throat, occasionally disappearing between the folds of fat: black, shiny, multifaceted beads. Why should he?

As Archie pencilled in the feathery fronds of Bertha's bonnet, his thoughts wandered wider than Walthamstow. Perhaps the grand mural was something that other impresarios, in other towns, would appreciate. Perhaps he should take his ideas further abroad…

He wasn't really paying attention to his sitter's prattle, which focussed mainly on old flames and new babies, with the occasional criticism of a passing shopper thrown in for light relief. 'See 'er 'at, did yer? Reckon you could bloomin' eat it.' And, 'Gawd, I'd give that kid a back'ander, he was mine!' She seemed content with his occasional input of 'Really?' and 'Quite so.'

21

'So are you going?'

'What!' Good Lord, was the woman a mind reader?

'Archie Price! For Gawd's sake! You ain't even listening.'

'Oh, I just didn't quite catch…' He looked around as if to blame the crockery merchant beside them for his clatter.

'Ida's wedding, you great lummox – you going? Getting married, ain't she? To that Fitzell bloke. Gawd, she's gonna be rolling in it when they tie the knot.'

'Rolling?' he muttered absently, thinking of Ida's pink voluptuous curves.

'Seeing as how his dad's been topped. Only child so it'll all come to him.'

'Will it?'

'Archie Price – what you like? His old man was that Jeremiah Fitzell bloke, lived up Forest Road in them big houses. Bit of a loner, but loaded, they say.' She waited but he carried on drawing. 'There's some as thinks it a bit, you know, funny, that nothing was took. Wond'ring why, you know, he was topped, and that. What d'you think?'

'They took something – they just don't know what. It was in the papers. The blood-streaked desk? The heavy sack over the wall?' he reminded her, flurrying the pencil over the fringe of her shawl in a series of exclamation marks.

He stopped, reminding himself to be careful, that he knew more than he should say. From what Tyrell had told him on the quiet, Jeremiah Fitzell had, since his wife's death, sought comfort in pornography, poor chap. Doing no one any harm, except his own reputation, if it got out. A churchgoer and magistrate, on the boards of this and that charity, and a member of the Primrose Club in St James's, he had been highly respected among the upper echelons of Walthamstow society. As Tyrell said, it would be a pity to destroy the man's good name. Better that than some other preferences he could mention.

Across the road, against the school railings, a cart drew up to stage another of Walthamstow's regular entertainments: the Saturday speaker. A bushy-bearded, bespectacled man leaned on a lectern and started haranguing a small crowd. Posters proclaimed that this was Councillor Sidney Crabtree of the Moderate Party canvassing for the coming local election.

'Do you ever stop to think who it was put in the gas and water pipes, provided these pavements for you to walk on? Who paved *all* the main thoroughfares in the town?' he began.

'You, was it, Sid? In yer shirtsleeves and workboots, wiv yer pick and shovel?' various voices heckled. 'Bloomin' roads are a disgrace! Bloomin' navvies digging 'oles every-bloomin' where!'

'See 'em, down the road, stringin' up them telephone cables. I ask you, telephone cables! Who's that for, eh? Where's the likes of us gonna get the money for bleedin' telephones?'

'Police station's got one and the hospital. Be the post office next…'

The speaker made a dismissive gesture. 'You'll all reap the benefit in time. The telegraph service will be a thing of the past. Everyone will have a telephone.'

'Get off!'

'That'll be the day.'

'You'll have gas to cook by, water on tap…'

'For the little woman to scour the pots,' shrilled a new voice, 'scrub the clothes, cook and clean and slave her life away…'

The men turned, frowning. What was wrong with that? Cheeky mare!

The councillor chose to ignore her. 'Your very own Ratepayer's Association is spending thousands bringing Walthamstow up to date, making your lives easier.'

'Not my life, Mr Crabtree! Nor any other woman's!'

'Put a sock in it, love!'

'Your elected council will…'

'Elected *by* men *for* men! When will women have their say?' Her cry was echoed by one or two other female voices.

'You tell 'im, gel!'

'That's right, ducks. Give women the vote!'

Archie stood up to stretch his back, to put an end to Bertha's interrogation and a face to the militant voice. Surely it was the young woman who'd recently moved in over the road? A slip of a girl, his mother would have said. A photographer who lived above the business.

He wished her well. She wasn't the only photographer in the neighbourhood, but from the work on display in her shop window she seemed to have a more artistic touch than the others. He could see the reasoning behind the images of shopfronts, but her other studies interested him more: her landscapes, views of the forest up the road and of the marshes down by the Lea, were charming, and her studio portraits quite the most imaginative he had seen. Customers were not clamped into fixed positions but were allowed to lean and loll and turn their profiles to the camera. Lips were parted as though they were caught mid-sentence. He imagined that improvements in shutter speed or plates allowed her to take photographs in seconds rather than minutes. Sometimes she dressed her sitters in theatrical costumes, as the Pre-Raphaelites had done, to make a historical narrative. A touch too sentimental, posing her subjects with flowers and pet dogs, draped over books and letters or gazing into candle flames, making him think of his early paintings from which he had, long since, moved on. Fair enough. There was still a taste for the mawkish, and it wouldn't do for them to be rivals.

But how brave of her to set up shop alone, how modern – a new woman, with a mind and will of her own. And a piano. Marches and popular ballads would tinkle out through the occasionally opened window. Though he never heard her singing, he liked humming along as he painted.

A kerfuffle broke out in the crowd. A plump, balding man twisted this way and that to examine the ground at his feet. 'Where's me wallet?' he yelped. 'Who's nicked me bleedin' wallet?'

Everyone stepped back, putting innocence between him and them. 'Come clean,' he pleaded, 'this ain't on. I'm a working man with a wife and kids to feed. It was in me back pocket and now it ain't. Someone's 'alf-inched it! Police!' he cried, with tears in his eyes. 'I bin robbed! Police! Stap me, where's a blooming copper when you need one?'

The cry went up. 'Police! Police!'

The councillor held up his hand in a vain attempt to keep his audience. He used his loud hailer to bellow over the increasing hubbub and confusion. 'Let's be sensible, gentlemen, ladies – just remain where you are until a policeman gets here.'

Some hopes. The crowd dispersed, men dragging away their wives, and vice versa, mothers their sons. *Goodness – was it that time already? They really had to get dinner on...* By the time two policemen came running up, only the victim and a handful of painfully honest citizens still remained.

Bertha, well pleased with her portrait, rummaged in her bag for her purse.

'Hello – Mr Price, isn't it?'

'Sorry? Oh yes, yes.' Archie snatched off his hat, taken aback by her boldness. 'Yes, I believe we're neighbours, Miss er...'

'Porter, Polly Porter.'

'Pleased to meet you, Miss Porter,' he smiled, thinking that perhaps he shouldn't draw her attention to the smudge of whitewash on her cheek. He ran his fingers through his red hair, realising that it might need a bit of a wash, and, come to that, he'd probably got charcoal on his own face. His hands were covered in it. Oh well, too late now to attempt to cut a dash. And why on earth was he bothered? It was only the girl over the road. 'You probably know your neighbour, Mrs Reeves...'

The women nodded coolly to one another. No love lost there, then.

'Would you like me to draw your picture, Miss Porter? Bertha's just going.' He couldn't help casting an artist's eye over her

25

unbecoming hat, her thick woollen shawl, her serviceable navy blue skirt and worn but polished black boots. No patches or darns, but no brooches, no fancy hatpins either. He thought he had her measure. Her hair was poker straight, scragged back in a bun like the Queen's, but a pretty coppery sort of colour. In his mind, he softened its harsh lines with pencilled-in flyaway tendrils. Her skin was milky and dusted with freckles. Her most interesting features were her eyes: large, black-fringed and glacially blue, almost without colour. He'd never seen such eyes.

'Ah, no,' she dimpled modestly. 'I don't think a portrait would do me any favours, thank you all the same. No, Mr Price, I've seen you coming and going and I thought I'd come over and introduce myself.'

'How are you settling in?'

'Well enough, thank you. There's a lot to do, sprucing up the shop and making people aware of the service and so on. The customers aren't exactly flooding in yet, but they will, I'm sure, as word spreads.'

'I've seen your window,' he said. 'Your pictures are very good. Have you ever thought of exhibiting? People will pay a lot for a good photograph. It might help you become established.'

She frowned. 'Do you think so, Mr Price? I'm not sure that people would buy photos as they would paintings.'

'They might. Depends what you charge for them.'

'But black and white? I mean paintings bring colour to a room, focus…'

What might have been an interesting, fruitful conversation was rudely interrupted by a man's cry of astonishment. 'Poll? My God, it *is* you! What the devil are you doing over this way?'

She backed into Archie, scattering the pennies Bertha had dropped into his palm, and didn't apologise for her clumsiness. Archie was fascinated, watching her change in the presence of this stranger. As every vestige of colour drained from her face, Polly mutated from the belligerent heckler, standing up for women's

26

rights, from the enterprising shopkeeper, and shrank, before his eyes, into a timid, one might even say *fearful* little mouse.

'Freddy! I, em…' Her pupils had dilated, her eyes foxholes in snow as they fixed on the newcomer's face. The man seemed quite gratified by her reaction, a triumphant smile playing about his lips.

She tried again. 'I didn't expect – em – oh –' She swallowed. 'I – I thought you were still in, em…' She glanced around, cleared her throat and forced a smile. 'Goodness, what a small world! I just came for the market, to get a few bits, you know. And you?'

He jerked a whiskery chin towards the railway. 'Came in on the train, Poll. Shopping like you.' The smile became a sneer.

Why was she lying, wondered Archie, and who was this ruffian who didn't believe her anyway?

Her brother, apparently. Miss Porter introduced him. Archie was nonplussed. This man was down-at-heel, shabby and unwashed, lacking a collar and tie and buttons from his coat. He looked, for all the world, as if he had been sleeping rough and smelled like a vagrant. Not someone you'd have associated with neat-as-a-pin Miss Porter. But it was the face that troubled Archie. He had a Grecian countenance, like Michelangelo's 'David', good-looking with a strong, regular bone structure, quite unlike Miss Porter's elfin looks. There was no family resemblance at all. That wasn't it, though. There was something Archie couldn't quite put his finger on.

'Don't I know you from somewhere?' he asked.

'Don't see how,' said the man rudely, paying him scant attention.

Mrs Reeves' eyebrows disappeared under her frizzy curls at his 'sauce'.

Archie wasn't put off. If he'd come for the market, where were his purchases, his weekend shopping bags? All he had was a heavy sack tied to his back. Not so unusual perhaps, many of the poorer shoppers carried sacks for their vegetables: that was the way of things in downtown Walthamstow. But Porter's sack wasn't knobbly with potatoes or cooking apples. It was much too regular. Shoes, perhaps? No, a bigger box than that.

The man caught his sister's arm. 'Let's have a cup of tea, Poll. Bit of catching up to do, I reckon.'

The girl apologised to Archie, nodded to Bertha, and went with him, looking very unwilling, leaving Archie to sign and date Bertha's portrait.

'There's more to them than meets the eye,' Bertha said, nodding like the dogs on the nearby Bakelite stall. 'Makes you wonder.'

'What?'

'Why she don't want 'im knowing she's set up shop up the road.'

'She'll have her reasons,' he said, and, as an afterthought, 'wouldn't blame her myself. He looks a rum sort of character. Bye, Bertha.' She was sharp, you could say that for the old girl. He raised his voice. 'Come along, ladies and gents, have your portrait drawn! Only a shilling.'

Five

'Remembered you and Ma liked to come to the market of a Saturday,' Freddy said as he shoved Polly through the doors of the tea shop, so roughly she nearly lost her balance. 'Long shot – lucky it paid off.' They sat down and he untied his sack and parked it under the table. He said, 'Why'd you never let me know Ma was dead, eh?'

She searched every cranny of her frantic brain for a convincing lie. 'But I did, Freddy – didn't you get my letter?' It sounded feeble. But she couldn't tell him that her first act of freedom when Ma died was to up sticks, run and hide, so that neither her adopted brother – her tormentor – nor his cronies could find her.

'No?' A frown rumpled his smooth brow and he sighed. 'Bleeding screws, they always had it in for me, sis. Not the first thing to go astray.' Reaching into his top pocket he drew out a half-empty packet of Wills Woodbines. He still smoked, then. She might have known from the stains on his fingers, the smell of him. He puffed smoke into the air above her.

'Oh dear,' she said, studying the broken, spent match in the ashtray, 'poor Freddy. It must have been a terrible shock for you when you... H-how, how did you find out?'

He told her he'd been released some weeks before, and gone straight home to Hackney. 'Imagine my shock and dismay, Poll – shock and dismay – to find Maybank Road empty! Locked and bolted, windows whitewashed! And not a word, Poll, not a word. Had to hear it from the neighbours that the old lady had snuffed it and you'd moved out. Well, I shed a tear when I heard, I have to say.'

Like hell, she thought. Freddy had never shed a tear over anything. 'I sent letters,' she lied. 'Lots of them. Those turnkeys!' She was even beginning to believe herself. 'I wondered why you didn't reply. I thought you were, you know, sulking. It wasn't my fault they arrested you, Freddy, honestly.' God, her tongue would drop out at this rate. 'I wanted to visit you, but it was hard – Ma was so ill towards the end, I couldn't leave her. Had to shut the shop and manage on what little we had.' Her hands were shaking so she could hardly hold her tea when it came, and she slopped some onto the pristine tablecloth.

'They might have let me out for the funeral of me own dear old mother – did you think of that, sis? Tuddy could have arranged for me to disappear!'

'No, I – it never occurred to me.'

'Anyway, I'm out now.' Switching on a smile, he reached across the table and took her hand between his calloused palms. She tried not to flinch. 'Well, ain't this nice, eh? I missed you, Poll. No wedding ring yet, I see?' He winked. 'Been a good girl and waited for me?'

Her heart lurched. 'Don't, Freddy…'

He grinned. His teeth were terrible, crooked and decayed. 'What's up, girl, don't you love me no more?'

They both knew it wasn't a joke. *'You'll never get your filthy hands on me again, you animal!'* she'd said, with a flat iron held out in front of her like a red-hot shield, while Ma had gurgled in her wheelchair.

'Course you do. You know what side your bread is buttered. Just as well, 'cause I got a job for you.'

There it was again, the assumption that she was his slave, at his beck and call. How would she ever break free?

'What sort of job?'

He took a moment to suck on his cigarette. 'Well,' he said,

blowing smoke in her eyes, 'it's like this, darlin', when they let me out of clink I had a bit of luck, see. Found something of value.'

'Stole it.'

He stiffened, looking round at the other customers. No one could hear over the clink of spoons, the clatter of crockery and women's chatter. 'Never you mind. You just listen and I'll tell it, right? See, there were complications and…'

'Are the police after you?'

'No, course not, what d'you take me for? I'm looking after something for Tuddy. No, don't make that face. He's been a good friend to me. At least he came to see me in the clink,' he reproached her.

'He came to see me, too, time and again. After money that he said you owed him. He was the reason I moved out of Hackney when Ma died.' The other reason.

'Right,' he nodded. ''Course, he'd've been after the inheritance.'

'Inheritance?' she repeated, bewildered.

'After Ma. From the sale of the house, the shop…'

'You're joking! I had to mortgage them when Ma took ill, to pay him off and your other debtors – the wine merchants and victuallers, the gaming house, people you'd played at cards. They kept coming round, month after month, threatening us, wanting more each time. "Interest" they called it. Mother and me, we nearly went to jail because of – of it.' She swallowed. The worry of it all had made Mother ill, desperate. 'There's nothing left.'

'So you still owe Tuddy?'

'I gave him what he asked for but it wasn't enough, apparently.'

'And what's left for me?'

'You?'

'They were my Ma and Pa, too. They adopted me out of all the little bastards on the street, promised me when the time came they wouldn't leave me short.'

'I – I'm afraid it didn't work out like that. They were both a long time sick and sickness is expensive.'

'What about your new place? You can sell that.'

'No, I can't, Freddy. It's – it's rented. Not mine to sell.' She couldn't disguise the faint note of triumph in her voice.

'No nest egg put by?'

Silently, she shook her head.

'Don't give me that!' he snapped, making her jump. Was he going to strike her, here, in public? 'You got money coming in, all right. You didn't get that,' he flicked her hat brim and she flinched, 'down the workhouse. And look at this shawl – it ain't fancy but it's quality, anyone can see that. Who you working for, Poll?'

Avoiding the question, she said, 'If you need money so badly, why don't *you* get a job.'

'I got one, thanks.' He puffed on his fag. 'Anytime I want.'

'Working for Tuddy? Oh, Freddy, you can do better than that.'

'No one will employ an ex-con, Poll,' he said simply, and she almost felt sorry for him.

'So what's this job you want *me* to do?'

'It's just minding something for a spell.'

'Until the heat dies down, you mean.'

He narrowed his eyes at her. 'Careful, Poll, or you'll say something you'll regret. No, this is Tuddy's, but he's not in a position to take it right now.'

She had done this before, as had Mother and Pops, minded his stolen goods until the hue and cry was over. 'What is it?'

'You mind your own and I'll mind mine.' Oh God, how she hated him and his big talk. 'It's in the sack. I'll be busy for a week or two, but then I'll come and pick it up.' He smiled in that horrible way he had, with his mouth only. 'So I'll need to know where to come, won't I?'

She set her mouth in an obstinate line.

'Come on, sis, give…' Smiling all the more, he rested his cigarette in the ashtray, slid his dirty hands along her wrist – and twisted her flesh in opposite directions. Hard. A Chinese burn he'd called it when they were younger. She turned her head away

32

to hide her smarting tears from the people on the next table. 'Don't you tell me no, you little cow.'

He wouldn't stop. She writhed. Her skin would tear. She tried to breathe evenly, without crying out. 'Don't, Freddy, please…'

'Do as you're bleeding told, then,' he hissed through grinning teeth.

'All right, all right!'

He let go. She rummaged in her shopping bag, mainly to hide her face, and she came across an old envelope with her shopping list on it. She tore it along the folds, turned it over, and, while he was sorting through her purse, began writing, daring to suggest, 'If you tell me where *you* live I could bring it round there.'

'My name's Billy, not silly.' He emptied her purse onto the table. A ten-shilling note, silver and copper coins. He shook his head, disgusted, but still took the note, a half-crown and a florin. 'No,' he said, 'the least you know the better. Don't try opening it, either. You won't like what's inside. And no tricks this time. No police. Friday week, right, and if you're taking me for a mug I'll do for you, sis, I swear, no skin off my nose.'

Pocketing the money, he left, and she sat for a long time, staring at his cigarette stub squashed in the ashtray, unchecked tears dripping off her nose and chin, plopping into the tea leaves in her cup. What future lay there unread?

She dried her face and picked up the sack. It was so heavy! What was it? Silver, jewellery? She guessed he would be outside somewhere, hiding, waiting for her to leave so that he could follow her. He didn't trust her and with good reason. She looked in her purse. What had he left her? Barely enough.

She crossed the crowded street. Archie Price was still there sketching, quite oblivious that her world had come crashing down. It had taken all her courage to speak to him, and what must he have thought of her and her rude, dishevelled brother?

'A whole dinner service, ladies, not two bob, not one and six. Come along, ladies, who's gonna help me out here?'

33

No one at all. She was on her own.

She walked down past the school, the heavy sack on her back, aware of him behind her, shadowing her every step. Through the back streets she went, across by the coal yards to the railway station, where she bought a return ticket to Hackney Downs, and caught the first train out.

Six

S he didn't get out at the next stop. Nor the next. Perhaps she was telling the truth. Now the guard was bawling, 'Hackney Downs!' as the train pulled in to the station.

Doors slammed down her end. He released the window to peer down the platform, letting in the cold, which upset the other passengers. They exaggerated shivers and gave him dirty looks.

'You getting out or not, young man?'

Ignoring the question and the old girl with a face like his horse, Freddy hung further out. Yes, that was Polly, bent under the weight of the sack. Careful, darling, you'll do yourself an injury.

He glanced down at the address she'd given him again: *119 Church Street, Stoke Newington, London.* So that was why she was getting out here. He knew Church Street. Other side of Clissold Park. He'd done a couple of shops there, years ago. Her lodgings must be over one of them. Of course, she'd need to change here for the Rectory Road train or maybe she'd go on to Stoke Newington itself. Fair enough.

He brought his head in and sat back down, lit up a fag.

'Shut the window, please!'

'Tch! I say, young man…'

He, too, could look daggers, and he could throw them, what's more. He smiled to himself, imagining their shock and surprise if he stuck them with his blades, the old bat with her ridiculous hat fallen over one eye and blood running down her nice lacy front, and old bulldog face, with his fat throat cut. He'd have nothing to lose. You can only hang once. Only now, he had everything to live for. A regular job, working for Tudd again, and a home with Poll. And no Ma or Pa to give him grief.

He'd been grateful once, long ago, when, desperate for a child of their own, they'd taken in the dirty little urchin they found at their shop window, held there by the bright 'fireworks' of chemicals igniting in the tray. But they'd wanted too much in return: honesty, loyalty, good manners. Too much, too much…

An office-type got in, smart dresser, top hat, off with his attaché case to town, slamming the door behind him. 'Anyone mind if I shut the window?'

'Not at all, sir.'

They smiled at the newcomer, giving Freddy the evil eye. What did he care? He sucked down the healing smoke, thinking that once things got back to normal and he had a few quid in his pocket, he'd move in with Polly. She'd look after him. Mend his clothes, darn his socks, cook and clean, buy his fags. Oh yes, he'd be in clover. They'd all be doffing their caps to *him*, calling *him* 'sir'.

At the next station he got out, crossed the bridge and made his way back to Hoe Street, handing in his platform ticket in all innocence.

Back in Walthamstow it was heaving: everyone pushing and shoving to get to this stall or that. He headed down the street to where the crowds were thickest, dipping into baskets as he went, sliding into pockets and bags, unencumbered now by the box. She'd look after it, wouldn't dare not to.

His horse was where he'd left it, tied up to the rail outside the Penny Bazaar, looking cold and bony but still standing. A couple of nights feeding on winter grass and holly didn't seem to have done her any harm. If the forest was good enough for Dick Turpin and Black Bess, it was good enough for Burglar Freddy and Whatsername. As for a nosebag of oats… Tuddy could moan all he liked: if he'd wanted the horse looked after he should have subbed him. Hah – that'd be the day!

And how was he meant to get the damned box up to the far reaches of Essex on this poor old broken-down nag? Look at him, having to stoop to dipping pockets to tide him over. Pity that last job went wrong. He could've done with a valuable souvenir or two to pop in a pawn shop. *'Smarten up, boy,'* Tuddy had said. *'Can't 'ave you looking like a bleeding ex-con. This is quality we're dealing wiv. You gotta impress, mate. You can talk the talk all right, but not like that! Next time I see ya, I wancha looking like a proper gent. Hair cut, shave and clean boots.'*

Passing by Cattermull's, the tailors, he checked out the three-piece suits in the window. Jesus Christ – fifty bob or more? But he could well have made that much by now: the hem of his top coat was really quite heavy. He went in the shop and took it off, laying it neatly on a chair while he chose his new clothes, but it slid to the floor, chinking loose change. He quickly put it on again, thinking he'd take his choice of clothes to the fitting room, and sort out some money at the same time. But a snooty junior whispered across the rail, 'You're joking, aincha? Sorry, pal, we only serve legitimate customers.'

'Give you cash—'

The boy assistant wrinkled his offended nose. 'But you'd have to try things on and you ain't exactly savoury. Perhaps I could recommend the public baths up the road…'

'Fuck you!' Another candidate for knifing. But he had a better idea. He picked up two or three grey jackets and when the assistant turned away again, he sliced the buttons off and pocketed them, poking them through the hole and into the lining to join the purses and wallets already there. Outside again, he felt smug with satisfaction. Teach you, you toffee-nosed git.

A few yards down the road he was assailed with the fragrance of newly baked bread and buns. Irresistible. He hadn't eaten since that bag of chips last night. He had money now, but he couldn't reach it, not without attracting attention. He joined the queue at Collen's the Baker's and, just before his turn, reached over to the tray of sticky buns in the window and took one. At the very same moment the hand of the law fastened on his collar. In the doorway, the snooty boy was creaming himself with excitement. 'That's the one, officer! I saw him in the mirror, damaging expensive goods. If I were you I'd look in his coat. He's a thief if ever I saw one.'

Archie was surprised, a few hours later, by Detective Inspector Tyrell tapping him on the shoulder, the walrus moustache trembling with excitement. His forefinger touched his bowler in greeting, as it had his helmet in the past.

'There's a turn-up, Arch!'

'What's that, then?'

'We only got 'im! Fitzell's killer! We was looking for a pickpocket and found us a murderer – him off your poster!'

'Never!' They'd found someone to match his drawing? Unbelievable. As he pictured the face, he realised where he might have seen Miss Porter's brother before. 'Name of Porter? Freddy Porter?'

'Porter? No. Billy Maggs. I've telephoned Scotland Yard, to see what they have on him.'

Archie frowned – he wasn't often wrong about a face. Billy Maggs? Of course, it could be an alias. But it was disagreeable to link a criminal's bloodline with that trim little body and the turquoise eyes. 'You have him in custody?'

'That we do. Got his horse, an' all – had the poor old thing hitched to the rail outside the Penny Bazaar.'

That evening they had the farrier carefully remove the shoes from the horse, not before time. Dark threads of woollen cloth, such as that used in the making of a policeman's uniform, had worked their way around the nail-heads and were caught up inside the right back shoe, together with traces of human skin and dried blood.

Seven

She dipped the brush in the bucket of whitewash and climbed back onto the chair. That was the ceiling's second coat nearly done, just that patch overhead, where a shadow of ingrained soot and smoke showed through. She had to be careful or it would drip in her eye. Slap, slap, and back a little further, if she could stretch that far. Dab, dab. She could hear the barrow boy packing up outside, people walking past, a trill of birdsong down the chimney…

Oh no! The chair tipped. Off balance she clawed at the air, crying out in surprise and fear as she toppled down.

Ooph! The landing punched the air out of her lungs.

Polly lay on her back looking up at the newly whitewashed ceiling, waiting for her heart to beat normally again. Well, that had nearly solved all her problems! If she'd cracked her head on the mantelpiece or the fender on the way down, that would've been her out of the picture.

Rubbing her sore head, she berated herself for clambering about on chairs in skirts, even with the back hem drawn between her legs and tucked into her front waistband. Served her right – trying to do everything herself. But what choice did she have? There was no money left for hiring painters and decorators. Besides, she was proud of what she'd achieved. Since moving in she'd chopped up the old counters for firewood and dispensed with the overhead cash tracks, chucked out the fossilised rat she'd found in an inglenook, and scoured the room from top to bottom. The shop looked entirely different now, almost as she'd dreamed it might be. Having disposed of the silverfish and the damp carpet in her bedroom, torn it up in lumps like rotting meat, and scoured the floorboards with carbolic, she could take her time about redecorating up there.

As she crawled across the floor to sit on a chair free of wet paint, her brain twanged like a Jew's harp. What damage had she done? She was more shaken than hurt.

A wisp of dried grass floated down into the empty grate. They were trying to build a nest up there. Stupid birds, didn't they know that it wasn't safe, that soon a roaring fire would roast their tiny tails?

A wisp of grass, though? If she were superstitious she might take it as an omen – the last straw.

She stared into the fireplace and a now uncertain future. Come on, Polly, no tears, girl, you're made of sterner stuff. Thank heavens the men hadn't yet put up the signboard. *Polly's Photos*, still leaning against the parlour wall, would tell Freddy exactly where to find her. How long would it be before he shoehorned his way in, demanding a share in the business? He might claim a brother's rights and take over the house and shop entirely. What could she do? Change the sign? Move out? Start up again somewhere else?

She heaved herself up and trudged over to the dark corner where she'd dropped the brush. If she left it the paint would dry hard and she couldn't be forking out for a new one. Sunset made the light orange and dark at the same time and it was impossible to see what dust or spider husks were stuck to the wet bristles. But she wouldn't light her lamps yet. Now that she'd taken down the curtains for washing, she was quite exposed to curious eyes – what would Archie Price think, seeing her in Mother's awful old wrapper? Her hand automatically removed the frightful headscarf and patted the flying ends back into place. He was a widower, she'd been told, an artist, a romantic. But she feared she'd made a poor impression. Her wretched brother!

Oh God. Freddy! If *he* should pass the shop and spot her!

Please, she prayed, albeit hopelessly, let him have believed her when she'd said she was in Walthamstow just for the market. But why should he? He was used to her lying to him. Perhaps he knew damn fine about the shop. Perhaps he was spying on her even now from across the road. She watched the greengrocer's queue: just the usual housewives holding out shopping bags to have potatoes and carrots tipped in. She saw Archie Price angled at his upstairs window so that the light fell on his easel, auburn hair flopping over his strong forehead, lips pursed, tawny eyes focused on the painting emerging under his clever paintbrushes. He had a sitter up there, a girl; she'd seen her go in, and was unreasonably jealous.

She didn't see her brother but felt his presence, his eyes on her shop, saw his tongue flicking out to lick his lips, waiting his chance to strike.

Oh, she could cheerfully wish him dead.

She'd assumed he was still in Pentonville, serving out a ten-year sentence. Neither she nor Mother had visited him there. She'd dared to hope she had shaken him off for good. How had he managed to find her? She'd told no one in Hackney where she was headed and, as he'd said, she'd left no forwarding address. How then? The removal people were the only ones who knew. Was it them? Maybe one of his cronies had been watching Maybank Road, seen the furniture being humped onto the cart, the name written on its side, and told him? Or the neighbours? Or someone here? Or was he telling the truth and had just come to market on the off chance?

Oh God, would it never stop, the what ifs, the worry?

Since the Saturday before last, the box had sat on top of her wardrobe. She'd put it off and put it off, knowing she had to get it to Stoke Newington by Friday, to that address she'd given him, so he could pick it up and go away. Leave her alone.

Tomorrow, then. In the morning.

Yes. Get rid of the wretched thing.

It was a very old tin box, with German or Dutch words engraved across the lid. Intriguing. When she went to bed she stared at it, dreamed about it when eventually she slept. Never far from her thoughts was that mythical box, the one Pandora had opened, releasing all the ills of the world, leaving poor little Hope tucked away at the bottom. She knew how Pandora must have felt.

A moment later she was upstairs lighting an oil lamp.

She spread a spare sheet on her good eiderdown then climbed onto a chair. She heaved the black tin box onto the bed and stared at its rusted bottom, wondering why it was just the bottom that was rusty.

She felt for the lip of the lid. Hesitated.

It had to be something damnable, judging from Freddy's secrecy. Important documents or bundles of bank notes? He said it wasn't money, but you couldn't believe what he said. That was how he'd survived on the streets before Pops adopted him. Lying and stealing. He couldn't stop now.

She eased it with her thumbs, this side and that, and, at last, the lid flipped back. As she sat staring at the contents, her hand flew to her throat in some relief. There, tightly packed, neatly stacked on end, were three long rows, not of bank notes, but of ageing postcards.

How interesting, and how unlike Freddy to steal something that didn't glitter. How surprising that he even knew there was a market in antique postcards. Was he becoming more discriminating in his old age?

Her fingernails were short, rimmed with whitewash. She didn't want to damage something precious so she found a pair of tweezers in her dressing table drawer and carefully, carefully drew one of the postcards from the middle of a stack.

What?

Oh no.

Oh Freddy, you vile … you nasty piece of … you – you…

42

Tears sprang to her eyes. These were old photographs of a kind no woman should be privy to; no man either. How awful. She took a look at another card. The familiar smell of sepia turned her stomach. Oh, God, she was going to be sick.

No, Freddy, no. This was too much.

She couldn't stop shivering. Downstairs, the grate was already laid with paper and kindling. She put on another few sticks of chopped up cheese counter and lit the paper, opened the damper, and, with shaking hands, covered the fire front with a double sheet of the local *Guardian* to make it draw. It was old news. Two or three weeks since publication. Among the other stories was the latest in a murder case. She had been so busy decorating she hadn't had a chance to read it before, just spread it on the floor to catch the drips of whitewash. Now a headline caught her eye. *'Have you seen this man?'* And there was a drawing of her brother!

Oh dear God! She snatched the paper away just as it was scorching and sat down heavily in a heap on the floor to read it. Her heart was galloping. It *was* him. *She'd* seen him, for one, Archie Price for another, and Mrs Reeves from next door, for a third. How many others? Freddy was for it now!

A policeman caught up in the tail end of a robbery – no, a *murder* – had described him to the police artist. She read quickly. An intruder had climbed up the wall of a big house in Forest Road, Walthamstow, in order to burgle it.

Well, that was Freddy's *modus operandi*. She had seen him in action, one dark summer night, when they were children. She had hidden around the corner to watch. She'd rubbed her eyes to see her brother climbing sheer walls, clinging on as if he were glued.

This barefoot burglar had been disturbed and had stabbed the owner of the house, a Jeremiah Fitzell (aged 67) in the head. That was Freddy's weapon of choice – a knife! How many times had he threatened her with one? He and his horrible friends used to practice throwing them at tin cans or birds in the garden. He'd even killed next door's cat and made her bury it under the lilac

43

bush. And one time he'd made her stand against the door while he threw knives around her! She had been wetting herself with fear. *'Little scaredy cat!'* She could hear Tuddy's cackle now. Her brother hadn't been able to resist skewering her arm. She still had the scar. Now they were saying he'd almost killed that policeman, Constable Tomkins. Freddy! A policeman! God, that alone was a hanging offence. And for what? So far as the police could tell, nothing of value had been taken, though they said there were indications that something like a box had been dragged out of the dying man's hands. A box! This one! That wasn't rust on the bottom. It was blood!

She sat transfixed, gibbering to herself. *Freddy, you bastard. Oh, oh, Freddy.*

What should she do? Well, she knew what. She should pop down the road to the police station and hand in the box. Shop him. She'd done it before. But this time she would kill him. He'd hang.

And what about her? What would they do to a receiver of stolen goods, a harbourer of criminals? They'd put her in prison. And if not, the gang would come for her. Punish her in their own way… Her head was spinning. She crawled out to the kitchen and poured herself some water. Drank it too quickly and coughed. Drank some more and waited for her head to clear. She would take the consequences, she always had. She'd survive. Unless they killed her, of course. She wouldn't be the first. Oh, hang and be damned, Freddy.

She put on her hat and shawl and was about to leave the house. It wouldn't take a minute. She might even say she'd found it. In the cellar downstairs, perhaps? Yes, she could have been clearing out the cellar and found it. Somebody could have broken in from the tunnel down there, thinking the shop above was empty and left it to collect later. She put the box under her arm, balanced on her hip. Heavy. Her hand was on the doorknob.

No.

She couldn't go to the police. What was she thinking? She couldn't do that to him. He couldn't help what he was.

She would get rid of the evidence. Freddy would be grateful.

Back in the parlour the fire had caught and was roaring up the chimney. She fed it with postcards, one by one. It was no use putting on a pack at a time: they would just kill the fire.

One at a time, she saw plump and naked limbs blacken and curl into flame, lascivious smiles and winks shrink and shrivel, the card become lighter-than-air black residue that floated harmlessly away up the chimney. The sweet sugary smell of the burning cuttlefish ink made her retch.

No, not this – a child! How could they? Poor little… Look at her eyes; so dull, the eyelids drooping. Perhaps she was drugged. Mother used to look like this on laudanum. Perhaps the poor little soul had no recollection afterwards of what she had been forced to do. Polly hoped not.

She turned away, her eyes blurring with smoke and tears. Dear God, those people should be horsewhipped, the cameraman shot. Vile, vile man.

The cards came out of the box easily now they were looser. The gap grew bigger as she removed twenty, forty, a hundred postcards and dropped them into the fire. Still she was only halfway there. This was going to take all night.

Goodness knows what Freddy had been intending to do with this collection. Sell it on, presumably. Or, more likely, he was working for Tuddy. Freddy had no reason to steal somebody else's pornographic prints when he was quite capable of developing his own. Pa had taught them both every aspect of photography: how to develop negatives from the exposed plates, how to fix them, how to use the enlarger to turn a negative into a print with sepia toner. But Freddy, the warped apprentice, had turned the wonderful, creative thing their father had taught them into a dirty, shameful business of his own. There were a couple of boxes of his ghastly glass negatives in the cellar downstairs. She'd been tempted to throw them away when she moved but knew that he was quite likely to turn up, wanting to print them out again. *'You what, you little slag! You threw them out?'* (She could almost hear his growling voice; see the flicker of the fire reflecting on the blade that he'd hold to her throat.) *'I'll slit your gizzard, little girl, cut you up and feed you to the dogs.'*

Fear goose-pimpled her shoulders, despite the heat from the flames. He would, too. If he were working for Tuddy, and he probably was, he'd have to kill her when he discovered what she had done, rather than lose face with his master. Never mind her good intentions, there was no chance at all that he would understand or forgive her for destroying evidence that could get him hanged.

She sat back on her heels. The box was still half full. He could probably get away with it. Tuddy wouldn't know any different. What if she put the lid back on the box now? Did as she was told? Would it save her?

Never.

He'd be after her like a shot.

He'd come back to Walthamstow High Street, where he'd seen her last, and ask around. It wouldn't take him five minutes to find her. Never mind whitewashing her ceiling; it would be splashed with blood if she didn't look sharp. There would be an end to Polly and her shop. She couldn't stay here.

She threw another mucky postcard into the flames, and another and another, blinking through a blur of determination. She would not let him win. The beginnings of a desperate plan were forming in her brain. As the last postcards flickered and flamed and Freddy's cruel spoils were reduced to a mound of curling black ash, light as feathers, Polly knew what she would do. She would disappear, leaving him the empty box. Go somewhere he would never think of looking.

Eight

Jungle drums in the distance, mosquitoes whining past his ear. He was greasy with sweat. A snake slithered purposefully up his leg and his cry of fear and revulsion woke him, just in time to stop his sheet sliding to the floor.

Archie lay as still as a stone while his heart slowed to something like normal. It was still dark, far too early to get up.

What was that about? Anxiety? There was nothing he was worried about, was there? He'd packed his bags, ready for off first thing in the morning; he'd arranged for Bob Cheshire to look after the mule, given him sufficient rent to cover two weeks' absence, though the Lord alone knew how long the trial would last, or when he'd be called to give evidence. Generally, hearings were local. People knew him and his drawings of suspects were taken as read. But Billy Maggs' trial at Chelmsford was an important murder case and the lawyers needed him to vouch that James Tomkins' description of his attacker could be trusted. He'd made a sandwich for the journey and gone to bed early. Bad dreams were the last thing he needed.

Perhaps he was anxious about his work: it simply wasn't selling. No matter how important and realistic his paintings of poverty, potential buyers – those with enough money to spend on art – would never buy work that pricked their conscience.

George Whittaker had had three of Archie's most recent pictures in his shop for two months and no one had looked at them twice. 'Too dark and depressing,' he had said, giving them back. People didn't want beggars and prostitutes hanging in their hallway for their visitors to see. Britain was supposed to be great, wealthy, head of an empire. Archie's paintings showed its rude underside.

He had to change his style, climb out of his rut and experiment. Again. Other artists, those on the Continent particularly, where it was warm, were trying all sorts of new things, painting outdoors with broad brushstrokes and thick bright colours. People bought their sunny people and landscapes to make themselves feel better.

In the summer, then. Soon, soon.

'Ar-chie!' Lizzie's voice held a note of warning. *'Prevarication, Archie!'*

Was she his conscience now? All right, all right. He got the message. Lighter subjects, brighter colours. Then, perhaps, he would get more commissions.

He'd start as soon as he got back from Chelmsford. He fluffed his pillow, rolled over and pulled the covers up to his ears. He must get some shut-eye or he'd fall asleep on the train and go past his stop.

Frank Tyrell had been thrilled to bits when Jimmy Tomkins, swathed in bandages and propped up in a wheelchair, had singled out Billy Maggs in the line-up. He praised Archie's divining powers or whatever it was that had helped him pick Jimmy's brains.

'I wasn't convinced,' Archie had to admit. 'I thought Jimmy was fobbing me off.'

'You should have more faith in yourself, boyo,' Frank had said. 'And don't mention your doubts in court. Jimmy may have been half-dead, but he gave us the description that helped us nab his attacker.'

Billy Maggs was being sent for trial by jury at the Chelmsford Assizes. The other witnesses – Jimmy, his doctor and a nurse were going up with Tyrell and Beckett in a hired carriage. The constable's bones and stab wounds were on the mend but they didn't think him up to travelling on the train. Besides, the policemen could protect Jimmy better in a carriage: they didn't want their charge nobbled, or to endanger other passengers. They had bags of incriminating evidence now: Maggs' knives stained with blood that matched both Tomkins' blood group and Fitzell's, the scrapings from the horse's shoes, a sack on the horse that had grounds of glass matching that on Fitzell's garden wall. That had all been sent on ahead in an armoured car with the scene-of-crime officers. There was no room for Archie: he had to go by train. Fitzell's housekeeper and the night-soil man were also making their own way there. But whatever had been dragged from the dying victim's grasp had disappeared into thin air.

On the railway platform he transferred his weight from one miserable foot to another, feeling the squelch of water between his toes. His head was heavy. He watched raindrops pocking the puddles and he hunched his shoulders against the dribbles down his neck. Other travellers were keeping dry under sensible umbrellas or in the waiting room. He'd seen little Miss Porter ducking in there out of the rain. She wasn't carrying a brolly. Her hands were full, with a tripod and what had to be a field camera in a wooden case, and suitcases. Archie might not have known her but for her tripod: she wore a veil and an all-concealing shawl. What was it about her that had attracted his attention? Her posture? That straight back and confrontational chin? She had a directness about her that he liked. He hadn't liked her brother, at all. Nor had she, apparently. He guessed Freddy had some sort of hold over her. What could it be?

A sort of sixth sense was lowering brollies and drawing people from shelter, readying themselves. And there was the train coming into view, smoke and steam bundling into the air. Standing room only. He had to fight to find room for his bags and easel among all the cases and briefcases in the luggage rack. There'd been no question of leaving his painting materials behind: an artist never knew when an opportunity for painting might present itself. He'd brought sketch books galore. They might even allow him to sketch in court.

He settled into the rocking motion of the train, his long, lean body swaying with it, the muscles of his feet adjusting to each shift of balance, his head full of the coming trial.

So much depended on his drawing of Billy Maggs. The prisoner would deny everything else. He'd say it wasn't his horse. Where would he have got the money to hire a horse? He'd found it wandering in the forest a few days before he was picked up in the high street. He'd certainly not trampled any policeman. If he'd robbed a house, where was the booty? Why would he need to resort to picking pockets and stealing buns on market day? He would say he wasn't even in Walthamstow on the night in question. There was a woman in Hackney, apparently, willing to swear the man had spent the night with her. Yes, Archie was very much afraid that there was no concrete evidence against Maggs.

He knew the defence would contest the drawing. They'd do their utmost to prove Jimmy Tomkins an unreliable witness: too ill, too traumatized to remember anything in detail, and too willing to please his good friend, the artist, at a time when he really only wanted to be left alone. How could he have seen his attacker? In the dark? From a position face down on the ground with stab wounds front and back, or from under a horse? No, the witness's testimony couldn't be trusted. He'd pulled that face out of thin air. Even the artist had been known to express doubts. It mattered little that Jimmy had picked Maggs out of the line-up. A jury might think he was swayed, in turn, by the drawing that had appeared in the local newspaper while he was still in hospital, the one headed: *Have you seen this man?* No, Archie would do his very best to see that justice was done, but he wouldn't be at all surprised if they found Billy Maggs not guilty.

Nine

Such kind hearts they had in the Walthamstow police force. The way they treated their guests! Nothing too much trouble to preserve a person's dignity.

Fucking filth.

Never even lent him an umbrella. A hat would have been a start. They'd given him back his coat for the courtroom, but the pockets were empty. No fags, money or blades, of course, and he was soaked to the skin. They'd take shortcuts to make it quick, they said, to spare him. But by the time he'd traipsed through a muddy 'rec', children's swings all chained up like him, through the marshalling yards, thick with coal dust, and over the railway line onto the station platform, he was chilled to the bone. Not to mention limping from the clubbing they'd given him! But they weren't getting a confession out of him! Lucky he had a thick skin after six years in Pentonville.

Filth.

Of course, it was more for beating up their mate than for knifing that old perve, but what was he supposed to do? Let one bastard copper nab him? Anyone would do the same. Tuddy's way was to knife first, ask questions later. Otherwise, where would you be? Slammed up in the choky and no way out. As he was. Tuddy would have made sure the copper was dead. *'Careless, Freddy,'* he could hear Tuddy saying. *'Dead men don't tell tales.'*

It was slow going, handcuffed, hobbling along in the gutter, with bloody great iron cuffs round your ankles, carrying your ball and chain and everyone eyeballing you. The filth had nice warm uniforms, helmets, hobnails and capes to keep the rain off, but even *they* were moaning, and they weren't off to the assizes and an all but certain hanging.

He didn't have a leg to stand on, they told him. But he was buggered if he was pleading guilty. If he stuck to his story he might get off with the pickpocketing charge; that was his only hope. Otherwise he was for the drop, and who would shed a tear?

Tuddy perhaps, for old times' sake. Or not.

Poll? Would she miss him? He was all the family she had now the old lady was gone. If he came through this, he'd hook up with her and no arguments. Might even put a ring on her finger. Now there was a thought. They weren't blood relations. She said she hated him, but you don't hate your own brother, do you? Yeah, she'd mourn him, all right. She wasn't cut out to be alone. No woman was.

Leaving her with the box was a risk, but what else could he have done? Buried it in the forest until the fuss blew over? He'd never have found it again, and God alone knew what havoc the damp would have played with those valuable postcards. They'd be worth nothing with mildew on them.

He hoped that bent copper had got hold of Tuddy, given him her address in Church Street, and he'd got the box from her. Perhaps then they'd be grateful. They should be. If he was right and the postcards were original Hans Vosses they were worth more than gold.

But now, oh fuck, he was off to the assizes. For the thousandth time he kicked himself for letting the cops finger him that day in the market, for pickpocketing, of all things. Another day or two and he would have bought his posh suit, had his hair cut and taken the box up to Tuddy. He'd've put on his posh voice for the mark or the dealer or whatever he was, done the deal, and by now they'd all have been living the life of Riley. But that day in Walthamstow he'd been down on his uppers, desperate, so what could he have done?

When the train came in, the copper they called Bradford, the big bruiser, and the other one, Foskett, shoved him in the compartment, shut the door and kept it shut, all the way to Liverpool Street, where he had to cross the concourse for the Chelmsford train. What a circus act! Chains clanking, police with shooters in their belts, people calling him names and gobbing! Lovely. Just to make him feel better they slid open the door of the guard's van, and booted him in there, like he was some old sack of rubbish. Anyone wanting to stow their luggage had to put up with him glaring at them and the filth pretending to be deep in their newspapers or their mugs of tea. Ages it took to uncouple the engine that had brought the train in, while, up at the other end, they put on a new engine, one with fresh water in the boiler and coal in the tender.

When he'd done all his flag-waving and whistle-blowing and the train was pulling out, the guard hopped back in the van with the boys in blue and Freddy boy for company.

The things a railway guard had to put up with! Livestock in the van, dogs and cats and canaries, all in cages and baskets, but that didn't stop them pissing and messing, yowling like demons. Freddy hated dogs especially. For weren't they the bane of a burglar's life? The guard had his own privy if he was taken short, which he let the cops use. Cats and dogs and convicts had a drain.

There was all sorts of stuff on the move: parcels going to Colchester, a door someone was sending to Ipswich, chairs to Seven Kings, bicycles. Packets, parcels. Milk churns.

If they wanted to sit down, there was only the floor, swilling with dog pee, or the guard's seat, or they could perch on one of the trunks, which they did. Foskett lit a lantern and suggested a card game to while away the hours. Needing a fourth for whist, Bradford and the guard, Edgar, reckoned the prisoner ought to take a hand. Still wearing his handcuffs and hobbles? Why the fuck not? What difference would it make to a wretched convict on his way to meet the hangman? Jesus.

Sitting up there, next to Bradford, wondering whether to play his ace when the geezer next lay a heart, or to grab the big man's pistol from its holster, he let his eyes roam over the luggage. The battered suitcase in the middle was addressed to *The Rev. Geoffrey Norris;* the one Edgar was on belonged to *Lady Tindall,* of *Ham House.* Could be milady's fox fur and tiara in there, only needing a jemmy to get at them. There was a tasty-looking trunk addressed to *Miss Florence Anderson* in Colchester.

He saw an old cardboard suitcase very like the one the Porters had used for their holidays in Broadstairs, the stain on it where Polly's ice cream might have dropped many years before when he'd tried to wrest it from her hand. He could still remember the seagulls swooping down for it, the noise they made, greedy buggers.

'You looking at my cards, you slimy bastard?'

Just stretching his back, he countered. He couldn't believe his eyes! The label actually read *'Polly Porter, c/o Left Luggage Office, Chelmsford Railway Station',* in her handwriting.

Well!

Good old Polly! She was only on the train, going to the assizes to cheer him on. Maybe she'd even say a few words in his favour. He played his ace and took the trick, earning himself black looks all round.

It was almost worth the trip to the gallows knowing she was on side. Perhaps she loved him really. Perhaps he *would* lift the shooter. It was his only chance of getting out of there. Should be easy, like picking pockets.

He had to do it before Chelmsford. Chelmsford would be too late.

Doors banged and there was a hiss of steam from away up the platform. The side of the van slid open. A woman, come to collect her pooch, a goggle-eyed, long-eared idiot, sliding and skittering over the wet floor as its owner tugged on its lead.

'Diddums think Mummy had abandoned him, then?'

The door slid shut. More doors slammed and the whistle blew. Edgar came back to play his hand – he'd put his cards in his pocket to save them getting nobbled while he waved his flag – and the train got up steam again.

Ten minutes went by at a steady lick.

'My trick I think,' said Bradford. 'Five of clubs trumps your king.'

The wheels clattered over the points, regular as clockwork. *Chuff, chuff, chuff* went the engine. Then the sound dipped as it plunged into a tunnel. The lantern flickered. Now he should do it, if he was going to. Last chance to get that gun.

But maybe she was going to the assizes as a witness for the *prosecution!* Maybe she was going to grass…

An enormous jolt flung him to the floor.

They all went tits up, the luggage slid about, bikes fell over, and the cards scattered.

'Fuck!'

With a lurch and a shriek of metal the train moved on another twenty yards or so before coming to a stop with the guard's van half in, half out of the tunnel.

Very quiet.

They all started crawling about or staggering to their feet when, from outside, came the sound of crunching gravel and a dull ring of metal as though someone was climbing on the wheel. The van shuddered.

The door slid open and a friendly face looked in.

'Hello, Freddy.'

Ten

The sounds – the ear-splitting screech of metal, the passengers screaming, the hiss of steam and that deafening explosion, breaking glass, the puncturing of the carriage walls – were nothing compared with the awful sense of powerlessness. Polly was tumbled about, bashed against walls and floors and luggage racks and bags and people – like a rag doll in the hands of a two-year-old throwing a tantrum. When it was over, when everything stopped and she realised that, however hurt she was, she was not dead, she heard something small hit the floor, spinning, clattering to stillness. A coin.

Nobody moved. She couldn't either. Her body was saturated with fear. Heavy with it.

Quiet stole in like marsh mist. The only sounds were her own heart pounding, a whispering hiss of steam, and the patter of rain. There was a sour smell of sulphurous smoke, hot metal, burnt grass, and bodily excretions, mixed with a woman's sweet perfume. Strangely, there was also a faint whiff of peppermint.

At least she was breathing.

Cautiously, she peered through her lashes.

Butchered humanity lay about her, damaged bags and boxes, bashed hats and broken brollies, a sticky paper of humbugs. And blood.

Ah-ahh! It hurt so much! As she pulled back from the horror, searing pain shot through her arm from shoulder to wrist.

She was lying on the floor, squashed against the wall with her right arm caught behind her, unnaturally twisted. She desperately needed to straighten out, but someone, a woman, was lying heavily across her. It was her perfume she could smell, sweet Lily of the Valley, strands of *her* hair that Polly now carefully removed from her mouth, trying not to vomit.

'Uh – excuse me, would you mind?'

As she shifted, the woman slipped off her lap and her head hit the floor with a thud. But the wax-doll expression in her blue-glass eyes didn't alter; her head lolled. 'No!' Polly cried: the woman was dead!

Polly's own trapped arm still wouldn't move of its own accord, and pulling it into a more normal angle was excruciating. Waves of darkness stole over her. No, don't give in.

'Help!' she croaked, trying to ignore the ringing ache in her temples. Seeing an open window she called again, 'Help me!' But there was no answering cry. Perhaps she was the only one left alive. Perhaps the world had come to an end. No, don't be silly, she scolded herself, not the world, just this train you're in. There's been a crash. Someone will come.

The entire carriage must have been flung off the rails and rolled down the embankment, helpless as a sheep on its back. What *had* been a planked floor littered with crushed apple cores, sweet papers, cigarette ends, was now a scuffed and muddy ceiling. What was *now* the floor was strewn with a crumpled waste of passengers.

She wracked her aching brain, but she couldn't, for the life of her, remember anything beyond the last few minutes. She knew who she was. Didn't she? Well, of course. Come on…

She saw, of all things – through layers of fog or steam – the old tin bath in front of the fire and Mother kneeling there, singing: '*Little Polly Flinders sat among the cinders…*' No, Mother had changed the words: *Little Polly Porter, Addie's little daughter, washing her pretty little toes…*' She couldn't remember the rest – the nasty bit, when Mother tipped the jug of cold soap and water over her head. Something about troubles and bubbles and soap going up her nose. Polly Porter. That's who she was. *Polly's Photos* was the sign she was putting over the new shop.

And yes – she patted her shoulder bag – she still had her plates. The leather bag had remained strapped across her body throughout her journey. It must have swung about during the tumbling, but her clothes, her shawl and her bustle must have protected it from harm. Wonderful.

She remembered telling the girl – the Lily of the Valley, blonde one – about her new studio. They'd introduced themselves, soon after the train pulled out of Liverpool Street, over a twist of humbugs that another passenger had handed round. Her name was Florence Anderson. They had discussed her namesake, Florence Nightingale, famous for nursing soldiers in the Crimean War, and the fact that every fourth girl at Polly's old school and hers had been named Florence after the heroine, while she, Florence Anderson, was named after the Italian city. Interesting.

Florence was an only child and an orphan, since her mother, her only living relative, had recently died of consumption.

'Mine, too,' Polly had been moved to tell the girl. 'What a coincidence.' Why not? What did the *exact* truth matter between strangers? Especially when the exact truth did not reflect well on one?

Florence had confided in Polly that, rather than live alone in the echoing family house, she had sold up, put the money in the bank and answered an advertisement to take employment as companion to a single lady in Colchester. It was an adventure, a risk, but it was better than living alone.

What would happen to that lonely single lady now that Florence Anderson was dead? Polly tried pulling her shoulder into a more comfortable position. Intense pain could be almost bearable, almost sweet, even though it brought tears to the eyes. What would happen to the money in the bank? Florence had no heirs; she'd said she was all alone. Such a pity they couldn't swap. Then Polly Porter would have died in the crash and her odious sometime-never sort of brother would stop looking for her. She sighed. If only...

Where was she? Wet grass and the fiddle-furls of young cow parsley poked in through the top of the upside-down door opposite. It was raining. She became aware of boards creaking. She wasn't alone!

An elderly gentleman with a saucer of baldness on his head, edged with whitish-grey wisps of hair, crawled out of the mess, muttering to himself, and pushed a sturdy hatbox under the door opposite. By climbing up and hanging onto the dangling leather window strap, the old gentleman could now reach the door handle. *'Dear Lord, save your people...'* He was praying. The dog collar registered, and she remembered that he was a vicar. No, not a vicar, he'd told them all – a minister of the Methodist faith. He'd been passing the humbugs around.

The door on Polly's side seemed to be rammed up against a dripping gorse bush. No escape that way.

'Excuse me!' she called. 'Could you help me, please?'

The man turned. Polly remembered him telling them that he'd just come from a ministry in Tottenham. He'd been on his way to Colchester to Saint Saviour's or Saint Simon's or somewhere, and said he was looking forward to staying with his married sister who ran a lodging house.

But now the man's eyes held no recognition, none at all. Perhaps he was concussed. Or perhaps he simply didn't see her. She was used to being invisible.

'Watch out!' she shouted.

As he'd turned, he'd twisted the leather strap so that the hole was slipping off its brass stud. He tried to hang on, but as he fell, the heavy window came crashing down, glass splintering, and he landed on his back in a tangle of legs and arms. His face was smeared with blood and dirt – Polly's was probably no different. His ministerial dog collar hung off his scrawny old neck, his spectacles had a lens missing. His eyes, meeting Polly's, momentarily showed the whites and then abruptly closed.

She had to do something. Move. Holding onto the luggage rack at knee level, she struggled to her feet. Oh God, her head was splitting, the compartment was spinning, her ears buzzing. She couldn't... She had to... Simply had to...close her eyes.

A long time later, she heard a murmur of voices and was aware, to her immense relief, that someone was taking care of her. Struggling up to investigate, she found an arm gently pushing her back to the floor. Somebody was kneeling beside her. A man cleared his throat and spoke in a soft Scottish burr. 'Rest easy, my dear, you're safe now. I'm a doctor, and this is my daughter, Effie.' There was another person behind him, a girl with dark curls. 'I'm Duncan MacKay, and you are?'

She couldn't stop herself.

'Effie, dear, did you get that? That man, Spratt, from the *Chronicle* is taking names. Tell him Florence Anderson, from —?'

'Lewisham,' said Polly, remembering an earlier conversation.

'Miss Florence Anderson from Lewisham is a survivor,' he reiterated.

Why had she said it? She was Polly Porter, the photographer's daughter and dyed-in-the-wool liar. Too late now to take it back.

So, in for a penny... 'The young woman who was killed,' she said, compounding the lie. 'Fair hair. I think her neck may have been broken in the crash. She said her name was Polly Porter.' She had no control. It poured out. 'She said,' she went on, 'she said it was a tongue-twister, like Peter Piper – you know, Peter Piper picked a peck of pickled pepper.' And, unaccountably, she burst into tears, mourning her own death.

'Oh there,' said the girl, handing her a handkerchief, 'you poor thing,' and when she had wiped her nose, 'Polly Porter, you say?'

'Yes,' she sniffed, 'I'm sure that was it.'

'I'll tell them.' The girl with the sympathy and curls left the compartment to make it official. Polly Porter was dead.

She closed her eyes. Oh God, what was happening? She had to

60

get a grip, keep her head. 'I, em, I imagine they'll mostly find out who died by checking the labels on the unclaimed luggage,' she suggested. 'Process of elimination.'

'Very likely. Or people will report it when their expected visitor fails to arrive.'

'Yes,' said Polly. She fervently hoped that the single lady in Colchester wouldn't make a fuss if her companion failed to arrive.

'Now then, Miss Anderson, I'd better explain. I think your shoulder is dislocated. This is a filthy place,' he kicked away a cigarette butt, 'but the longer we leave it the greater the risk of permanent disability, so I'm going to attempt to put it back now.'

'Whatever you think,' she whispered, horrified. She should be grateful, she told herself firmly. She'd got off lightly.

'Right you are, then,' said the doctor. As he moved into the light of a hurricane lamp burning beside them, silver glinted in his side whiskers. The man was older than she had taken him for, probably in his late forties. Looking around, she realised that the other passengers, dead and alive, and every bit of baggage had been removed. She must have been unconscious for some time.

'We'll just wait for Effie to get back.'

'You don't happen to know where, em – have you seen my camera? It was here earlier, on the floor by the window, in a wooden carrying case with a collapsing tripod. Did someone take them?'

'Don't worry, Miss Anderson. Everything's safe, I assure you. All the cases and boxes have been loaded onto a wagon while we decide where you are to be billeted. There are a number of injured and no hospitals within easy reach.'

'Oh. I wonder – could someone fetch my camera for me now? This is such an opportunity.'

'What!' He leaned away to get her into focus. Clearly, he thought her either mad or heartless. 'I'm sorry, Miss, but that is unthinkable. Apart from the shoulder and a nasty bump on the head, you are covered in cuts and bruises. You are probably in shock, or concussed, or both. We have to be careful.'

'I will be, I promise. I'm not a ghoul, I'm a photographer. This – the crash – is news. The man from the *Chronicle* will write it up and I can supply a photograph to go with his article. It's my duty as a responsible citizen.'

Reluctantly, he called to Effie through the broken window to fetch the mahogany carrying case and the tripod.

'My other things are in the guard's van. A trunk, hatboxes…'

'Yes, yes, my dear, my daughter's gone to identify them. They *are* labelled, I suppose?'

She nodded quickly, wincing as marbles rolled around in her head. 'Miss Florence Anderson, Colchester,' she said, mentally crossing her fingers. Her own battered suitcase, she hoped, would eventually find its way to the left luggage office at Chelmsford. Oh dear, all this intrigue. The future looked complicated.

'What – what happened exactly? To the train?'

'Landslip, my dear, brought down a tree and a quantity of debris, mud, rocks and so forth, onto the line. The train coming out of the tunnel ploughed straight into it.' He paused to place gentle hands on her shoulder, squeezing, ignoring her yelps. 'We've had so much rain the ground's saturated – trees down all over the county.'

He described how the engine must have hit the debris and reared up at full speed, before rolling down the side of the embankment, taking the first passenger carriage with it and derailing the one behind. Its death throes were heard for miles around. There'd been a fearsome hissing of steam as the pressure built and built and then a deafening explosion as the boiler burst, spewing gallons of scalding water and flinging live coals about. Polly didn't remember any of this, just the tumbling turmoil before she passed out for the first time.

The doctor removed his jacket and rolled up his sleeves.

'Were many killed?' she asked him.

'Three in this compartment. The young woman you spoke of.'

Polly bit her lips.

'And another lady and a child, a boy. An older gentleman, a Methodist minister, has head injuries, like yourself.'

She reached up, for the first time. Her hat was gone and her hair seemed clumped and sticky. The slightest pressure hurt.

'He has damaged an eye, but he should pull through.' He nodded, as though trying to convince himself.

'How many others,' she asked, 'altogether?'

'Dozens injured, still more in shock, eight dead, including the fireman, poor chap.'

His large busy fingers prised the cork from a small stoneware bottle and poured a tincture into a spoon. 'Chloroform,' he informed her. 'You won't feel a thing.'

'I'd rather be conscious, if you don't mind. I really must take that photograph. It'll probably be the only first-hand record of the disaster, and I'll need to have my wits about me. I can probably manage it with an assistant or two, if you wouldn't mind.'

She caught the smell of rain as Effie returned, lugging the heavy camera case, the tripod tucked under her arm. There was no alarming chink of glass. The girl looked sick.

'The guard's van – apparently there was another sort of accident in there – the police won't let anyone in there yet. It's – it's like a blood bath. All the luggage has to be wiped down before they'll let us take it. But your trunk is there, intact, Miss Anderson. They told me that much.'

'We must hurry, doctor. Would you please reach into my pocket for my glove? Thanks. It's leather. I'll bite on this while you do what you have to. I promise I won't make a fuss.'

They helped her from the train, down a makeshift ramp of planks, and, while the doctor went to tend the people in the next compartment, Effie and the *Chronicle* reporter, Bartholomew Spratt, walked Polly down the embankment, into a squelchy field where she set up her camera. The smoke was now blowing away on a light breeze and the rain had reduced to a fine drizzle. Not the best conditions for taking photographs, but if she used her glass plates – by far the best for clarity – a wide aperture, and took the train in two halves, it should be possible to stitch them together to show the full panorama of the disaster. It wasn't easy, one-handed – the doctor had insisted she wear a sling – with wobbly knees and her good hand shaking, but with Effie holding the tray of flash powder and Spratt checking that the tripod didn't sink in the mud, they managed.

Her carriage was at an angle, upside down on the embankment, wheels in the air, like a stranded beetle. The broken locomotive still emitted pathetic little puffs of steam. The next carriage was upright but half on, half off the rails, and the rest of the train was hidden inside the tunnel. Dazed passengers were being led out into the light.

The wounded sat or lay about on the wet grass, bandaged here, there and everywhere. Some were being tended by fellow passengers, or draped with coats and shawls, awaiting transport. The railway police and local farm workers lent a hand where they could.

'Damnable sight!' a man's voice brayed, his vowels tight with breeding. 'Came too damn fast through the tunnel, I'll warrant.'

Lifting the blackout cloth and straightening, she saw a group of gentlemen gathered a little way off. The one who had spoken – a tall skeletal fellow in frock coat and topper – adjusted his monocle and acknowledged her presence with a leer and a nod. One of his companions, a smaller olive-skinned man, spoke with a foreign accent and waved his hands about a lot.

'You think any train can stop for alla this trees and rocks and mud? It is, how you say, without hoping.'

'Impossible,' agreed their companion, a windswept man, more appropriately dressed for the mud and outdoors in cap, waistcoat and wellingtons and a coarse sort of driving coat. 'There simply wasn't enough time. No, he should have started slowing down well before the tunnel if he'd known there was an obstruction on the line. Which, of course, he didn't. He couldn't see.'

'If you say so, Gifford. Now then, what's happening to all these people? Do we know? I suppose they'll have to be carted off to Chelmsford by road, seeing as the trains can't get through?'

'Out of the question, sir. Their injuries would be compounded by the rough journey to hospital. Some of them wouldn't survive. No, we'll find billets for them in the village, and the doctor and Miss McKay here will see to their medical needs. Lilian and I can take a few, and there's room at the vicarage. I suppose we couldn't impose on…'

'No room at the inn, I'm afraid, old chap. We have Signor Marconi with us all this week. But if there's anything you need, sheets, blankets, beef broth, that sort of thing, don't hesitate to ask.' The cut-glass voice, honed to penetrate, paused and took on a calculating tone. 'I suppose we might perhaps find a small cubby hole for a really needy case. What about you, young lady – do you have somewhere to stay?'

Polly realised with a start that he was talking to her.

'No, no, I'm not, sorry, Mr, em?'

'Beasley, my dear, Lord Beasley.'

'Lord? Oh. I don't think there's…' She turned to Effie, appealing for a sign. The doctor's daughter widened her eyes in warning and gave the very, very, slightest shake of her head. 'No, I don't think there's any need,' Polly continued. 'My shoulder was only dislocated. It's not too bad now. If you could point me in the direction of the nearest coach depot I can continue my journey…'

When the lord had wandered off, Effie said, 'Nonsense, Florence! Your shoulder is the least of it. You're in no condition to travel, particularly on your own. Papa was adamant. If Richard – Mr Gifford will –'

'Of course, of course,' the windswept man said, 'we'll be glad to put you up, Miss…?'

'Anderson. Florence Anderson.'

Eleven

Sledgehammer to crack a walnut, the old man, old Jonas Porter, would have said. Crashing a train to spring a burglar? Whose idea was that? Tuddy's? Lemmy's? Nobody was saying. They hadn't thought that far ahead, imagining that the train would brake gently, stop, and they'd get him off between stations. They knew it was a risk, with an armed escort and that, but it was all supposed to be managed quietly, in an orderly fashion. They hadn't thought people would die.

And Tuddy did try, give him that. As the door slid back, revealing him in all his ugly, ferocious glory, his blade poised in his fingers, the coppers should have known, should have taken heed. Tuddy was a force to be reckoned with.

'Now, then, lads,' he said, quite pleasantly, quite reasonably, as Lemmy and Curly crowded in behind him, 'if you've got any sense you'll just throw those shooters out the door and let us do our business quiet like. Then nobody will get 'urt.' They'd even brought gags and ropes to tie the buggers up.

But the guard couldn't do as he was told. He only put his train whistle to his lips! Jesus, men with whistles! Jumped-up little pipsqueaks. Because, of course, Curly's blade flipped through the air, faster than the eye could see, and parted the geezer's eyebrows, neatly and forever.

And then the trigger-happy copper, Foskett, had taken a shot at Curly, hitting him in the arm. No need for it, and so Foskett got it in the neck, right in the Adam's apple. Fountains of blood

66

everywhere. And the racket: dogs barking, cats screeching. Not quiet, like Tuddy wanted it, not at all. That left just Reggie Bradford, who had looked very surprised when Tuddy topped him. He'd been counting on them letting him go, him being so cooperative, delivering messages to and from the lock-up, but with knives flying about you couldn't pick and choose.

The van was awash with blood. Freddy was covered in claret, none of it his, thank God, by the time Lemmy managed to remove the cuffs and shackles.

He drew their attention to Polly's suitcase. The box was too big to be in it, but perhaps she had brought it with her. If she was on the train, she'd be able to tell them where it was.

'You gonna look for her, are you?'

'Em, I don't…'

'No, me neither. Think about it – if she's coming up for the trial she won't have brought it with her, Freddy. Where's the sense in that? No, she's left it at home in Stoke Newington's my guess. We'll call in there. First things first. Get you away and then we'll see. Come on, we ain't got all day.'

As they all climbed down, from the footplate to the wheel to the ground, the tunnel ahead filled with a horrible noise, of moaning and wailing, and for a moment he felt bad. If Polly had been on the train she might be hurt. But he was alive and free. That was all that mattered.

Onas Shipton was keeping an eye out.

'Got a fag, have you, mate? I'm gasping.'

'I have so,' said Onas, dealing them round. 'Would ye be wantin' a tot o' poteen to go with the smoke, mebbes? Well, get a move on, then.'

Tuddy had five mounts waiting up the track.

'Where are we going?' Freddy asked him as he hoisted himself into the saddle. He felt sticky with blood and sweat. He'd have given his eye teeth for a bath and a change of clothes.

'Onas's place.'

'Oh, what?' he whined, flicking his dog-end away in disgust.

'It's 'andy.' The old man was in no mood to argue. The carnage back there had upset him. It hadn't gone to plan. 'Beasley won't put us up at his place. Too risky and too many servants to blab. 'Sides, e's got comp'ny 'e's trying to impress. Gypsy camp's the best I could do at a pinch.'

Really? Onas Shipton's camp was a collection of dirty old caravans, offering neither comfort nor refuge. Onas was all right; it was Tuddy. Gypsies brought out the bully in the man, like no others. He hated them. There were some who thought Onas was another of his bastards. Who would know? In any event Tuddy had taken reluctant charge of Onas as a child, when his mother was jailed for soliciting. But he was more than happy to give the kid back when she was released five years later. Onas would run away and hide when it was his turn to climb in a fanlight and open the door for the big boys.

Now, it seemed, Tuddy was calling in favours, making Onas turn people out of their vans for the duration, while the gang prepared to do this deal with the geezer over at the big house and fetched Freddy off the train. Anyone didn't like the Lunnoners' presence, or the idea of doing anything that risky – and many didn't – well, they could just fuck off out of it.

When the riders reached the camp, only a mile or two from the railway line, on a bit of scrubland by a river, there was tinkers' stew, hooch, a smoke and a change of clothes to take the sting out of what they'd done. Apart from a warm welcome, there was everything they needed.

Curly was leaking everywhere and Tuddy was beside himself. When Shipton's missus, Lavinia, suggested he should see the village doctor, he smacked her, hard, round the head.

'You wan' us caught, do ya?' he snarled. 'Bleeding quack's gonna ask himself where a London geezer managed to get hisself a gunshot wound round 'ere, inne? Eh? Eh?' and he shoved her so hard she fell back against the caravan steps. Tuddy snarled and spat out of the side of his mouth, sizing her up. He was tempted to take her, you could tell.

Shipton reared up, very protective. 'Don't you touch my wife!'

'Why?' said Tuddy with a nasty smile. 'What you gonna do about it, eh? Eh?' And he smacked the husband, as well. The other gypsies held back, muttering and giving him the evil eye. Gypsy curses were powerful, everyone knew that. But Tuddy didn't give a toss.

From nowhere his razor-sharp blade appeared in his hand, gleaming in the rain. 'You wanna make sunning of it, yous lot? Nah, didn't fink so. Now get sunning on my boy's arm, bitch, 'fore I slice that pretty neck o' yourn. An if 'e croaks, *you* will. Got it?'

A bruise forming on her face, and limping a little, Lavinia tied a bandana tight around Curly's upper arm, threw some home-made hooch over the wound to prevent poison setting in, and patched him up with a mashed-nettle poultice held in place with ragged bandages, and a sling made out of a kiddie's shawl or something.

Freddy felt guilty. If it hadn't been for him getting nicked, Curly wouldn't have got himself shot. He felt sure Tuddy blamed him. Mind, the old boy still hadn't explained why they'd saved his neck. Not for love. Tuddy loved nobody but himself. Not even Curly. So did they think he'd grass them up at the trial? No, they knew him better than that.

He hoped it wasn't another job. He was off burglarising for a bit, he explained to them. Properly shook him up, had Forest Road.

Tuddy's lips pursed in anger. He'd upset their apple cart, knifing the geezer, he said. Last thing they needed was cops on their tails.

'But he'd eyeballed us, Tudd! And he would *not* let go of the bleeding box.'

'Didn't have your mask on, did ya? How many times I 'as to tell ya, Freddy?'

'Blimey! I got us a box of Hans Voss porn. Voss was the master. Worth a mint, I reckon.'

'Yeah,' said Tuddy, 'so Beasley said. 'E's some sort of expert, and 'e's very interested to see what's in the box – "erotica" he calls it – but o' course, he can't, seeing as 'ow you've left it with your sister. Lucky 'e don't mind waiting. Ask me, 'e's got a screw loose, but that ain't our problem. Long as 'e sees us right.'

Twelve

As he came to, Archie realised he was being moved. Bumping. He could hear a continuous skirr of wheels and the clop of horses' hooves on some wet and muddy track. So, he was out of that damnable train compartment, at last, with its stench of burning and death, out in the drizzly fresh air. He was lying flat on the dusty bed of what seemed to be a four-wheeled hay cart and that was something to be glad about. They must have freed his stupid foot from the luggage rack. But, by God, the pain was no less. His leg hurt, his head ached, and every tuft of grass the wheels ran over, every stone, rut and pothole, made him wince. Perhaps he should have taken the jollop the doctor had offered him, but he'd seen laudanum addicts and they weren't a pretty sight.

Where were they taking him? Opening his eyes made him blink in the fine rain, but he was able to make out bare branches overhead, a pewter sky and crows, disturbed, cawing and flying about. He tried to sit up, and moaned.

'You'd best lie still 'til we get there…' A man's voice. Archie squinted and made out the dog collar of a dishevelled clergyman, sitting above him, his hand covering one eye. His bony old knee trembled and his heel ticked rapidly against the wooden floor. 'Or you'll disturb the strapping. He's used anything that came to hand, looks like. Legs of an artist's easel!' He giggled. 'The doctor says he'll put proper splints on your leg when we get where we're going.'

What! He felt down his leg and discovered pits in the bandages where the peg holes were. Damn. His easel destroyed? Now what was he going to do? These things were expensive. Perhaps it could be mended. 'Where's the rest of it – the easel?'

'It's probably coming separately,' he said, though it was perfectly clear that the poor old man had no idea.

'Where are we going?'

'You may well ask. Just have to put our trust in the Lord, young man. We're way out in the sticks, that I do know. Rural Essex. Chelmsford is miles away in that direction.' He waved a stiff hand. 'Ingatestone was our last stop and that's way back there.' His voice quavered as the cart jolted. 'We're miles from anywhere with hospitals, so they're taking us to a place we can rest up and recover. The luggage is coming behind in the trap with another injured passenger, a young woman who was in my compartment. Pleasant person. Polly, I thought, though I could be mistaken. There were two young women and one died. I'm not sure which one. You're the only survivor from yours. Next to you, that's the engine driver, poor chap.'

Archie followed his nod and realised that what he'd thought was a bundle of dirty rags was a lump of charred human flesh tucked under the opposite seat, the head turned away. He smelled of smoke. 'I'd've thought he'd, that he, em…'

'No, though there's not much hope, poor lad,' the older man mouthed. 'Scalded near to death when the boiler exploded. Wet cloths,' he patted his face and various parts of his anatomy to indicate where, 'to try and ease the pain … they've given him some sort of knockout drops. I've asked the Lord to intervene, but His Will be done…' He wagged his head, his sigh filling his lungs. 'We're all in His hands now,' he said, before pointing out a second bundle on Archie's other side, another human form, its head covered with a coat. 'Young man, I believe.'

Archie flinched. His shoulder, his elbow and his leg were *touching* a dead man. A shudder ran through him. He was lying between the dead and the dying. If he moved he'd hurt one but not the other. Oh Lord, this was horrible, horrible. His instinct was to shift, get clear of them both, sit up; if only he could get the necessary purchase on the truck floor, but his leg was useless. He scrubbed at tears of frustration and fear that ran past his ears, but he was too weak to be manly.

'Take it easy,' cautioned the old man. 'You'll hurt yourself. We're dropping him off at the church.'

'Dropping him?'

'They're putting all the fatalities in one place for ease of identification. The relatives will want to see them.'

'Yes, of course…' was all he could say.

They weren't the first. There was quite a queue of horses and carts waiting to enter the churchyard. *Saint Andrew's in the Parish of Little Nessing*, Archie read as their cart trundled past the noticeboard. Sombre yew trees now, winter dark, grey sky, greyer stone, Gothic-stained glass. At last they came to a halt beside the church porch where concerned people were unloading bodies, muttering instructions ('Third pew on the left') and carrying them inside, one at the head, one at the feet. Archie's companion sat with his hands clasped in prayer. There was a jingle of harness and Archie looked into the face of the carthorse following, a blinkered grey. It tossed its head as it moved back a pace or two, whickered, and blew steam into the air.

'Just the one, is it?' The tailgate dropped and two men, one in the black garb of a priest, began tugging at the feet of the body to Archie's right.

'No!' Archie said. 'Not him, he's not dead.'

'You sure?'

'He's just unconscious.' He felt among the dirty rags for the man's wrist. There was no pulse. 'Actually,' he said, his voice catching, 'I think you may be right.'

A slow procession trundled back out to the lane. It was a while before anyone spoke and, predictably, it was the preacher. 'Bad business, bad business,' he said. Then he smiled brightly, his thin face grey with shock. 'The local bobby wants to question us all, being eyewitnesses of sorts.'

'Yes.' Archie coughed. He had difficulty enough finding his voice, leave alone conversation. There must have been a dozen or more bodies, people who had set out this morning on a journey, who would never reach their destination. Carts and carriages passed, carrying shocked and grieving relatives and friends, most of them with injuries. They would be billeted nearby. It seemed the entire village was opening its doors to strangers. 'But, the bobby – I would have thought it was more than one man could manage on his own.'

'They'll have policemen up from London, I shouldn't wonder. Or down from Chelmsford.'

Archie thought, with sudden clarity, *Tyrell and Beckett and a few of the others will be up there already, booked into the Swan Hotel.* He was supposed to meet them there, ready for Maggs' trial that was scheduled to start in the morning. He should try and get word to them.

'I don't suppose they'll know where to find us…'

'The doctor's left word at the – at the *site,* apparently. That was his trap behind us. He lives out this way, too.' The preacher frowned. 'He *did* tell me his name.' His parchment-like fingers twined together as if for another prayer. Did God ever intervene, Archie wondered, particularly in something so trivial as a doctor's name? 'Now what was it? Mac something – McGill, Macrae? I – I can't seem to…' He gulped, then leaned across Archie and tapped their driver on the shoulder. 'Excuse me – *where* did you say we're going?'

'Gifford Lodge,' the man tossed back at them, against the wind in the trees, the trotting hooves and creaking wheels. 'Not long now.' Long Essex vowels, Archie noted, but the consonants were pronounced, the aspirates sounded. 'Educated,' his mother would have observed, having been a teacher before she married his father, the Welsh butcher.

The clergyman confirmed that this was no country yokel driving them. 'This gentleman says he heard the sound of the boiler exploding from two miles away,' he informed Archie. 'Came down to see if he could help.' He turned back to the driver. 'Sorry, I know you told me but I—'

'Gifford, Richard Gifford.'

'Oh. Same as the – you own the, em…'

'Gifford Lodge has been in the family since my grandfather took on the tenancy in the twenties.'

'Ah. Well, I must say – and I'm sure I speak for this young man – it's very good of you to give us succour.'

'*Succour?*' He seemed to find this amusing.

'Like the Good Samaritan.'

'Not at all. My wife and I are rattling around like peas in a bucket since our children left home. We have the room, why shouldn't we give crash victims "*succour*"? And we're not the only ones shoving up to make room. All the villagers want to help.' He shook the reins, clucked the pony. 'How are you doing, young man? Not jogging you about too much?'

'No, no, I'm fine, thank you, er, Mr Gifford.'

'I'm so sorry, young man,' the clergyman addressed Archie. 'Didn't catch *your* name.'

He told them.

'And I'm Geoffrey Norris,' he said. 'Methodist preacher from Tottenham. Itinerant, you would say, like a gypsy. I was just off to my next port of call: Saint Stephen's in Colchester, for Easter, putting up at my sister's for a couple of nights. I may have mentioned that already,' he said to the driver. 'I'm a bit of an old windbag. You'll have to forgive me.' He gave a nervous hiccup, meant as laughter. Mr Gifford nodded affably. 'I don't know how I'm to get to Colchester by nightfall. My sister won't know what to do if I'm not at the station at six. Is there a coach or bus I can take?'

'Not tonight, sir, I'm afraid. In any case, you're in no fit state to travel.'

'But it's imperative—'

75

'They'll announce the crash at Colchester railway station when news gets through.'

'Do you think so? Oh dear, she'll be so worried and I have to get word to Saint Stephen's.'

'And tell Information where survivors can be found.'

'Can you get a message to her tonight? Mrs Hilda Sutton of Brierly Road.'

'There's always the telegraph. If you write down what you want to say I'll get someone to take it to the post office.'

'Oh dear, she'll be – she doesn't like telegrams. They're always bad news, but I suppose—' His exhalation of defeat held more pain than a mere sigh. 'Oh.' He gulped. 'Oh well.'

Archie thought that was what he would do too. Write a note to Frank Tyrell, care of the Swan Hotel.

The rutted ground gave way to a smoother driveway, the line of trees to a blackthorn hedge in bloom. When they reached a turning circle, the minister touched Archie lightly on the arm with the toe of his boot and, when he'd gained his attention, rolled his eyes. Archie got the impression all was not lost.

A couple of sturdy lads came round the side of the house to help. Their boots were muddy, their hands ingrained with dirt as they unbolted the tailgate. ''Ave a care, Dick, they'm in a right owd state,' one said. 'Easy does it, gen'l'men – gaw', ee seen some trouble this day, en'ee?'

Archie tried to ease himself up but his leg wouldn't cooperate. He leaned on his elbows. He did feel rough: bruised in every part, his right leg singing with pain, though his foot was numb. The same doctor who had tended him on the train appeared at the front door, wheeling a bath chair.

'What happened to the burns case?'

'He didn't make it, Duncan,' their host informed him, dropping the reins and climbing down. 'We left him at the church.'

'Oh.' The doctor covered his despairing sigh with the fingertips of both hands. 'I said we shouldn't have moved him.' Shaking his head, he wheeled the bath chair to the back of the cart.

The preacher took the opportunity to whisper in Archie's ear. 'The doctor came on ahead, he and the girl – brought another casualty back in their trap.'

Archie nodded. His head felt most dreadfully heavy, now that his neck had to bear its weight. He lay back down. He couldn't be bothered to pay attention to this annoying old man, who was now fussing that he didn't need a bath chair. He gave in, however, without a noticeable fight, sitting fiercely upright and putting his hand over the eye that seemed to be giving him trouble.

One of the lads saw to the horse while Gifford and his wife, who introduced herself as Lilian, very gently helped Archie down from the cart, mindful of the strapping on his leg and averting their eyes from his torn trouser-leg flapping in the wind, displaying ragged winter combinations. Gifford, he saw, was carrying his other boot. Though they invited him to lean on them, he tried to take his own weight, hopping and dragging his foot and wincing with pain. Both his supports were slenderly built, and he was a head and shoulders taller than either of them.

Richard Gifford had the face of a hunting bird: aquiline nose and deep-set eyes with long salt-and-pepper hair tied back in the old way. His ruddy complexion spoke of an outdoor life. Auburn-haired Lilian was about the same age, with wind-burned cheeks. Her brow was furrowed.

'Oh dear, oh dear, what a terrible thing!' she mourned, her bony hand trembling under Archie's elbow. 'It just never occurred to us.'

'Sorry?'

'*Lilian*—' The man's voice was sharp as flint.

'Aren't we to blame, though, Richard?' she insisted. 'Was it not negligence on our part? Allowing trees to grow so close to the line. We could be cast as the villains of the piece.' She bit her lips. 'They worked so hard to clear the land, the navvies, all those years ago. Some died making the line safe, sinking piers in the marsh, building viaducts and digging tunnels and – and we've let them down. The trees were seeds blown on the wind, those sycamores seed everywhere, and we, we paid them no mind.'

'The railway owners are responsible for the maintenance of the line, not us. Wouldn't you say so, Mr Price?'

He shrugged agreement though he was hardly listening, wondering when he could write the telegram. He was never going to be able to testify in court tomorrow. He'd let poor Tomkins down, and Tyrell. All of them. Without warning, he found himself shaking, on the verge of tears.

His human props paused to exchange pitying looks. The woman, rubbing sympathy into his arm, murmured, 'It's all right, dear, you're in shock…'

Archie glanced down at her as he straightened. It might have been his mother speaking. She too had a soothing contralto voice, though Eliza Price had stubbornly retained her London accent through forty years among the Welsh, and Mrs Gifford spoke with a faint Essex twang. His mother was taller than this woman, but she was also a fading redhead. Archie took his looks and height from her.

He explained where he should have been, and they assured him that they would see to it. His friend at the Swan Hotel – Mr Tyrell? – would get his news soon enough.

The burden lifted, he could look around, get his bearings. Beyond the old house and this turning circle were the outbuildings, barns and sheds of a farm. He could smell animal dung and hear the lowing of cattle and a raucous cockerel stretching its neck. Functional ploughed fields and pastures dotted with cows and horses and their young spread all around. Thick hedgerows, encrusted with white blossom, hemmed the fields with stitchwort embroidery – his fingers itched for paper and pencil. The farmhouse itself must have been built hundreds of years ago. It was a timber-framed, brick and thatch hulk, with mullioned windows and studded Gothic doors, standing four-square and surveying the seasonal growth with quiet complacency. A ginger tom stretched its front paws and jumped off a windowsill into wild garlic.

The house was of the enduring kind, built to last. Trees on the railway line, modern disasters, were of no consequence.

He frowned, trying to think. There was something he'd missed, something odd. But his brain was a mishmash. It was too hard to try and organise his thoughts.

He concentrated on putting his best foot forward and hopping on the other. He just wanted to reach a place where he could sit down, anywhere.

'Let's get you settled in,' Lilian said, reading his mind.

Archie recognised, when Lilian lifted it, his old carpet bag. Poor thing, it had seen better days: threadbare in places, spotted and streaked with paint, with darned patches that bore testament to Lizzie's needlework. She had sewn a strap to the sides so that he could sling it across his shoulders. The original handle was fingerprinted with dried paint. It smelled disgusting, of oil and turpentine and something like stale socks. 'You're an artist, are you, Mr Price?' Her hand flew to her mouth. 'Oh. They said they'd found an easel and, oh dear—' She glanced at his leg. 'I believe they broke it up to make your splints. Don't worry, we'll fix it. Is this wooden box yours?'

He shook his head. No, going on the shape, that box was more likely to contain a collapsible field camera than paints. Whose was it, he wondered? Was Reverend Norris interested in photography?

The Giffords had been very thorough in a very short time, providing a haven for injured and traumatised crash victims, taking responsibility for their luggage and their peace of mind.

As Archie made to take his bag from her, her husband said, 'Leave it, Mr Price. Maud will take the things to your room. That's your suitcase, is it, the smaller one?' At the mention of her name, a buxom maid in a cap and apron appeared, bobbing a curtsey. 'We'll put you on the ground floor to save your leg. Is the bed made up in there, Maud?'

'Nearly finished, Mr Gifford, sir.'

Lilian handed her the bag of art materials, while she went to attend to other business. Archie ducked under the lintel and, as his hair brushed the ceiling, was aware that the house had been built for smaller people. His host helped him down the corridor to his room.

Inside was an iron-framed bedstead with brass fittings, flower-sprigged curtains at tall casement windows, a writing desk, a washstand with ewer and basin, and, most pleasing, a plump and sprawling armchair beside a newly lit fire. 'It gets a mite chilly on this side of the house,' explained the maid, but he was hardly listening. His legs folded under him, and he collapsed into the chair's soft embrace. Gifford got down on his knees to unlace and remove Archie's remaining boot.

'Oh, please don't,' he begged. 'I can do that.'

'I doubt it.'

It was true. Archie bent his head, and cymbals clashed, drums rolled, and the room flitted past his eyes a few times before settling. He allowed his host to ease off the boot, exposing a malodorous sock knitted by Mam and seldom washed. A big toe peeped through a hole. Archie was mortified. Gifford made no comment.

While Maud pottered about, dumping his bags, arranging his boots under the table, removing pillowcases and towels from a cupboard, and putting the finishing touches to the bed, Gifford helped him off with his greatcoat and hung it on the back of the door.

'Now I'll leave you in peace. There are drawers and cupboards for your things, and Maud will fetch you some soup and bread to be going on with. Just ring the bell if you need anything.' He indicated a bell pull beside the bed. 'And don't worry about the telegram. I'll see to it personally. Now Doctor MacKay prescribes complete rest, so if I were you, Mr Price—'

'Archie…'

'And you must call me Richard. Now, if I were you, Archie, I'd hop right into bed.'

When he woke it was dark. He was still sitting in the armchair, now with a cushion behind his head and a footstool under his stockinged feet. He did not recognise the socks. His leg, he noticed, was now encased in shaped wood, two sides fitting his calf and shin and bound with clean bandages, while the easel supports leaned wearily against the windowsill, having served their purpose. A small table and oil lamp had appeared beside him, and in the lamp'a soft light sat a plate of sandwiches, another of cake, a pot of tea (still warm under its cosy), a cup and saucer, teaspoon, milk jug, and sugar basin. The shutters were closed. Leaning against the chair was a pair of crutches for *his* use, he realised with a start. People must have come and gone all night without disturbing him. Such kindness…

When he next opened his eyes the shutters had been folded halfway back, allowing fingers of sunlight to poke through. His face and scalp were sore to the touch, and when he moved his head, every bone, every vertebra, his very skull seemed to creak. He was still in the chair. Someone had put more coal on the fire, with tongs presumably, because he hadn't heard them. Lord, he felt rough. But he had to relieve his aching bladder. He heaved himself up and staggered to the bedside, cranking himself down to where the chamber pot discreetly winked. Although he could bend his knee – just – his ankle was in a wooden brace and movement was difficult.

'Just a minute,' he called out a minute later, when a knock came at the door. He'd had to urinate into the pot while sitting on the bed.

'If you'm done, I'll clear away, sir.' It was a young man's voice.

'Clear away?' Now he noticed that last night's sandwiches and cake had been replaced with eggs in china cups, a rack of toast, butter, and a jar of jam. The teapot was wearing a different knitted cosy. 'Em…'

'Thomas, sir.'

'Give me a few minutes, would you, Thomas?' He was famished.

The young manservant returned as Archie was about to pour his second cup of tea. Of middling height, the lad was simply dressed, not in any sort of servant's livery. Straw-coloured hair was slicked back from a ruddy face.

'I'll do that for ee, sir,' he said, his brawny hands fastening around the teapot. 'You'm meant a be a-bed.'

'There's no need,' Archie protested.

'Oh, I don' know 'bout that, sir. Doctor reckons you'm to stay there for a few days. You'm bin right knocked about. He'll be in presently to check on ee.'

'He's here already?' When he consulted his pocket watch he found it wasn't as early as he'd thought. Just five minutes shy of ten o'clock.

'Ay, sir. He'm upstairs wi' the young lady.'

'Young lady?'

'Miss Anderson, as broke her arm or summat.'

How many invalids did they have in the house? It wasn't that big a building. One or two guest rooms beside their own living quarters? They were really putting themselves out, these good people.

Before the boy left with the breakfast things, he helped Archie off with his clothes and poured hot water from an enamel jug into the washbowl, stropped a razor and mixed up lather in a mug. He was all for helping him shave, but Archie assured him that he could manage on his own. That said, his ablutions seemed to take forever, and he was exhausted before he towelled himself dry and donned a crisply ironed nightshirt. As soon as his head touched the pillow, his eyes closed. An insistent something wanted to tug them open again, but it was no use.

If the doctor looked in on him he did not disturb him.

Thirteen

As Effie MacKay had been standing by to assist her with the camera shot, Polly had had to give the name Florence Anderson to the reporter. He took her slide to the *Chelmsford Chronicle*. Bartholomew Spratt had been travelling on the train, further back, and been stuck in the tunnel for ages, not daring to get out in case the train started off again. He wasn't hurt, he told her, apart from a bruised knee as he fell, and the crash had more than made up for it. What a scoop! A tragedy, but a scoop! And to have a photograph as well! After helping Polly, he sat on the wet grass and wrote his column while waiting for local transport to take him and other uninjured passengers on to Chelmsford. He was very put out that 'they' didn't simply send down an engine from 'town' to pick up the other carriages of the train. What were they thinking? Surely, if they'd simply re-coupled them and towed them away they'd have saved a few score passengers a lot of delay and inconvenience? Apparently, though, someone else told him, the police were refusing to let the guard's van go anywhere. It was a crime scene, they said. 'What crime?' he'd asked, but they wouldn't tell him. Ridiculous, this secrecy!

The *Chelmsford Chronicle* would publish her photo. Their engraver would make it printable, and they would need to know where she was staying, to reimburse her. Effie MacKay told the reporter that Miss Anderson would be staying at Gifford Lodge, Little Nessing, for the next week or two, at least.

Polly's relief to know that her given name would appear in the list of fatalities was immense. When Freddy went hunting for her in Walthamstow, her neighbours would tell him his sister was dead and he'd have to accept it. She would never be bothered by him again.

But she might have known her good luck would not last. When the walking wounded trooped in for high tea on their second afternoon, their hostess let it drop that they had an artist staying with them, an Archie Price, who had been in another compartment and had concussion and an injured leg, which he was presently resting. They hoped that Mr Price would join them for meals when he was feeling better. 'Miss Anderson' choked on her ginger cake.

There could only be one artist called Archie Price, and he knew her. He would betray her. What could she do? Tonight she was safe, but tomorrow?

She tried to lose herself in the teatime clink and chatter, smiling, faking interest in Minister Norris's description of the young man who had shared his lift back to Gifford Lodge. His picture of a well-built Welshman in his late twenties with auburn hair was exactly how she would have described him herself. Perhaps she would have added deep-set, whisky-coloured eyes and a bluff way of speaking. But he didn't seem to have said much to the preacher – he must have been in too much pain. Their hostess told them that Mr Price had been going to Chelmsford to testify at the assizes. He was a police artist, apparently.

Obliged to hawk his wares in the Saturday market to augment his income, Polly added, silently.

Mrs MacKay, the doctor's pretty young wife, pounced on this scrap of information, announcing that she, too, was an artist, self-taught, and that she would welcome a 'real' artist's thoughts on her efforts.

Polly was the only one to spot Effie, the garrulous woman's even more talkative stepdaughter, lowering her eyes to chase cake crumbs around her plate with a fork. Embarrassment had turned her pretty ears pink.

'Do you also paint?' Polly asked the girl.

'I don't,' she said, 'though I do have an interest in photography.

It seems an admirable pursuit for a creative person, who has neither the time nor the patience for painting.' She quickly added, 'Nor the talent, needless to say. I was intrigued, the other day, watching you work.'

'I couldn't have done it without you.'

'It must have been hard with a dislocated shoulder.'

'Your father had fixed it, Effie – it was still painful, but I could have used it, at a pinch. I was lucky to have you. And I had to take the photo, didn't I? If they publish it there will be a cheque in the post soon.' A delicious bubble of excitement made her cup wobble and the tea spill. She put the cup down smartly.

'It's all right,' said the girl. 'It's just a drop and the napkin caught it. It would be a shame to spoil such a lovely dress. Did you have it made or is it off the peg?'

Polly murmured something about a shop in Lewisham. Oh dear, the lies were still flowing. It was shameful. It was also difficult to be consistent. 'Your parents seem very friendly with the Giffords,' she said by way of diversion.

'They grew up together,' Effie explained. 'My mother and Lilian were best friends. Mabel is my stepmother.'

Lilian Gifford beamed across, hearing her name mentioned. 'Yes, she said, 'we were all great friends as children, playing together every chance we could. It was an idyllic time, before the railway came. This part of Essex was a wonderland, particularly in high summer. I remember playing crazy games of hide and seek in the hayricks and having picnics among the buttercups. When we were too hot with running about there was the river to swim in – along with the frogs and dragonflies. And Membury Woods down there,' she waved her arm at the French doors, 'was made for children. We built dens and climbed trees. At the end of summer,' the middle-aged woman put her finger to her lips, pretending to look around for eavesdroppers, 'there were apples to scrump and cobnuts.'

They had all attended the village school until they were fourteen, when Richard was sent off to be turned into a gentleman farmer and Duncan's mother died. His father, the village doctor back then, packed him off to his grandparents in Edinburgh to continue his schooling up there. In time, Richard returned from agricultural college to take over the reins at Gifford Lodge and, a few years later, married his childhood sweetheart, the schoolteacher's daughter. 'Me!' she said, with an air of triumph.

Duncan qualified as a doctor, came back to help his father in his practice, and married the fourth member of their childhood gang, Effie's mother, Agnes Olsen. Sadly, her dear friend Agnes had died giving birth to Effie's little brother, who also died, and it was some few years before Duncan could bring himself to look at another woman. But, when Effie was thirteen, the irresistibly sweet and pretty Mabel Dunwoody moved into Little Nessing with her parents, became friends with Lilian through the church, came to tea at Gifford Lodge, and met and bewitched the lovely Duncan, who married her and gave Effie two little brothers and a sister to love and spoil.

Effie smiled at this. She clearly had great affection for her stepfamily.

Polly said that she, too, had been an only child, that her father had been a photographer who had died a few years before her mother. That much was true.

Everyone turned to her with expressions of sorrow. 'You poor thing!' said Mrs MacKay. 'All alone in the world.'

Polly put on a brave face and said she was a fully trained photographer, that when her father had died she had taken over the shop. She had been on her way to stay with an old school friend who had married and moved to Colchester.

Effie declared that it was good for a woman to have a profession, to exercise her intelligence and her management skills. She had always helped her father with his patients, she declared, glancing over at him fondly. She was adept at bandaging wounds, she said, lancing boils, rolling pills. She had even extracted a tooth or two.

Wincing, the older women and the clergyman began comparing the merits of oil of cloves as a stopgap cure for toothache. The minister said he had never had a tooth extracted, even though he was partial to a sweetie or two. The Lord had blessed him with good strong teeth. 'Like a horse.' He scrubbed them night and day with a charcoal and clay mixture, the recipe of which he would be happy to share with them. Now his eyes, on the other hand…

Sitting beside Polly, Effie regaled her with stories of children with beads stuck up their noses or in their ears, of barefoot labourers scything off toes.

Polly shuddered, the reference to bare feet having struck a nerve.

'Oh, I'm sorry,' cried the girl. 'I didn't mean to distress you. I was brought up to speak my mind and I'm afraid I sometimes say too much.'

She forced a smile. 'You seem very young to be taking on so much responsibility.'

'Not at all, Florence, I've been helping Papa since I was small, and I shall continue as his right hand for as long as he finds me useful.'

'But you're far too young and – and vulnerable. What if someone doesn't like your diagnosis? Suppose they turn nasty? A girl in a surgery by herself…'

'Oh, I don't do diagnoses, Florence, just run-of-the-mill stuff, if Papa's not there. Things that your mother would do for you, or a nurse – yes, I suppose I'm a nurse, really. When I am properly qualified – and I'm going to begin my studies this autumn – if I have any trouble I'll produce my trusty revolver.'

'Heavens!'

'I'm a crack shot! My father insisted I learn to shoot.'

'One of my stepdaughter's many talents,' Mrs MacKay interrupted with a laugh. Their talk of firearms had infiltrated the general discussion on spiritual healing and made Effie's stepmother nervous. She soon stage-managed the girl onto the piano stool to play for them, a couple of pieces by Schubert and Chopin, played in a choppy, almost military style. The sheet music was on the stand from her last visit.

'Do you play, Miss Anderson?' the doctor enquired as Effie came to the end and returned to her seat. The minister had already dropped off to sleep, a beatific smile on his face.

Oh dear. A young woman of Florence Anderson's standing would be accomplished in all sorts of ladylike pursuits – watercolour painting, embroidery, singing – to entertain company. She may even have had her own music teacher. Polly had to confess that she didn't sight-read at all but could play a few melodies 'by ear' if they could bear to hear those. Certainly they could. So 'My Grandfather's Clock' got an airing, along with 'Marching Through Georgia', 'The Camptown Races' and 'The Londonderry Air'. Not the most sophisticated repertoire in the world, but they all seemed to enjoy singing along, and even the minister woke up to join in 'Silver Threads Among the Gold'.

That night, Maud, a plump, good-natured girl, undid the buttons on the fine wool dress and, as Polly stepped out of it, asked if she would like it sponged and pressed. Such luxury! Two days ago, the police had released Florence Anderson's trunk and Maud had unpacked for her, putting away whalebone corsets, bustle supports, silk petticoats, camisoles and bloomers in the chest of drawers, with lavender bags, and hanging up all the fashionable dresses and jackets in the big wooden trunk. Polly had found it hard to hide her surprise and delight.

Among Florence Anderson's luggage were three hatboxes containing frothy concoctions Polly had only seen before in shop windows, and there were all sorts of accessories and toiletries. There wasn't much call for pretty things on a farm, but Polly wouldn't be staying here much longer, she was sure. Her injuries had been slight, and she would soon be well enough to go home. She had taken Effie's words to heart. A gun was the answer to a girl's problems. She would purchase one as soon as she could. With a revolver in her pocket, she could keep all predators at bay. No need to go further into the Essex countryside to 'lose' herself. The rural life didn't suit her. Pigs, cows and chickens were best served with potatoes and gravy.

'The missus en't one for dressing up, 'cepting for church,' Maud said, brushing out the complex hairstyle she'd given Polly that morning. 'Not like her girls. They liked me to try out the new hairdos they see in the magazines. It's nice to 'ave another lady to do for.' Polly had never been one to fuss over her appearance, and was pleasantly surprised by what corsets, fine clothes and a lady's maid could achieve. Staying at the farm was more a holiday than a convalescence, and, although she felt like a malingerer, she would take what perks were on offer. Besides, her shoulder still hurt if she sat for too long. Her head wasn't quite right yet. There was a lump at the back and she still had dizzy spells and bad dreams.

In the trunk Maud had also found Florence's books. Did madam want to have them beside her bed or on the bookshelf? There were freshly bound novels by the American lady, Louisa May Alcott, as well as older copies of novels by Harriet Beecher Stowe, Thomas Hardy, Charles Dickens and Arthur Conan Doyle.

'On my bedside table, if you wouldn't mind, Maud.'

She could hardly contain her eagerness. The best she'd had at home were penny dreadfuls she'd read to a bedridden mother, night after night. She was starved of good literature. What a luxury! She made a start on *Uncle Tom's Cabin* straight away and was soon engrossed in the trials of the poor black slave at the mercy of the vicious plantation owner, Simon Legree. Thank God that sort of slavery, at least, was a thing of the past, and Englishmen and women were educated to believe that no man could own another. People were not property. Servants and labourers were paid for the work they did, of course, not very much, perhaps, with room and board thrown in, but they were free agents to come and go as they pleased.

Only wives had no choice. They were supposed to do what they did for love, and Polly rather doubted that things would change very much when and if women were allowed to vote. When she thought how her mother had toiled to keep the house clean, to keep them all fed and clothed, to provide the unpaid labour her father had needed in the shop, when she saw how Lilian drudged about the farm, and kowtowed to her husband, she was determined never to marry. She relished her freedom, such as it was.

This evening though, once Maud had gone, Polly worked up the nerve to look through Florence's personal papers. In a journal which she found at the bottom of the trunk, Florence wrote about a life of sheer idleness – or so it seemed to Polly – endless tea parties, shopping trips, visits to the theatre and opera houses, galleries, and holidays abroad. How could she have been lonely? She seemed to have plenty of friends. Yet she had agreed to become a servant – well, lady companion – to another woman, someone she had met on a recent cruise, to whom she had become singularly attached. She referred to the older woman as Hermione. By this time, Florence should have been installed in Hermione's house in Colchester, making pleasant conversation, playing cards, reading to her, and preparing to travel with her around Britain and Europe, visiting watering holes and making the grand tour.

Florence also had a bank book giving the bearer access to an annual income of two hundred pounds, and a nest egg of eight hundred and fifty pounds that had recently been paid in from the sale of 44 Wyndham Close, Lewisham, London. Polly was aghast. All she had intended to do was take on another woman's identity, not her bank balance.

What would she do with all this money?

If she could perfect signing her name, as Florence M. Anderson had done so neatly on the flyleaf of each of her novels, if she could convince a bank manager that she was one and the same Florence M. Anderson, she would be set up for life and could go wherever she pleased. But first, she must have a word with the painter.

Fourteen

A telegram arrived from Tyrell, lying next to a newspaper on the breakfast tray.

STOP WORRYING BOYO STOP CASE DROPPED STOP EXPLAIN LATER STOP ROOMING AT SWAN HOTEL INDEFINITELY STOP FRANK

Case dropped? Good Lord! Surely his testimony wasn't that important? And why, if the case was dropped, was Frank staying on in Chelmsford? Well, that settled it – Archie would get the train home as soon as he could. He certainly didn't want to go trudging round music halls with his leg in splints looking for work.

He shook out the paper to view a large image of the train disaster. Someone, with an eye to scooping a rich reward, must have delivered the photographic plates to the offices of the *Chelmsford Chronicle* while the police artist was dozing by the fire in his comfortable room in Gifford Lodge. A missed opportunity, Archie. Not good, boyo.

He had to admit it was an impressive view: panoramic and rich in detail – photography at its best.

There was a tentative knock and, thinking it was the maid to take away his breakfast tray, Archie called out, 'Yes, come in!' When he realised whose yellowing skull was pushing round the door, he lowered his newspaper, inwardly groaning.

'Poetic justice of sorts,' the minister said, as he folded his tall frame into the chair beside the bed. 'They've found the rest of your easel, and reckon it can be mended, but they've lost my suitcase, did they tell you?' He presented a droll figure, in an ancient pair of corduroy trousers, several sizes too big, that someone, presumably Richard Gifford, had found in the attic. They smelled of mothballs. He sat clutching his wire-framed spectacles, with a piratical eyepatch over one eye. 'Sent it to the wrong house, I expect,' he sighed. 'Mustn't complain, but it did contain my Bible and daily readings. Mrs Gifford has kindly loaned me one of hers, but it's not the same. Mine is annotated and is very dear to me. O-ohh,' his sigh was deeply felt, 'it's all sent by the Lord to try us, I suppose.' He templed his long, tapering fingers. 'Well, my boy, look at you, with your leg in splints. I'm disappointed. I fully expected to see you at breakfast this morning.'

Archie shrugged. 'The doctor insisted I stay in bed,' he said. 'I've been concussed, he says.' He told the minister how he had been flung about while attached by one foot to the luggage rack, and that Doctor MacKay was surprised his skull hadn't smashed like a boiled egg with a spoon. His leg had been twisted to the point of breaking, and one of the bones below the knee may have been cracked. The Achilles tendon had been stretched abominably, which was why he needed the leg-shaped splints he was wearing now and strapping, to act as a brace. 'Quite unnecessary, I'm sure.' However, he had been advised to rest for a few days. When he felt well enough to get up, he was supposed to try and keep his weight off his leg for a good few weeks. No stairs, no unnecessary walking.

'A few weeks!'

'I know – I can't possibly impose on our hosts for so long. I need to get home, earn some money.' As he shifted in the bed, he groaned.

'Are you in pain, young man?'

Archie's grimace was rueful. 'A little,' he admitted, 'but it's not that. To be honest, I don't have much money. I don't know how

I'm going to repay the Giffords for their kindness, or the doctor's bill, for that matter.'

The grey teeth appeared like a row of lichen-splotched tombstones. 'I understand you're an artist,' said the minister. (Oho, so Archie had been the subject of gossip around the breakfast table!) 'You could offer to paint their portraits. That would be something they might appreciate. Personally, I'd find having to look at myself on the wall every day something of a trial.' He tittered, implying that Archie shouldn't take him seriously, and, in fact, if Archie were to offer to paint *his* portrait…

'It's an idea, certainly. I'll bear it in mind. But how are you doing, minister?'

'Having a bit of trouble with my sight,' he confessed. 'Quite apart from the damage to my specs – a missing lens – I must have hit my head in the crash. I don't remember anything about it. The good doctor says something has come adrift in my eye, the other one, wouldn't you know?' He could read and write only by wearing his spectacles upside down so that the 'functioning' eye got the lens.

'Why don't you change the lenses around?' Archie suggested.

'Change the – oh, do you think that's wise? Suppose…?'

'Give them here,' Archie said. He rolled the telegram into a sturdy tube and used the thin edge to loosen the screw keeping the lens in place. Swapped it over. 'How's that?'

'Oh,' said the clergyman. 'That's perfect. Necessity is the mother of invention, eh?' he snorted without humour. He tapped his eye shield, still in place under the missing lens. 'But I mustn't use this eye. The doctor could give no guarantees, but thought that rest might help.' He had walked down to the village, yesterday, he said, to send wires to the good people of Saint Stephen's in Colchester, and another to the 'superintendent' of his diocese regretting that he could not preach there this Sunday or for a good few Sundays to come. 'And I sent one to my poor sister, who must be frantic with worry.

'It's not much more than a glorified crossroads, is Little Nessing,' the old man prattled on, 'but quite picturesque. There's that rather nice church we passed, Saint Andrew's. The, em, the deceased have all been taken away now. There are a dozen or so farm workers' cottages, clustering around a village green. There's a public house, of course, the Crown, and there's a school, a smithy, and this rather quaint little shop, selling everything from paraffin to postal orders. And newspapers, though not necessarily the current issue.'

'Yes, this is yesterday's,' said Archie, indicating the one on his bed. 'They're not very clear as to the cause of the crash.'

'You mean whether it was an accident or an act of sabotage?'

'Sabotage? You mean someone deliberately—?' It hadn't occurred to him. 'Surely not? That's terrible.'

'Well, if the mudslide was not an act of sabotage, Mr Price, it must have been what they call an act of God. And He must have struck minutes before the train was due, which shows an appalling sense of timing, even for Him.'

'That's rather cynical for a man of the cloth.'

'Not at all. I'm simply saying that perhaps the Lord is being blamed for something that wicked men did.'

'Have you *seen* the papers, the sketch they did. Did you notice how close that tree was growing to the tunnel exit? The preceding train, rumbling through the tunnel, could easily have shaken the tree loose. God doesn't come into it, nor wicked men.'

'Or a loose tree is a gift for saboteurs.' The long bony nose turned towards the door as though sniffing out someone listening. He leaned forward and Archie caught a strong whiff of eggy breath. 'You know their man Thomas – mine of information! Apparently, his brother, em, Edgar or Edwin, the stable lad at the big house up the road—' The older man scratched his scaly pate. 'Elder something? A tree of some sort. Elm? Elmscott Hall? No, Elmscott Place.' He nodded. 'Large estate encompassing all the land around here, two or three villages. Anyway, this lad was

94

giving a hand clearing the line, yesterday, and found a place high up on the fallen tree where a rope had been tied and pulled, damaging the bark, breaking twigs, scuffing branches. And, further back along the line—' He drew an invisible railway line with his fingernail on Archie's eiderdown. 'Further back,' he repeated, 'where the tree and muck had *originally* fallen, because, of course, the engine pushed the tree a good few yards before it derailed—' He paused to take an almighty breath. 'Further back,' he said again, 'they found signs of *activity*! Prints of horses' hoofs and other, you know, signs – manure and what have you, several piles, in fact.' He cleared his throat. 'Now, I ask you, Arthur—'

'Archie,' he said automatically.

Norris regarded the invalid with his one mad eye. 'Archie – I ask you – riders on horses, dragging trees down with ropes? What does that tell you?'

'They may have seen the tree overhanging the tunnel and tried to pull it down, remove it, before the train came – but miscalculated.'

'And realising the devastation they'd caused, they're now keeping their heads down? Yes, that's a possibility. I think it more likely that these were simply village louts, spotting an opportunity for vandalism.'

'Surely not? I mean, to *deliberately*—' Lord, it beggared belief.

The old man shrugged. 'They probably didn't foresee such dire results.'

The old man was dangerous, spreading such rumours. 'Has Thomas's brother mentioned this to the police?'

'Naturally. He, the village policeman, told him to keep it to himself for the time being.'

Until he is sure of his facts, he assumed. 'So Eddie tells Thomas, who tells complete strangers—'

'You can't blame the lads, Arnold, they don't get much excitement out here.'

'That's no excuse.' His head was thumping like a piledriver.

95

The old man inclined his head. 'You mark my words, Arthur. That was no accident.'

When his visitor left, Archie lay back on his pillows, his forehead creased, his eyes squeezed shut. There was some scratchy little something beyond the headache, at the back of his brain, something connecting to the minister's revelations.

What could he remember of the journey immediately before the crash? It was like walking into a room and finding you've forgotten why you came. It's no good, all you can do is retrace your steps till you remember.

So, thinking back, there'd been mile on mile of wet cow parsley dancing by in the rush of the train. 'Queen Anne's lace' they called it back home, for its delicacy and its pretty white tracery. Like Lizzie's bridal veil three years ago, he'd thought. He'd pulled out his sketchpad and pencil, his preferred way of killing time and blinked away the tears. No, he wouldn't draw her again. Not here. Allowing for the jolt and jiggle of the train, dark tunnels, and incoming and departing passengers at stations, Archie had given himself up to lightning sketches of platforms, porters, signal boxes, distant woods and wild acres, voluminous skies, farmland, and fields where cattle sat stoically waiting out the rain, or carthorses hauled ploughs through the wet curds of heavy soil. Towns and villages flashed past at forty miles an hour – too fast, too fast – and eventually, he'd given up and simply stared, committing his impressions to memory.

He'd noted a farmhand, leaning on a gate, a dog in a yard, yapping at the train, a single magpie on a fence, harbinger of sorrow, a blur, and then the long tunnel and thick smoky darkness, a deceptive cocoon. There'd been no preparation at all for the shattering streak of daylight at the other end, the nerve-splitting shriek of brakes, and oblivion.

Go back, go back. What was that – that something he'd seen just before the ear-stopping plunge into the tunnel? Colour, was it, or movement? What?

Something by the track. People.

Whoosh…

Go back, go back again.

Three men, maybe four. Were they the vandals Norris had talked about? What were they doing? Standing, simply standing at the side of the track. Railway employees waiting to continue some sort of track maintenance? Or perhaps they were the men who had brought the tree down, hoping to shift it off the track before the train came along. If so, what were they doing on this side of the tunnel?

Who-o-osh…

He borrowed pen and writing paper and sent a letter to Frank Tyrell, care of the Swan, Chelmsford, describing what he may or may not have seen. He didn't want all and sundry to read this in a telegram, setting hares running. In telegraph-ese, between those STOPs, it would have looked so much more solid than it really was. Four men, in dark clothing, standing in the rain waiting for – for what? The crash? He drew a picture. The faces were shadows under their hats, blank. They'd gone by so quickly. Too quickly for him to remember details.

Other letters went to Clara, his little stepdaughter in Clapton, to Ida Sutton whose wedding he had missed, and to various music halls advertised in the *Chelmsford Chronicle,* including the Variety Playhouse in Chelmsford itself. He sent lightning sketches of artistes they should have heard of, the likes of Dan Leno, Marie Lloyd and Little Tich, that he'd done as posters for Percy Reeves. He got Thomas to post them.

Trying to recall the features of the men he'd seen kept him awake at night, and when he did, eventually, manage to drop off, nightmares of the crash woke him again. His cries brought anxious knocks on the door.

'You awright in there, sir? Anything I can do for ee?'

But there was no sleeping draught the doctor could give, no

old wives' remedy that Lilian or Maud or Norris could suggest that had any effect on the nightly visions of screeching metal and screaming people, the lung-puncturing feeling of being helplessly flung about with bags and suitcases, lengths of knitting, books and papers. Dogs and cats and even birds flew by, and stranger things: Whistler's mother in her chair, a butcher's boy on a bike, Lizzie stirring a saucepan, Bertha's beads…

Awake and wet with perspiration, his trapped heart rattling at his ribcage, his leg aching worse than ever, he tried to draw what he'd seen. It might act as a sort of catharsis, telling his brain that yes, this had happened but it was manageable. He drew scraps of dream or memory, like a student's mindless scribblings in the margins of an exercise book, adding some cross-hatching, curls and squiggles to give the impression of movement, panic, fear.

He filled one page after another. Flying objects were all over the place, higgledy-piggledy, overlapping, at odd angles, topsy-turvy, back to front. But that was how it was.

And he still had the nightmares.

Of course, he told himself, he was limited by pencil. The reality and the nightmare were not black and white. He really needed to paint, but what would he paint on? Paper was of no use with oils.

The next day Thomas found him several large flat pieces of wood in an outhouse that had been cupboard doors. Primed with whitewash they were perfect for painting on. Then the dear fellow mended the easel. He screwed on some new hinges he found in a drawer and set it up beside the bed so that Archie could sit to paint.

Wood was a new medium for him. Primed, there was no surface resistance and the easy flow of the paint gave him enormous pleasure. It was almost sensuous. This was painting in a very different way, there being no image to copy, except the one in his head. If he didn't like the way a particular hand opened or closed he could paint over it. If he wasn't happy with the way a book juxtaposed a bag or brolly he could move it, play with it, until he had a composition to his liking. He could paint in whatever colour he liked, with whatever thickness of brush; he could highlight and shade, add perspective when he felt it was called for. He could look at a suitcase from two different angles and paint them both. One form seemed to inspire the next and the painting grew almost organically. Colours blended or clashed as his mood dictated. This was artistic licence gone mad.

His brain was teeming with far too many images for one picture alone. When he had covered one cupboard door, he signed it, dated it, and started on another.

Fifteen

The weather improved. It was still cold but sunny. Narcissi and hellebores appeared in the garden outside his window. Archie put on last Christmas's thick Welsh sweater and scarf under his faithful old painting smock and, with crutches, hopped from his room, up the corridor and onto the terrace, out of the wind. Thomas brought the easel and Archie's bag of paints, and the artist sat for two hours, undisturbed, bringing his nightmares to life.

He became aware of Maud staring wide-eyed at his painting from behind the closed glass doors. When she met his eyes she gave a nervous smile and came through with coffee and biscuits.

She cleared her throat. 'That what it were like on the train, Mr Price?'

'Something like. I've not quite got it yet.'

'Oh, I would say you 'ave, sir. It's terrifyin'. Things flyin' about, and people gettin' hurt.' She whispered, '*Dying…*' She took a deep breath. 'And the ol' train turnin' over and over. I ent never seen nothing like it.'

He stood back, trying to see it with her eyes, telling himself he shouldn't be surprised that she had been moved by his picture. She was a sensitive little soul. Several times she had anticipated his needs and turned his pillow, brought in bedsocks, cups of cocoa, books, a jug of spring flowers without being asked. And she was right about his painting. It was different from anything in the galleries – too different, perhaps. It would never make him famous. He was, he actually was, working out his own feelings – fear, pain, helplessness – in paint.

Good.

Last night he had slept better, only waking once. That may have been because he was working again and was properly tired, or it may have been the cathartic effect of painting out his trauma.

He drank his coffee and looked up when a young woman sat at the table beside him. The girl from the room upstairs?

'You've caught it exactly, Mr Price.' She gestured with her cup.

'Oh, of course, you were there. Travelling on the train.'

'In the next compartment to yours, with Minister Norris.'

He put down his brushes and palette. Gave her his full attention. 'Where were you hurt?' What an idiotic thing to say. He was taking longer than usual to come out of his painting trance.

'Um – my shoulder was dislocated – it's better now. My head is still all over the place, though. Your picture – it – it brings it all back.'

He knew her. Knew those eyes, the irises the palest smoke, with perhaps a hint of turquoise; out here in the sunshine her pupils looked like – like frog spawn? He couldn't place her. Perhaps he'd seen her standing on a station platform or something. Hoe Street Station in the rain, but wearing a dowdy old dress, a shawl, and a hat with a veil – very different from now, in her stylish woollen dress with a bustle and white lace collar, her hair braided and waved by the maid, a pretty locket about her throat. 'Of course, it's Miss Porter, isn't it? I hardly recognised you.' His eyes creased against the sun's brightness. 'You look –' He hesitated. 'Different.'

She put down her cup and saucer and put a slender finger to her lips. She looked around, checking for open windows and eavesdroppers. Lowering her voice, even though they were the only people on the terrace, she murmured, 'Mr Price, I am not Polly Porter any more. I have taken the name of a Florence Anderson, who died in the train crash and doesn't need it any more. Oh, don't look so disapproving. Please, hear me out. I know it's wrong, but I also appropriated her travelling trunk. These clothes were hers (we were of a size, luckily), and it is Florence Anderson who now seeks your help.'

'Forgive me,' he frowned, 'I'm not sure I follow…'

'You are the only one here who knows my true identity, Mr Price, and I am begging you to keep my secret.'

'But why? I don't understand.'

'No, you wouldn't,' she said. She paused and took a long, shuddering breath. 'I wonder what you would paint if I told you my story. It's not as dramatic as a train crash perhaps, but dreadful, nevertheless. Life-changing. I think I will find you sympathetic.'

She had certainly caught his interest.

She told him an unhappy tale of a family brought low by an act of kindness. Some twenty years before, Miss Porter's then childless parents, the Hackney photographer Jonas Porter and his wife Adeline, had taken an urchin in off the streets, intending to provide him with a home, an education, and a trade. An act of charity. No sooner had they got Freddy used to sleeping in a bed than Polly was conceived. Poor Adeline always said she didn't know which child was the more trouble, the six- or seven-year-old (they were never sure of his age) or the newborn.

'According to Mother,' Polly said, settling into her story, 'Freddy took forever to learn to eat with a knife and fork and shielded his plate as though someone was to snatch his food away. He screamed at bath time, refused to have his hair brushed, his face washed. And he *hated* wearing shoes. As for using the privy properly…' She threw up her hands. 'Mother told me later that the only way they could get him to do what they wanted was by bribing him with the flash pan.'

'The what?'

'The pan of chemicals you ignite when a photograph is taken. The white flash drew Freddy to the shop in the first place. He loved it. The "fireworks" he called it.'

'I suppose he would. This Freddy is the chap you introduced me to in the market that day?'

'It is.'

She described how Freddy had started his apprenticeship as her father's 'flash boy', holding the tray of magnesium and, at a signal from Jonas, touching it with a lighted spill to create the dazzling explosion. He was a fast learner. By the age of eight, he could clean his teeth, spread dripping on his toast, recite the six times table, and use the bellows camera. By the following year, he had mastered long division, cleaning his boots, opening doors for ladies, and developing and enlarging images in a darkroom – everything he needed, in short, to turn him into a professional photographer and to enable him to 'pass' in civilised society.

'*Pass?*' asked Archie.

'He was still a barbarian at heart, Mr Price. Always will be.' Her tone was bitter. As he grew older, the 'fireworks' lost their attraction; photography became a chore. He wanted action and adventure and went out at night with his old friends from the Roost, the rooftop slum on the Hackney Road where he'd been living when Jonas took him in. 'He was never formally adopted. I think, officially, he was Pops' apprentice.' He attended the local board school but tended to fall asleep at his desk after a night on the tiles. He played truant and the school board man was always at the door. 'I remember Pops marching him back when he was still small enough to drag by the ear.' He was always in trouble, making the worst sort of friends. His teachers beat him, but it made no difference. Tuddy, an older man on the Roost, had beaten him black and blue, apparently. By the time he left school at thirteen, he was out of control. 'My parents couldn't cope – he ran rings around them.'

He found it impossible to obey rules or to believe in their love and loyalty. He was violent, abusive, broke their furniture in fits of temper and frustration; he stole, lied and cheated, came and went as he pleased. Things were pretty bad when Polly was growing up, but after her father died (of a broken heart, her mother always said), they were worse. Freddy, now a young man, was a law unto himself, bringing home his awful friends, treating his mother and sister like slaves. 'He did as he pleased.' She took a deep breath. 'My poor mother tried to kill herself.'

'No!'

'She threw herself in front of a train at the level crossing. It knocked her aside, but she was badly injured, losing the use of her right arm completely. A nasty bang on the head disfigured her and affected her in – in other ways.' Her eyes looked inwards, replaying dire memories.

Lord, thought Archie, this sounded horrible. To be desperate enough to want to end your life, and then to mismanage it and to have to live with the consequences! Poor woman. Poor *women,* both of them. His heart went out to them.

'She needed constant looking after,' said Polly, 'and she wore me out. She was a heavy woman, and moving her from her bed to the commode, or to the wheelchair to take her to the shop, was exhausting. I had to work – it was our only source of income. I couldn't leave her at home with *him*. He, well, he was unkind to her. Hard times…' She ran her finger round the rim of her coffee cup, before lifting salty eyes to his. He could see she was preparing herself to tell him something awful.

'One morning – I'd just taken Mother her breakfast, I remember – Freddy dragged himself through the front door, in a bad way, blood soaking his coat. "Quick, shut the door," he said, in a state of real fear. "If anyone asks, you haven't seen me." I thought there'd been a gang fight. It wouldn't have been the first time I'd had to pick up the pieces.

'He was lucky to be alive, he told me. He'd been seeing some woman whose husband had come home unexpectedly and attacked him with a knife. He'd managed to escape via the bedroom window, climb down the wall and away. I took that with a pinch of salt, seeing his bulging pockets and the sack over his back, but you didn't argue with Freddy unless you wanted a fat lip. I cleaned him up as best I could, sewed up the wound in his

104

shoulder and put him to bed.

'The next day I saw in the paper that a Colonel Wilfred Culpepper and his wife, on the other side of town, had come home from a regimental dinner and disturbed a burglar in their bedroom. The old soldier had lunged at the intruder with his cavalry sword and pierced his shoulder, but had been wounded in turn, with a knife. His wife described an intruder of about twenty, with regular features and bare feet, who had made off through the bedroom window with a haul worth at least a hundred pounds.

'Freddy stayed in bed for a week, Mr Price, in a fug of cigarette smoke, waiting for the fuss to die down and it did, eventually, as old Colonel Culpepper recovered. But Freddy made the most of it: "Fetch this – empty that – get my breakfast, dinner, tea – go round the corner for a jug of ale, half an ounce of baccy…" I was running around after him, trying to look after Mother and keep the shop ticking over, taking and developing photographs to put food on the table, cleaning the house – I was exhausted. When he wanted me to take a package round to Tuddy Skinner, his mentor, I dug my heels in. He knew I couldn't stand the man. Tuddy … he took liberties.

'"Do it yourself, you lazy toad!" I said. "You're not getting me mixed up in your shady deals!" I knew it had to be some valuable trinket from the Culpepper robbery that he wanted Tuddy to turn into cash. When I refused, he knocked me to the ground with his good arm.'

'The devil!' cried Archie. 'And did you go to this, this Tuddy?'

'Eventually, yes, when I came round.'

'My God! He knocked you unconscious!' She nodded. 'And did he, this Tuddy, did he, em, molest you?'

She turned away.

'But you should have gone to the police!' he cried.

'I did, but not for that. They'd have said I'd brought it on myself, asked for it, knowing what the old man was like. No, I – I told them about Freddy. Shopped him. Not the sort of thing a girl does to her brother, but I was past any sense of loyalty, Mr Price. I told them where to find him and that the loot was either under his bed or at Tuddy's or in Busy Leslie's pawnshop on Commercial Road. And I took Mother round to the shop while they did what they had to do.

'At the trial, Freddy was convicted of robbery with violence and packed off to Pentonville Prison for ten years. The trouble was, Mr Price, they released him early.' Tears threatened again and she swallowed them quickly. 'He found me, by accident, the other day in the high street. I don't think he knows about my new shop, but it won't be long. Mr Price, when the 8.39 drew into Hoe Street Station that morning, I couldn't get aboard fast enough. I didn't know where I was going, just that I had to get away from him.'

'But your shop, it's untended – you must have left valuable equipment behind, besides all your furniture?'

'I know, I know,' she mourned. 'The cameras are irreplaceable, particularly the studio camera. It was Pops'. The prints it produces are so sharp, distinctive, you know, even in sepia. But it was far too big to bring with me.'

'I thought I saw a camera among the baggage, when we first arrived.'

'Not a studio camera.'

She studied Archie over the rim of her cup. 'That picture in the *Chelmsford Chronicle* – the one of the wrecked train – I took that with Pops' old Hare field camera,' she said with obvious pride. 'Effie MacKay, the doctor's daughter, acted as my helper, in lieu of a left arm.'

'It was you! Excellent work!' He was aware of his lukewarm smile. He couldn't rid his head of the images of all the poor girl had been through. He changed the subject, saying that in the bottom of his suitcase he had a small Kodak camera of his own, a wedding present from Lizzie. She'd thought he could use it to take photographs of his models, to refer to if they couldn't make a sitting – a good idea had it worked.

'You wouldn't do me a great service, Miss Porter?'

'No, no, Mr Price, please, I'm Florence Anderson now. I've told the lie and must stick with it. I know it's despicable, and I'm not proud of myself, but it's too late now to tell them the truth. Perhaps you could call me Florence, or Flo, if that's easier. Florence is a bit, em, formal, isn't it?'

'Flo, then. And I'd be glad if you called me Archie. And don't worry – your secret is safe with me.'

There were tears in her eyes as she beamed her thanks. Poor soul. It must have been so hard for her to tell him, a complete stranger, all those intimate details. She must have been desperate. 'Look,' he went on, 'I've had an idea. Since you're more mobile than I am, I wonder if you'd mind fetching that newspaper, the one with your photo in? And a magnifying glass, if the Giffords have such a thing. Thanks.'

She laughed as he spread the page on the table and examined the photograph with the lens. In fact, two photographs had been cleverly pieced together to make a panorama. 'I didn't have you down as a narcissist, Mr Pri – em, Archie. Are you really looking to see yourself being stretchered out to the Giffords' wagon?'

'I'm not, am I? Oh, I see, you're joking. No, Geoffrey Norris said that someone was behind the crash, that the train was stopped deliberately. I wondered if we could actually see anything.'

'Yes, I've heard his theory. I don't think there's anything, just passengers and helpers of one sort or another. I think any hanky-panky must have happened before.'

'Yes, that's what I think.'

'Of course, there could have been something happening out of sight on the other side of the tunnel.'

'I – I think there was.' And he told her about the flash of humanity he'd seen before the crash. 'As if they *knew*. As if they were expecting something of the sort.'

'You can't remember what they looked like?'

'Sadly, no. I'm beginning to doubt I saw them at all. I can't imagine there are really people who would deliberately cause a rail crash.'

'Oh,' she said, lifting an eyebrow, 'you'd be surprised…'

He turned back to the newspaper. 'Oh, look just here, em, Florence, you can see where the tree was growing, up on this higher ground.' He pointed to a large crater on the wooded embankment, some way back from where their carriage lay scuppered. 'That's where the root ball was torn out.'

'So it must have fallen across the track just *here* originally.' It was her turn to point. 'May I have the magnifying glass, please?'

As they craned over the newspaper Archie was very conscious of her warmth, her perfume – a sweet Lily of the Valley. Lizzie had used it. Had that come from the purloined baggage?

'Just here,' she cried, tapping a finger on the page, next to the track. 'There's certainly a lot of disturbance just here. It's impossible to tell if it was caused by men on horses or by the tree being shoved along by the train.' She chewed her lip. 'If only I'd thought to take a shot from the other side.'

He was about to tell her that no one could think of everything, that she'd done remarkably well. He turned and met her startling eyes, which, like water, seemed to reflect the grey sky.

'What I would like to do now,' she said, very seriously, 'is to go down to the crash site and have a proper look around. It might help answer a few questions, put a few spectres to flight.'

'I'll come, too, if you don't mind.'

'Are you up to it?'

'Possibly not, but I'm going crazy sitting around here. Em, perhaps we can persuade Lilian to come as well.'

'She's a very busy lady, with far too much to do to have to chaperone me, as well.' Good Lord, she could read his mind! 'Besides, Archie, I'm a working girl, well past the need for chaperoning.' Now what did she mean by that? She looked up quickly and saw his frown. 'No, I've always taken care of myself, Archie,' she reassured him. 'But thank you for thinking of it.'

108

Sixteen

Any awkwardness soon dissipated. Polly, or Flo, as he was learning to call her, was good company. He minded that his game leg, even with a walking stick in each gloved hand, restricted his pace and prevented him helping her with her folding camera and tripod. She didn't seem to mind and didn't draw attention to his difficulties, allowing him to go first along the footpath and pottering along behind quite happily.

She was delighted by the cows in the next field, and the wild flowers beside the ditch, wanting to know the name of lady's smock, red campion and stitchwort. 'So pretty,' she cried, clapping her hands like a child, 'like little stars.'

He pointed out the blossoming blackthorn, the real harbinger of spring in his view. 'They'll have sloes here in the autumn. Have you ever tasted sloe gin? My wife used to make it. Sheer heaven!'

She didn't drink gin or any spirits. Their effect on her was immediate, and she didn't like the feeling of being out of control, especially when her brother was around.

Ah, he thought, dead wives and evil brothers... Effective chaperones in themselves.

Just beyond the cow field they came to a swiftly flowing river, which they crossed by an ancient wooden bridge to rising ground with skeletal trees silhouetted against the sky – Membury Woods, according to Lilian. Archie paused for breath. This would need all his willpower and strength. Blasted leg.

They could hear the banging of heavy metal, and the raised voices of the workmen. Further chuffing and clanking suggested some sort of steam vehicle was being used for the really heavy work.

The enormity of the disaster struck each of them all over again. Why were they spared and others not? There seemed no rhyme or reason.

But they hadn't come to examine the progress of the clearing-up operation. When they came to a fork in the footpath, they took the track left through the trees to the other side of the tunnel. They continued on through leaf mould and puddles, skirting ancient tree roots, brambles and ditches, passing foxholes and cheery swathes of celandines and hellebores.

'So many bluebell shoots,' he said, pausing to rest, hoping it wasn't too obvious. 'Another fortnight and the whole place will be a carpet of blue.'

'Really?' she said. 'Bluebells?' He realised that this town girl had probably never seen bluebell woods in her life.

They exchanged greetings with an old woman gathering firewood. Yes, he supposed, the villagers would rely on these woods for fuel and perhaps food as well. There would be blackberries in the autumn, and sloes and crab apples, mushrooms and herbs, if you knew where to look. Not to mention rabbits. Polly – Flo – was enchanted by them, with their noses twitching, eyes wide to the whites, disappearing into bushes and long grass the second Archie and Polly seemed too close.

A couple of hefty black and white pigs were grubbing for beech mast and acorns between the tree roots. Polly gave a little squeal of terror. Lord, thought Archie in a panic, what could he do if they decided that she would make a better meal? What a useless escort he was. To his relief, the swineherd, a young boy appearing from behind a massive oak buttoning his fly, had the porkers on strings. Pigs on the loose could be dangerous.

'Good day!' he called as he came level with the lad. The boy touched his cap and Polly bobbed a sweet little curtsey. The walk was doing her good, he realised.

'Mister,' nodded the boy, 'Missus,' and then, with daring, 'B'ent you they Lunnoners off the train crash?'

They confirmed that they were and that they were staying with the Giffords.

'Lovely day to be out in the woods,' said Polly.

The boy said, 'Best mek the most of'n while us can, missus.'

'Why's that then?'

'His lordship's selling off the woodlands to some furriner.'

'Really?'

It was true, the boy assured them. He had heard the owner of the estate, Lord Beasley, and Farmer Gifford having a 'set to', on this very path. The 'furriner' was going to enclose the woods, chop down the trees and erect tall masts to 'cetch the wind or summat. Mester Gifford were agin' it.'

'I'm pretty sure this Beasley can't do that. Not legally. It's common land,' Archie said after they'd said goodbye to the boy and moved on.

'I met his lordship the other day,' Polly said, 'and the foreigner, an Italian, I think. I doubt the big man gives a tinker's cuss for legality. He seemed very high-handed to me.'

No doubt the boy had some, if not all of his facts wrong, but it wasn't without precedent for unscrupulous people brazenly to clear common land and build houses or fence off fields where their animals could graze. It had taken an Act of Parliament, only a few years before, to save Epping Forest from shrinkage by enclosure, he told her.

'Do you suppose, Archie, that people round here know their rights?'

'Probably not. Many of the older folk are unschooled, probably can't read. They just do as they're told.'

'Surely someone should tell them before it's too late?'

The question continued to occupy them until the trees thinned and they could see the railway lines stretching away into an empty distance. Theirs were the only footprints on this particular path, apart from the prints of small animals and birds. It was a pretty fair guess that the four men Archie had seen so fleetingly had arrived at the line by the road parallel to the railway on the other side. They had only come round to this side of the tunnel, through it, over it or around it, when they had finished their dastardly work further up.

The ground was still damp as they walked down through tussocks of grass. Archie prodded them speculatively with his stick before taking a step. He must look like an old man, he thought dismally, but a slip would do him no good at all.

They had to get round prickly bushes, helping each other, before they could climb over the fence and stand by the track. The police had cordoned off the tunnel entrance with ropes, after the guard's van and the three undamaged carriages had been towed away. The hollow sounds coming from the tunnel now were workmen dismantling the derailed carriage at the other end. There was no longer a police presence and Archie assumed that they had, long since, collected all the evidence they needed, leaving the muddy ground around the roped area mashed and churned. Of course, people would have been milling about here, removing luggage from the guard's van, setting up the cordon, helping passengers down from the last few carriages. It would be impossible to pick out the footprints of any bystanders who had been waiting, anticipating the crash.

He went to the open track and stood with his eyes closed, then open, trying to remember what he'd seen from the carriage: four shadowy men, standing well back from the track against the fence. His sleepless nights hadn't been entirely unproductive: he'd remembered that he had been looking at a church in the distance when his eyes had been drawn to them. Where was it? He wouldn't have been able to see it through these bushes and trees, so he walked up the track about twenty yards until the copse thinned. There! There was a steeple on the horizon, probably Saint Andrew's, in the village, where the train fatalities had been lodged only a couple of hours later. He paused a moment to reflect on life's terrible vagaries.

He realised, of course, his seat in the railway compartment had

112

been another six feet or so higher than his eye level now; he'd have had a far more complete view of the church. But it wasn't from this angle. He walked on ... nor this. This one. One of the men had been sitting on the fence just there. *Just there!* And, as the train went past ... there had been a flurry drawing his eye, distracting him. Something had happened. What? He shut his eyes again. An unexpected movement. The train had rushed past and ... the man's hat had blown off into the open field! It must have happened just about...

'Here!' he shouted to Polly, who'd been examining the track by the tunnel entrance. 'This is where they were when I saw them!' And here, this distance from the main goings on, there was little sign of police disturbance.

It wasn't hard to find the exact place by the fence where they had stood. Grass and flowers were flattened, stems broken and turning into hay. And here someone had knocked out a pipe. Archie patted his pockets, found an old letter and brushed some remaining strands of tobacco into the envelope. It was a long shot but someone might recognise the brand. Here was a cigarette butt, flattened and stained with saliva or rain. He imagined the smoker had worn the cigarette on the wet inside of his lip until it had gone out. He added it to his collection. And there – *there* – were the most beautiful prints of boots, left and right, impressed in the mud. Good old Essex clay. You could see where the tread was worn, down the outside of each leather heel. Looked like the wearer was bow-legged. Here was where the man had sat, transferring mud from his shoes onto the ancient strip of fence when he had hooked his heels over it. Polly pointed out broken bits of twig embedded in it, and a strand of sisal from the rope they'd used. Wouldn't it be marvellous if this was evidence that they'd pulled the tree down? Thank goodness it hadn't rained since the day of the crash or this evidence would have been washed clean away and lost.

'How close can you get your camera?'

'Very.' While she was setting it up, resting it on its own carrying box rather than on the tripod, he ducked through the fence into the field.

So the man had sat there, waiting, maybe emptying his pipe while he had the chance, and then his hat had blown away in the rush of the train. He would have twisted around to go chasing after it, leaving a thread from his coat or trousers on a splinter of wood, perhaps?

No, disappointingly, there was nothing. Of course, the police might have already removed it as evidence. But he had the feeling they had not been this far along the railway line.

Archie figured that the hat would have flown in a two o'clock direction, blown by the diagonal rush of air from the tunnel. Where had it landed? In the grass? In this cow pat? No, but it *had* bowled through it, leaving a brim stripe in the mess. There, look! This one held the imprint of a man's shoe! And it pointed towards – a gorse bush. This was where he had found his hat, all right. Just here, in the grass, was where the man had tried to wipe the green cow shit off his shoe before hurrying back to his cronies. Was he aware that he'd also got it on the rim of his hat? How had he wiped that off? A handkerchief?

He continued searching until he found it. A filthy scrap of paper stuffed deep into the scratchy gorse. And on the paper, something written in pencil – a number perhaps, 11 – almost obliterated by the mess of cow shit.

Should he try and clean it? Better leave it to the police. Carefully, he folded the paper over and put it in the envelope.

'Over here, Flo, and watch out for the cow flops!'

He hadn't been dreaming. There really had been people, waiting at the side of the track, one an older man who had written something on a piece of paper. A number *11*. Perhaps it was the time of the train? *11* something. It would be about right. Lord, what if it was? What if this were real proof that the man was waiting for the train?

Further up the track, hopping between the sleepers, he came upon a crumpled Woodbine packet and a sodden picture card of a pugilist. Whoever had dropped it wasn't a collector. Archie put the finds in his pocket.

He heard a quiet, *'Oh, no…'* from behind, and there was Polly, sunk into a heap between the rails, her skirts concertinaing under her, her face white.

'What? What's the matter, Flo?' He came over.

'Look…' Her finger waggled at something caught on the side of a rail. Something very small. A spent matchstick? 'Archie, I – I think my brother was on that train!'

'What!'

It took some while to convince her that many men did that to matchsticks.

'No,' she insisted, shaking, her eyes full of fear, 'it's his way, his signature. He always does that after he's lit his cigarette, and – and that packet you found – it's his brand.'

'His and thousands of others. For heavens' sake, Polly, you've got to stop this, you'll drive yourself mad. Why on earth should he have been on the train? It's a bit of a coincidence, isn't it?'

'Perhaps he's following me.'

'Why would he do that?'

She confessed that she had not told him the whole story, earlier on. On the day Archie had met him, her brother had given her something to mind for him, ill-gotten gains. She hadn't brought them with her, whatever they were, and, in any case, had given him a false address. But he'd be desperate to have them back and, discovering she wasn't there, might well try to find her.

He tried to put her mind at rest. Her brother probably had no idea she had travelled by train out of Liverpool Street, and, in any case, she was officially dead. If he couldn't find her he'd have to give up, wouldn't he? Eventually, she accepted his proffered hand and rose unsteadily to her feet, but apart from taking a few more photographs of a place under some trees where oats and bran and hoofmarks told of ponies being tied to the fence on the other side of the line, Polly's interest in detective work had waned. She just wanted to get back.

Burdened with dark thoughts and fatigue, their conversation on the homeward path was sporadic and brief. Perhaps the train had been carrying valuable mailbags for the Post Office or bank notes from De La Rue's? Perhaps a famous person had been kidnapped? Perhaps their finds, in Archie's pockets, would help incriminate some robber, now a mass murderer? What if Polly's photographs proved to be decisive pieces of evidence in a court case? She could easily develop them if she could only find an old cupboard or something to be her darkroom: she had brought small amounts of the necessary chemicals in the one suitcase they had salvaged from the wrecked compartment. Her other suitcase was in the guard's van, labelled Polly Porter, and she couldn't lay claim to that.

Slowly they climbed the hill towards Little Nessing, arriving back at the farmhouse as the smell of soup drifted from the open kitchen window. Despite the long walk, neither of them felt particularly hungry.

A small carriage was waiting in the forecourt. The Giffords had visitors.

'Archie, old chap! Good to see you up and about!'

Frank Tyrell sprawled in a wicker chair on the terrace, looking quite out of place in his sporting tweeds. Opposite sat a beaming Stanley, now Detective Sergeant Beckett, wearing a single-breasted grey sack coat and bowler. Very smart. And between them lay two empty coffee cups and saucers and a plate that might once have held biscuits. Gifford explained to the walkers, as they fell gratefully into chairs, that the Walthamstow policemen were here to interview survivors of the crash.

'But I see you already know each other, Archie,' he added.

'All right for some,' said Tyrell, directing his banter at Archie, who, exhausted, propped his lame foot up on a nearby chair and removed his gloves to massage some life into his bruised and aching hands. 'Thought you was supposed to be some kind of invalid! And what do I find? You've gone gallivanting off with a pretty young lady. Yeah,' he said to the others, while Archie rolled his eyes, 'we're old mates, me and Rembrandt here.' He gestured towards the oil-on-wood 'nightmare' painting, still on its easel, glistening in the sun.

'If you didn't want to attend the assizes, you should have said,' Beckett chipped in, with a wink. 'No need to go wrecking trains!'

The convalescents couldn't raise a smile between them, although he was an engaging young chap, Beckett, twinkling with bonhomie and enthusiasm, just lacking tact.

'So you're here at last,' said Archie. His throat was dry and his voice sounded as if it was being dragged over gravel. He coughed. 'I sent that letter ages ago!'

'Couldn't get away, old son. Paperwork.'

Tyrell explained that the train crash was taking up most of their time. While they were in the area they'd been helping the railway police and the Chelmsford constabulary, sifting evidence, taking witness statements from everyone who had been on that journey. His cheeks bulged like peaches in a smile his eyes failed to echo. 'That's our story…' He winked. 'Now then, Arch, aren't you going to introduce me to your friend?'

Must he? Oh Lord, what if they recognised her? Surely they would know the proprietor of the new photography shop in the high street? That would be her secret out of the bag. But there was no hint of recognition in their eyes as he struggled to his feet, leaning on the table to introduce them to the somewhat dishevelled 'Miss Florence Anderson' from Lewisham, who had been on her way to Colchester when the train crashed.

She blanched but, smiling gamely, shook hands with the detectives and, with only a slight tremor in her voice, responded to their enquiry about her health by complimenting Doctor

117

MacKay on how well he had put her shoulder back and the Giffords on their care and hospitality. In answer to their next question, she said that she had seen nothing out of the ordinary prior to the derailment. Her lips quivered.

Don't, urged Archie silently.

She had seen nothing, she said, through the rain on the window of the train compartment, to warn her that, in a few brief minutes, her life was going to be turned upside down, that she would experience unimaginable terror, that she would see people die, people maimed in the most obscene and horrific ways. She had thought she was going to die herself.

'No,' she said, to another question, she hadn't seen any railway signals and, if she had, she wouldn't have known what they meant and what could she have done, anyway?

Her eyes brimmed.

She jerked her pointy little chin towards Archie's picture. 'See that?' she demanded. 'Mr Price was painting it this morning and he has it just about right. The trouble is it wasn't a dream – it was real, it happened.' She shuddered. 'We've just been down there and saw where the people who caused it, who pulled the tree down onto the track, stood callously by and watched it happen. While the carriage rolled over and over, while we were flung about and dead bodies flopped into us, while severed limbs flew about our heads, they were standing on the other side of the tunnel calmly smoking! We were thrown about from ceiling to floor, from wall to wall, banged and broken. People, nice people, died because of a few – I don't know – vandals? No, that's too good a name for them – murderers! Mr Price thinks he can paint it out of his system. My guess is he never will. I know I won't – forget it, I mean. I can't read without ghastly images intruding. I can't eat, can't sleep. My mind is scarred, deeply scarred. And I am never, ever going to travel by rail again!' She was wringing her hands and tears were running unchecked down her face.

Gifford said quietly, 'Maud, take Miss Anderson to her room and make her comfortable, then I'd prescribe tea, hot and sweet.'

The detectives stared after the shivering woman, their expressions registering shock of a different kind.

'Poor show, Frank,' said Archie, his own eyes wet. He wanted desperately to go after the girl, give her a sympathetic shoulder to cry on, but it was probably better not to.

'Yes, I – I reckon I could have handled it better,' Tyrell admitted. He blew 'Sorry' through his moustache and shook his head helplessly. 'I knew it was bad but—' He cleared his throat. 'Poor girl.'

'What did you expect, guv?' muttered Beckett. 'These people have been through hell. They're still in pain.'

'Yeah, my fault,' said Frank. 'Heard so many harrowing stories about the crash, I'm getting hardened. A bad fault and I mustn't do it.' He scowled.

Gifford nodded. 'Tea all round, I think.'

'Mmm. Good idea,' said Archie. 'Probably better if we take it in my room where there's a fire. It's getting rather chilly out here.'

'Of course. I'll get Thomas to bring in your equipment. Good to see you're painting again.' He forced a smile, ever the good host. 'I take it this, em, this,' he gestured towards the easel, 'is an exercise to get the blood moving, as it were? Our friend, Mr Norris, suggested you might like to have a go at Lilian and me. But I hope you don't mind if I opt for a more conventional interpretation, not bloody bits of us thrown against a wall!'

'What you calling it, Archie?' asked Beckett. '"The Butcher Boy's Revenge"?'

The visitors seemed to find laughter cathartic.

Archie found his sticks. They'd given him blisters across his palms, and the struggle to get upright again was painful. He'd overdone it, and so had Polly, poor thing. Too much, too soon. Now he had pins and needles and couldn't bear to put his weight, even a little, on either the damaged leg or the one he'd been favouring all morning.

'Right,' Beckett announced, 'I'll go and get the reverend's version of events, leave you two to catch up. I'll be careful, don't worry. He's lost the sight of one eye, I gather.'

'Will you be able to manage the walk to your room, Archie,' said Gifford, 'or shall I fetch Thomas?'

'Thank you, I'll lean on my friend.' He glanced at Tyrell, who was now frowning and blinking, as though trying to remember where he had seen this man before. Archie kept quiet. Unless it became quite impossible, he was determined to keep his promise to Polly.

Seventeen

'So what's all this about you spotting a gang of wreckers waiting for the train to crash?'

'Good Lord, did I say that in my letter?'

'More or less, and I gather, from Miss Anderson's little outburst just now, you've told her all about it, an' all.'

'As a matter of fact, she and I both think the train crash was staged, that those men pulled the tree onto the line deliberately. As she said, we've just been down there and—'

'You could be right.'

'What! You think so, too? What were they after? Mail bags or something?'

'Or something… More precisely, some *one.*'

'A kidnapping?'

'Your Billy Maggs was being taken up to Chelmsford to stand trial for the Fitzell murder and they stopped the train to fetch him off.'

'No! He was on the same train as…?' He blinked. 'You kept that quiet. So the men I saw were waiting to get him off, were they? Where was he? Guard's van?'

'With Reggie Bradford and Gerry Foskett. The buggers killed them, and the guard.'

'Oh my God, Frank!' he gasped. 'Reggie and Gerry?' His hand over his mouth, he shook his head. He had known them both; they were both regulars in the Horse and Groom. It was dreadful to think they were gone, poor fellows. 'So that's why the trial was cancelled.'

'Yep,' Tyrell sighed.

'Perhaps they were in on it, Maggs' gang. The Fitzell burglary, I mean. Perhaps he would have implicated them at the trial.'

'Well, they're all wanted for murder now. Bastards!'

'Do you,' Archie swallowed, 'have anything to go on? Any idea who they might be?'

'Nothing. By the time the railway police arrived on the scene, they were long gone and the locals were helping get people out, carting them off to billets. Any trace of them villains soon turned to slurry in the to and fro of rescue work. The guard's van was awash with blood, from a dozen stab wounds between them, so no clear prints there either. Gerry managed to pop a shot at one of the buggers, bless him. We found his gun, standard issue, among some animal cages, and the bullet buried in somebody's suitcase, with blood and shirt fibres attached to it. But he couldn't shoot them all. They knifed him pretty early on, I'm guessing, and took his keys to free Maggs from his chains.'

'So what do you know about this Billy Maggs? Who does he run with, where does he call home?'

'No criminal record, Archie. The Met have nothing on him. As for his gang, that's why I'm here. Rather hoping you could put faces to them.'

'*Me?*' He shook his head. 'Oh, Frank, I've tried my darnedest to remember what they looked like, but they were only a flash of colour against the cow parsley, a hazy impression.'

The detective drooped, blowing out his moustache dejectedly.

Archie wanted desperately to help. He turned out his pockets. 'Look, we managed to find a few bits of evidence.' He took the various envelopes and twists of paper, handkerchiefs and boxes from his pockets and gently unwrapped them, spreading out their contents on the wide windowsill and explaining where each was found: the mud scrapings from the fence, the Woodbines packet and cigarette card, the broken match. 'And this.' He unfolded the piece of dirty paper. 'Sorry, it's not very salubrious, but I thought it was interesting. There's something written, see? Eleven something?'

Tyrell got out his penknife and scraped off the dried-on excrement. 'It's an address, I think, but such poorly formed letters, it's hard to—' He paused to turn the paper, bring it closer. 'Hmm, my guess is whoever wrote it is illiterate. They were probably taking dictation – it's misspelt, too. It's not eleven, it's one-one-nine, and I think that's meant to be Church Street. Where? Stock Newton?'

'Stoke Newington?'

'Well, it doesn't mean anything to me at the moment, but I'll hang on to this, if you don't mind. It may tell us something.'

'Keep the lot – they're no good to me. Tell you what, though, Frank – little Flo Anderson is a photographer. She took photos of any likely footprints and hoof marks, further up the track from the crash. She carries a tape measure in her camera case for the light or something, so we were able to jot down measurements against each item in her notebook.'

While the detective was going over the evidence again, Archie observed, 'You could take the photographic plates with you, I expect. She'd develop them for you if only she had a darkroom. She's brought all the necessary chemicals and things.'

Tyrell nodded. 'I'll have a word with Mrs G, tonight. She might not mind emptying a cupboard or something for the girl.'

'So one of the villains will have a bullet hole, you reckon?'

His friend sniffed. 'We got a bloody handprint on the doorsill of the guard's van and partials on the footplate and wheels. "Railway" took tracings and measurements, but it was raining on the day, see – the prints wasn't clear and they was almost gone by the time we got there. Any blood on the track from the gunshot wound was likely washed away.'

'Should be able to match a handprint to a hand, if ever you get them.'

'Always supposing I don't throttle the bastards first. Knifing our Reggie… Bright future ahead of him.'

So that was why Tyrell was still here, long after the trial had been dropped. It had been his decision to send Billy Maggs to Chelmsford. Because of that decision, the train had been wrecked, the prisoner had escaped, the escort had been killed; it was all down to him. His responsibility.

Poor sod. No wonder he was so distressed. Since joining the force, Reggie had lived under the same roof as Tyrell, at the section house. For the last three or four years, Emma Tyrell had cleaned and cooked for the young constable, washed his clothes, along with those of the other two policemen who lived there. The Tyrells always went to support him at wrestling matches down at the 'Royal Standard' pub on a Saturday night. Archie had gone along with them. It must have been like having a member of your family murdered.

'I blame myself,' said the detective. 'Shoulda packed Maggsy off to Pentonville or the Scrubs straight off, if only on the pickpocketing charge. I mean, that was a given. If you'd seen his coat, Arch, when the boys nabbed him in the Penny Bazaar! Jingling like Father Christmas's sleigh bells! I'd say a dozen poor souls went home that afternoon minus their cash. They found three purses and a wallet under the stalls when they packed up – empty, of course.' He licked his lips. 'Any more tea in that pot, Arch? And another biscuit wouldn't come amiss. Up early this morning; no breakfast.'

As Archie poured, Tyrell confessed that his pride had kept Maggs in the high street cells. He'd been determined to pin Jeremiah Fitzell's murder on him too. But that was proving more difficult.

'But Jim identified him?'

'He did,' said the detective, 'no trouble. But the bastard denies he was anywhere near the place. "No comment, no comment." Even with a little persuasion.'

'Would his alibi convince anyone?'

'Well, he says he was stopping with some brass, Sal Tucker, down Hackney way, and she corroborates. Mind, she was sporting a black eye when we talked to her, poor cow, and a broken wrist. Think he's a bit "handy" with his women.'

124

'So you packed him off to see what the jury made of it.'

'I did.'

'But why would anyone want to fetch him off the train unless—?'

'Exactly. Either they knew he'd break under questioning and implicate them, or he's got something they want. Remember Jimmy Tomkins described a sack landing with a thud.'

'A sack – yes, yes, of course.'

'Now he didn't have any sort of sack when we picked him up in the market, with or without a thud. My thinking is, if the gang ain't got them, he's stashed the spoils some place.'

'And only he knows where,' said Archie.

Eighteen

Next day, a Friday, Tyrell called back at Gifford Lodge, while Beckett and the village constable, a PC Philpot, gathered a few more survivor statements from the village. So far, all the injured passengers had been far too caught up extricating themselves from the wreckage or getting help to notice anything happening at the back of the train. Even those in the last few carriages had been drawn to the front of the train rather than the rear. Nobody had noticed the abduction from the guard's van. Some believed they may have heard a shot, or shots and cries, but had been too worried about themselves to investigate. The police were getting nowhere fast. The only person who had seen anything at all was Archie.

'Before we turned in last night, me and Stan went for a walk around town. I wanted to get you some canvas. Can't have you painting on wood – that ain't right. I'll fetch it presently – big roll of the stuff. Well, we saw these posters, didn't we, posters for the music hall? A proper Palace of Varieties.' Archie's ears pricked up. What was Tyrell suggesting? 'They was advertising this bloke – the Great Revilo – doing whatjecall-it? – hypnotism.'

Archie smelled trouble. 'No, Frank.' You wouldn't trust a man with a name like that, but perhaps Frank was pronouncing it wrongly. Surely it should be Revilo as in re*veal*, not revile? Even so… 'No, you are not getting me up on a stage for everyone's amusement.'

'Hear me out, boyo—'

'Frank, you know how these things are managed – they have plants in the audience.'

'But suppose there's something in it? Suppose we could get him to put you under so you could remember the faces of the killers you saw? Doesn't that sound like a plan?'

'No, it doesn't. Thanks for the canvas – much appreciated. I'll have to owe you. But I'm not having my brains messed about with, for you or anyone else. They're in a bad enough state as it is.'

'You did say you'd help in any way you could.'

'Frank!'

'Come with me tonight. I'll pay. You can judge for yourself.'

'No! Good Lord, how many more times? I shouldn't have done that walk yesterday – my leg's killing me, and you want to drag me out to see some fake hypnotist?'

The auditorium was packed when Archie limped in. Tobacco smoke stung his eyes and the aroma of fish and chips gnawed at his stomach. There had been no time for a meal before the long drive through the country lanes to Chelmsford's high street. The Variety Playhouse was a saloon bar theatre, not very different from the Horse and Groom back home, with an auditorium crammed with tables and littered with apple cores and chip paper, tankards and jugs of ale.

There was no foyer fit to take a mural.

The audience was noisy with anticipation.

'Oh, lookee, Seth, there be that hussy Maria Stone, all got up to the nines, bit o' rabbit fur round her neck. And who'm that wi' er, I'd like t'know? 'E'm a new one on me.'

'Jem! How be you, an' all? Fair flaked, I'll wager, arter all that hedgin'.'

'Right enough, Jarge. Bin stubbin' they tree stumps longside Barley Lane. Good turn out, ennit?'

Archie and the detective slipped into empty seats at a table near the back of the hall as the gaslights dimmed and the compère, a dapper little man with grease-slicked hair, centre parting echoed in a curled moustache, took up his gavel and demanded silence.

Archie hadn't been in a music hall since Lizzie died. The howls of laughter, the catcalling, the excitement did not fit his melancholy. But she had loved it. She knew all the songs, and he had loved to hear her singing 'Daisy, Daisy' or 'Two Little Girls in Blue' as she went about her work in the pottery.

The first act was one he'd seen before at Percy and Bertha's. Charlie Farnesbarnes, as he called himself, was a sporty-looking chappie in a striped blazer and a straw boater, telling jokes. He had the audience in stitches.

'I say, I say, I say, do you know the difference between Joan of Arc and a canoe? No? One is Maid of Orleans and the other is made of wood.'

Archie frowned. Lord, this was painful. Frank Tyrell elbowed him in the ribs. He was tickled, obviously, though he must have heard the joke a dozen times before.

'Have you seen my girlfriend's bonnet? I gave her that. Have you seen her jacket? I gave her that. Have you seen her eyes? Both black. I gave her those, too!'

While Archie groaned, his companion slapped the table and wiped tears from his eyes.

'Where are you going?' he demanded as Archie struggled to his feet. Lilian had wound a bandage round his blisters, but he had abandoned his sticks tonight and brought a crutch.

'Bar.'

'Fetch us a sandwich, mate, and another pint.'

After he'd paid the barman, it was as much as Archie could do to manage the crutch and one foaming tankard, let alone the full order.

'Let me help you, sir.'

He turned too quickly and nearly lost his balance. He knew that voice, the Irish lilt. His heart quickened. 'Good Lord – Kitty!'

'Archie? Be Jaisus, Archie Price!' She held his face steady to kiss his cheek and then spent a few moments wiping it clean of lipstick. 'What brings you to these parts?'

She was made up to the nines, her eyes and cheekbones exaggerated to be visible from the back of the auditorium where, like as not, they had no posh binoculars, or even spectacles to view their music hall idols. Her blonde hair was piled up under wafting turquoise ostrich feathers, and her low-cut silk gown, coloured to match the headgear, was swathed over her creamy breasts to reveal a deep cleft where once he had buried his nose. She had plumped out, and her fingers on his arm were dimpled and beringed. She was no longer the winsome Irish girl in green, singing folk songs to the fiddle's wail and a bodhrán beat. She told him that her erstwhile singing partner, Mary, had returned to Ireland, to sing in pubs and clubs in Galway to be nearer her mother.

Kitty announced that she was now married to Charlie Farnesbarnes, the comic.

That Charlie Farnesbarnes? Archie thought. *Good grief, Kitty, you can certainly pick 'em!*

'Not his real name, of course. Mrs Perkins, so I am. We have a wee babby we take around from job to job. He's sleeping in the dressing room right now or I'd bring you to see the little angel.' She took a sip of her Guinness. 'Just come out for a jar before I go on. Best drink in the world for a nursing mother,' she declared. 'Full of iron to strengthen the milk.'

Froth formed a cupid's bow on her upper lip and he offered her a handkerchief. She examined it, wrinkling her nose. 'I won't if you don't mind,' she said, producing something clean and silky from her reticule and dabbing at her lip. 'Sure an' I can see you're still painting, Arch.'

'Oh, sorry.'

She stood back to scrutinise him, and, for the first time, he was aware of his unironed shirt, the frayed collar, his too-long hair, the loose threads of his cuff, his worn elbows. He must look quite ragged. 'Lizzie not around, Arch?' she asked gently.

'Here in spirit only, Kitty, I'm afraid.'

'What do you mean?'

He had the sad task of telling her how and why he was alone in a strange town, down at heel, how his wife had died in childbirth, how he'd never get over losing her.

'Oh, Archie. I'm so sorry. Sure and that's the worst that can befall a body. You poor dear. And there was the little girl – Clara?'

'She's sad, of course, but she's doing well with her grandparents – learning a lot about art from him, and gardening, handcraft and baking from her. When I was last over there, for my birthday, she'd made me a pretty papier mâché cufflink box and iced a rather wonky cake, decorated to look like an artist's palette.' He couldn't help the pride in his voice.

'Goodness – she's how old, Archie?'

'Six, but clever like her mother.'

'She's lucky to have you.'

'She doesn't "have" me, Kitty. She doesn't think of me as her stepfather, though I am, of course. She's never called me Papa or Daddy, only Archie.' Kitty made a moué of sympathy, and he swallowed a lump of self-pity rising in his throat. In a more positive tone, he said, 'She has friends to play with on the Camden streets and she's doing well at school. It's a far better life than I could give her, though I try and see her as much as I can.'

'You're a good man, Archie.'

'No, I'm not, Kitty, I'm a weak and foolish man. I've let my work dwindle to nothing and I've no idea where my next commission is coming from. I was hoping to find work painting for the music halls.'

'Scenery, you mean?'

'It may come to that.' He laughed. 'No, my idea is to paint a big picture for the foyer that will include dozens of famous faces...'

She frowned. 'People in this trade don't want to be one of a crowd, Archie. They want to stand out. They might sit for a portrait if you asked them, one they can hang in their home or in the Portrait Gallery in London, to be seen by everyone. A bit of publicity is always good. You could do me, if you like, but not if I'm going to be a blurry face in the back row.'

'Never that, Kitty!' he laughed. But she was right. He hadn't thought of the back row.

'Or posters. You were always good at posters.'

'But I want to paint, that's my trade.'

'Well, paint a poster then, like that little French aristo. Or has he cornered the market?'

He shrugged ignorance. His leg was aching. He pulled another bar stool towards him to rest it.

'How have you managed to injure yourself?'

When he told her she threw up her hands, the greasepaint creasing with concern. 'Sweet Jaisus, you could have been killed, so you could. Sure an' we heard about the crash up in Colchester and were worried they'd close the down-line as well, and we'd be stranded.'

We, she said. He sighed. She might be married with a baby and therefore off limits, but she was still delectable. He heard the comedy act coming to an end, the final song 'Don't do that to the poor puss cat', and the audience singing back with gusto, '*Miaow, miaow, miaow!*' Applause and cheers unearned, Archie thought irritably. He'd better be getting back: Tyrell would be getting thirsty.

But she was up close, her hand on his arm again.

'So what are you doing here, Archie?' She cocked her head in that way she had.

He explained. 'The Great Revilo is the man I'm here to see. Frank Tyrell – remember him? Copper at the Walthamstow lock-up?' She nodded. 'Well, he's decided, in his infinite wisdom, that there's information locked inside my brain that he needs, and he thinks a hypnotist can help winkle it out.'

'You're *not* going up on the stage?'

'Not if I can help it.'

131

'I wouldn't. Some people don't mind making a show of themselves – they can't wait to get up there in front of an audience, but it's not for the likes of you. He can make you think you're a babby back at your mother's knee, get you crawling around on the floor and sucking on a dummy. He can make you think a walking stick is a snake or plain water something delicious, like wine, and get you drunk on it, too.'

'Really?' Just as he'd feared: the man used his audience for others' amusement. Nothing like Freud, who put his patients into a trance to find a cure for their obsessions, their hysteria. He and Frank had come to the wrong place. 'Aren't they planted in the audience, his subjects?'

'No, not at all. I wouldn't tell a lie!' she insisted. 'They're ordinary folk come out for a night's fun, just like you.'

'All I want is to remember something I saw only fleetingly and I don't want all and sundry knowing about it.'

'That bad, is it?' she teased.

'Who knows?'

'Well, he's your man, Archie. If anyone can do it, he can. He helped me to stop biting my nails.' She displayed her prettily painted finger ends for his approval. 'And my Charlie, who was afeard of heights, can now go out and walk along cliff edges without a qualm, not afraid I'm likely to push him off. Now there's a thought!' She rolled her eyes, and laughed. It was supposed to be funny. 'Revilo' – as Archie had thought, the name was pronounced 'Revealo' – 'is even helping my old man sleep through the night without hearing the babby crying!' This was an even greater joke, and she had to put down her glass and grab the bar for support. The tear she wiped away was one of laughter, surely? She sniffed and frowned herself sober. 'I'll ask him to see you privately. He won't charge you a penny, seeing as you're a friend.'

The barman gave them a tray and Archie moved his purchases onto it.

'He sounds a marvel, Kitty.' He eyed her empty glass. 'Another?'

She waved away his offer. 'No, I'm on shortly, after Oliver. He's clever,' she said, referring back to the hypnotist, as Archie opened the door into the hall. Lowering her voice, she added, 'And perfectly genuine, you know, not a quack or a fake.'

Tyrell jumped up when he saw Kitty with the tray, offering her his chair. 'Thank you, no, I must go and check on the babby, before I go on. Nice to meet you again, Mr Tyrell.' And with a swish of her bustle, she turned to go. She'd always regarded the police with suspicion.

The master of ceremonies brought his audience to order and announced the next act. It was indeed the Great Revilo, 'master of mystique', a tall streak of a man, with a small goatee beard and moustache, who swept on from the wings in a red silk-lined cloak and a top hat. Very theatrical, Archie felt, the very cliché of a ringmaster about to bring his troupe of wild animals to heel.

'He's not really Revilo,' came a whisper in his ear. Kitty was loath to leave them. 'He's Oliver Allsop. Olly. Revilo is Oliver backwards. He used to be a nerve doctor, but there's more money in this game, he says. More fun, too, than sick people. He's read all the books, Archie. He won't let any harm come to you – he has his reputation to think of.' The warmth and perfume receded. He turned, but she had gone.

Archie was impressed. Revilo invited volunteers to join him in what, he assured everyone, was not magic, but an experiment. Contrary to Archie's expectations, he did not put them to sleep with swinging pocket watches – their eyes remained open – but by the power of suggestion, he deprived them of the ability to speak, hear or see. Their motions were completely controlled, so that they could not stand or sit, except at his bidding. Their memory was taken away: they forgot their own names and those of their friends. They were made to stammer, to weep, to laugh, to believe they were out in a fierce gale or that their house was swarming with ants. When, at the end of the routine, the six volunteers were brought out of their trance, with no recollection of their antics, Archie was completely won over. These extraordinary experiments were performed without any trick, collusion, or deception.

'Very good.'

Tyrell agreed, applauding thoughtfully.

Next up was the 'Irish songbird, Miss Kitty Flanagan!' As ever, Archie was thrilled by the sweetness of her voice and her come-hither glances to the audience that seemed to settle on him. The lyrics were bawdier than he was used to hearing her sing, the innuendoes more obvious, but he guessed that was what her fans enjoyed. He joined in 'Who were you with last night?' When she announced, 'This next song is for a dear friend in the audience – he knows who he is,' Tyrell elbowed him and Archie blushed. He blushed even deeper when the orchestra struck up 'I was a good little girl 'til I met you'. It wasn't true at all. She had been a rich man's darling long before they'd met, but she still had the power to titillate: he found himself aroused for the first time in years. Hastily, he dug out his sketchbook and added another drawing to his collection of Miss Kitty Flanagan.

Act followed act: a troupe of girl cyclists, a magician, and another comedian, a big name from the smoke, whose jokes were slightly off colour but who sang songs they all knew and could join in with: 'It's a great big shame', 'Two lovely black eyes', and 'If it wasn't for the houses in between'.

Archie was sketching away and singing along with gusto when two people walked up to the table: Kitty had returned, bringing the hypnotist with her. Her dresser was minding the baby, she said. During the interval, while Kitty reminisced about old times and portraits Archie had painted of her, Tyrell and Revilo lowered their voices to discuss Archie's hypnosis, and Archie did his best to keep tabs on both conversations.

'He's pretty sure he's seen something that he can't remember clearly, that could have a bearing on a recent crime.'

'So Kitty said. It wouldn't have anything to do with the train crash, would it? He'll be pretty confused about anything that happened during his ordeal, I imagine.'

'No, this happened just before, just as the train went into the tunnel.'

'The best one was *Behind the Scenes at the Hackney Empire*, don't you think, Archie? Archie? Though *Two Irish Songbirds* was lovely – that one you did of Mary and me.'

Archie's antennae were twitching: 'Fra-ank—' he cautioned. The beer had loosened the detective's tongue. They'd only just met the man. Could he be trusted?

The hypnotist acknowledged Archie's concern and assured them that he was the soul of discretion. Like a doctor, he was under oath not to reveal to another living soul what went on between a client and himself. 'Rest assured, gentlemen, even this conversation will go no further.'

'We-e-ell…' Kitty murmured, behind her fan.

How soon could a consultation be arranged? The matter was quite urgent.

'Gifford Lodge? Isn't that in Little Nessing?' They confirmed that it was. 'Then perhaps I—' He frowned. 'Would you excuse me for a moment?' They watched him thread his way through the tables and chairs to where a couple of well-dressed gentlemen were sitting near the stage.

'That's Peregrine Beasley,' Kitty whispered. '*Lord* Beasley, so he is, of Elmscott Place. Hereditary, not earned. Fingers in a few unsavoury pies. Comes here often – great pals with Oliver. The other man's Italian, I think – Peregrine's after selling him the silk factory on Hall Street, to make some sort of electrical thingies. The girls are so pleased it's changing hands – Beasley's a real pest, touching them up, making lewd remarks. Oh, don't look so shocked – you know me – speak as I find.' She frowned as something occurred to her. 'Archie, he knows your work. That painting you did of Mary and me, *Two Irish Songbirds*? He's the one bought it – Perry, I mean, not the foreigner. Made of money, our Peregrine. Broke my heart to let it go, but we were desperate when Walter was born. I'm thinkin' it would do you some good to get to know him, Archie, him bein' an art collector an' all. But be careful. Your man's a bit of a shyster.'

'There'y'are, Arch,' said Tyrell, 'see if he'll take your brainstorm pictures.'

'My *Scribblings for a Disturbed Mind,* you mean? Too avant-garde for him, I'd have thought. For anyone, come to that.' The truth was, he didn't like the look of the hypnotist's friend: his hands were all over the waitresses, and his laughter at some of the last comic's innuendos had been too loud and too long.

Archie watched the way the hypnotist was conversing with his fine friend, cutting out the foreign gent by whispering rudely in Beasley's ear, and gesturing towards their table as though pointing out an area of interest to a visiting dignitary. Kitty was smiling at the whey-faced baronet, in a restrained sort of way. She clearly had her reservations. He and Tyrell nodded a greeting, but his lordship was listening too hard to Revilo to pay them heed. Eventually, after a deal of discussion, some sort of agreement was reached, and Revilo returned to their table. Beasley lifted his glass towards them and condescended to smile.

'That's Lord Beasley,' Revilo informed them. 'His place is just up the road from where you are staying. As luck would have it, I'm dining with him tomorrow evening. If you like, I could come to the Lodge in the afternoon and cut across there afterwards, killing two birds, as it were.'

'Oh. So soon?' It looked to Archie as if he wasn't going to be able to get out of it.

Tyrell said, 'How very obliging,' and it was settled: Allsop would arrive for a general consultation after lunch the next day.

'General?' Archie frowned. Tyrell tapped the side of his nose with his forefinger.

*

On the way home, the detective explained that if word got out that Archie had seen the hypnotist alone, and then subsequently people were arrested, it could put both his life and the hypnotist's in danger. 'So we'll invite them all to the entertainment – the Giffords and any guests they may care to invite – each to consult the hypnotist in Gifford's study, if he agrees. A sort of camouflage for the main event,' he said.

'Tch,' Archie clicked his tongue. Words failed him.

Nineteen

Next morning a letter arrived from Ida Sutton, his ex-model and the new Mrs Fitzell. She told him that because of his father's sad and cruel demise, Fitz and she had had a quiet wedding. As executor of the will and sole beneficiary, poor Fitz was now up to his ears sorting out the estate. He intended selling it all off, house and contents. *'Imagine, Archie,'* she wrote in her crabbed little hand, *'living in a house stuffed to the gunnels with outlandish things like monkey paws and shrunken heads! I would be scared witless. The place must be haunted, if only by Jeremiah himself? Think what a miserable ghost he must be, having died in that horrible way!'* Not that she and 'Fitz' believed in the supernatural. They were both thoroughly modern people. Give them fresh air and bicycles and they'd be content.

They were soon moving into one of the big new houses on the Woodford High Road. With Jeremiah's money they wouldn't need a mortgage. First priority, though, was to find his father's murderer. She had seen Archie's posters, and to spur more people to action they were putting up a £500 reward. That was the one good thing to come out of all this: they could afford to do that for poor Papa Fitzell. As for selling the collection, that was going to be a real 'bind!' She had offered her bookkeeping skills to help, but dear Fitz, bless him, wouldn't hear of it. It was a dirty job, he declared, and she wasn't to soil her pretty hands. She did have pretty hands, didn't she, Archie? Wasn't that one of the things he'd always complimented her on? She often thought of him and the times she had posed for him and hated to think of him so indisposed. *'Get well soon, Archie! Kisses, to make it better, from your friend, Ida x x x x x'*.

Archie's wet eyes, as he refolded the letter, were in memory, not of Ida Fitzell, whose paper kisses were meaningless, but of Lizzie who, to please her little daughter, used to kiss his injuries better. Lord, he needed her now.

'Oh, what a long face, Archie!' Mr Norris came in from the terrace to offer Archie a piece of toffee from a small crystal dish. He'd gained access to the kitchen the night before and made a tin of the stuff. 'Stick-jaw, they call it, back home. Don't do your jolly old teeth much good, but it lifts the spirits tremendously.' Archie couldn't refuse. 'Bad news?' the old man asked, licking his lips, his good eye devouring the kisses on the bottom of his letter as though *they* might be made of sugar.

'No, no.' With sticky fingers Archie refolded the letter and put it in his jacket pocket. 'On the contrary,' he mumbled with a full mouth, trying not to dribble.

The churchman waited, but when no more information was forthcoming, he carried on. 'I, too, am in receipt of a letter this morning. One-eyed or not, I am to give the Good Friday sermon at the Primitive Wesleyan Chapel in Boxstead, in lieu of Saint Stephen's, Colchester.'

'Boxstead? Where's that?'

'Next village up the road.'

'That's hard,' he said. 'Are you up to it?'

'The Lord will give me strength.'

He felt sorry for the poor old soul. 'How will you get there?'

'Oh, I imagine I'll be able to hitch a ride on a cart or something.'

'You don't want to be left stranded in the middle of nowhere by yourself.'

'God will provide.'

Archie had a sudden and inexplicable, instantly suppressed,

urge to offer to accompany him. He and religion were not good bedfellows. Jesus, the great teacher? Possibly. Religion and creeds and priests and all the other man-made trappings? Hell, no.

'You heard, of course, that Doctor Macrae has fixed up for me to be looked at by an eye specialist?'

'Doctor *MacKay* has? That's extremely good of him.'

'Indeed.' The older man patted his eyepatch. 'So I shall have a busy time of it. Whoever said life in the country is quiet? What's more, I hear we're in for a treat.'

'What's that?'

'Haven't you laid on entertainment for us?'

'No?'

'The hypnotist, the Great Ramondo or somesuch, is going to read our minds. I was speaking to your Inspector – Inspector—?' He raised his eyes heavenwards as though seeking help from the Almighty.

Did he do it on purpose? Surely no one could get the wrong end of the stick so often or be so forgetful? And why had Tyrell singled Archie out?

The Giffords had insisted on the detective staying the night after bringing Archie home from the music hall, and he had spent half the morning trying to persuade all members of the household to attend the 'entertainment' after lunch. Florence Anderson was keeping well out of the way, taking her meals in her room and claiming to have a headache. Poor Polly – Tyrell's interrogation yesterday had been the last straw.

'Ah, here you are!'

And here *he* was, peeking round the door like a naughty middle-aged child. Tyrell came in, beer gut first, and Archie put a slip of paper into Freud's *Studies on Hysteria* to mark his place. He was getting more out of it second time around. Norris offered Frank a piece of 'stick-jaw' before smiling and raising his hands in understanding as he backed out of the room. Old friends needed to be alone.

140

'What are you getting me into, Frank? Norris seems to think Oliver Allsop is some sort of clairvoyant. I think he sees us standing up and doing "turns" on the dining table like children at a birthday party.'

'Poor old soul. His mind was probably elsewhere when I was telling the others. We have several volunteers.'

'I see, and what's he getting out of it, Oliver Allsop?'

'Oh, he'll charge them two bob for half an hour.'

'I can't afford two bob, Frank!'

'No more can I, Arch. His usual rate is one and six. The extra will cover your consultation.'

'That's not fair!'

'Shh!' He looked around the drawing room as if expecting someone to pop out from behind the fire screen complaining about being overcharged. 'That was his price for coming out here. If they want a longer session they can make arrangements to see him in town. Don't worry, Arch, this way no one will suspect you of being any different from the rest of us.'

'I don't like it, Frank.'

'Needs must.'

'For all we know he could be a scoundrel! Your case depends on my lost memories. What if he's a charlatan, delving into people's subconscious to find out their secrets in order to blackmail them?'

'You've been reading too many novels, boyo. No, he's on the level. I promise I won't let anything untoward happen.'

'The whole damn thing is untoward!'

Lord, thought Archie, as his so-called friend left the room, do I really trust either of these tricksters?

Twenty

The first time he'd gone upstairs, to borrow a book, he had shuffled up and down on his bottom. Now, carrying his crutch, he hauled himself from stair to stair, using the banisters on either side to save putting weight on his leg. The walk yesterday had done no lasting damage, and he should probably be thinking about getting back to Walthamstow in the next few days. At the top, he and his crutch lumbered up a slight incline and he was reminded that the house was an ancient one, timber-framed and slowly sinking into the Essex clay. Few floors were horizontal.

Along the passageway he met Polly closing her door and realised that she had the room above his.

'Hello, Archie!' She looked better.

'Missed you at breakfast … and lunch,' he said, smiling back. 'How are you?'

'Happier, thanks. Did they tell you, Lilian's given me an old pantry off the kitchen for a darkroom, so I've been developing yesterday's photos? It's good to be working. Takes my mind off my other problems. But what about you? You must be excited. This hypnotist Lilian was telling me about – you're finally going to be able to put faces to those men you saw. It *is* for your benefit this has all been laid on, isn't it?'

''Fraid so, and I suppose I am excited, in a way. More nervous about the actual hypnotism, actually. Are you going to try him out?'

'No, I'm waiting for the photos to dry, and I'll give them to Mr Tyrell to take back with him. I'm giving the hypnotist a very wide berth. He might find out I'm not who I say I am and tell Tyrell.'

'I think you should be honest with Tyrell, Flo. Tell him what you told me. I'm sure you'll find him very sympathetic. I'll speak to him if you like.'

'Please don't. He may be your friend, but he's also the law; there's no changing that. I've told lies and harboured stolen goods. Aided and abetted criminals. He'll have to put me in jail once he knows what I've done! Won't he?'

'I don't *think* so,' he said, but she took no comfort from that.

Having once been the West Lodge of Elmscott, the farmhouse was large enough to boast a small library. As Archie pushed open the door, he saw that almost every bench and chair was occupied. A layer of tobacco smoke swirled about peoples' heads. With that and the woodsmoke from the fire, Archie found his eyes smarting.

'Sit by me.' Lilian Gifford patted the space beside her on a high-backed wooden settle next to the fire. 'Here, let me get a footstool for your poor leg.'

He didn't argue. It was good to be fussed over.

Richard Gifford sat on his wife's other side, looking apprehensive. It wasn't often he had so little control over what went on under his roof. Opposite, on a couch, separated from her husband by Geoffrey Norris's skinny behind, sat Mrs Mabel MacKay, a pretty, plump, rosy-cheeked matron, whom Archie had met a day or two earlier, when she had visited Lilian to show off her new baby boy. She beamed at Effie, who had her nose in a medical book and didn't see her. Mabel had persuaded Archie, with dimples and rather fine brown eyes, to show her his first 'nightmare' painting. She had studied it, finding it rather perplexing, she said, never having seen anything quite like it before, though the pure hues reminded her, in a strange way, of a

Mister Kandinsky, whose work she had seen in the National Gallery. Did Archie know him?

She'd told him that she was a watercolourist herself, self-taught, using her pictures to illustrate a small book she had written about the local flora and fauna, in between caring for little James and his older siblings. Now she reminded Archie that he'd encouraged her to bring her work to show him, next time she was over this way. And here she was, complete with her little book (she patted her reticule), *sans enfants,* who were at home in the tender care of the nanny. Perhaps later, after the 'entertainment', there would be time for Archie to give her his honest opinion.

He smiled, but said, so that everyone could hear, 'Mr Allsop is not here to entertain us, but to offer help, for any problems you may have. I am hoping he can give me some relief from my insomnia. But you might want to consult him about other things: bad habits, cravings, fears, secret longings – I don't know. As well as being the Great Revilo, Mr Allsop is a registered doctor of neurology, and it is in this capacity that he is joining us today. He is honour-bound to respect his patients' confidences.'

Lilian Gifford turned to the doctor. 'Duncan, dear, I suggest you go first. As a medical man you can judge, better than the rest of us, how good this man is. Meanwhile, do please, everyone, make use of the library, while you're waiting. Read or talk as you will, or there's a chess set and jigsaw puzzles and several packs of playing cards.'

Maud and Thomas handed round tea.

Having drained his cup, the minister tinkled on it with his spoon and asked if anyone would join him in a game of cribbage. Frank Tyrell pretended not to hear, concentrating on writing up his notes. Eventually Stanley Beckett obliged.

Archie and Mrs MacKay went over to the window to discuss her flower paintings. They were prettily done, and he murmured appreciation of their delicacy and freshness. But watercolours were watercolours, not his cup of tea, and he could not give her his full attention. What was going to happen? Tyrell was relying on him to solve a crime, and he wasn't sure he could.

Doctor MacKay returned, frowning. 'The man's genuine enough,' he replied to Lilian Gifford's 'Well?' but he would give no further clues. He went straight to the shelves and took out a book. When Archie passed, he saw the doctor had chosen the Freud volume he had just returned.

Lilian went next, to judge for herself, and came back looking perturbed. 'He told me my mother's name, where I was born, and the book I was reading, and when I asked him who had told him, he said I had, myself. He had put me to sleep and asked me the questions and I had answered him. But I don't remember him asking me anything at all. It's rather upsetting to know that someone can have that much power over you. I wonder if he's married. I don't envy his wife. Goodness, you'd never be able to trust the man. He could put you to sleep and make you do anything he wanted.'

Archie bit the soft skin inside his mouth. Why had the man given up doctoring in favour of the entertainment business? It smacked of a lack of gravitas and grit. And care. Doctors cared, didn't they, for the wellbeing of the patient? Entertainers did not.

The card players wanted to finish their game, and Mrs MacKay did not have any bad habits that she wanted cured, so Archie went in next.

'Mr Price! Look at you, man – your shoulders are up by your ears. Relax. No harm's going to come to you, I promise. I'll just explain. I'm going to try and slow down the events of that train ride. But first I want you to tell me what you do remember, so we can set the scene. Were you reading or talking to another passenger or simply gazing out of the window? What was the weather like? What were you thinking?'

Because he had been over and over his journey, night after night, this part came easily. The hypnotist took notes.

'I saw a flash of humanity and then darkness, a muffling of the ears as the train rushed into the tunnel, and then…' He frowned. 'And then…'

'Stop there, Archie. We don't want to remember what came next, but what came before. A "flash of humanity"? A person or persons standing at the entrance to the tunnel. They were standing in the rain. We'll work on that. The human brain is capable of absorbing far more information than you give it credit for. We may be lucky. So, first let's do some deep breathing to get you in the right frame of mind. Close your eyes, please, and breathe as slowly as you can. In – and out… In – and out…' The man's voice slowed with the words, became more intimate, impossible to deny. 'Your feet, Archie, the toes, the arches, the instep, the heels, are relaxed and heavy, quite without sensation.'

And so they were, as were his ankles and his calves when Allsop mentioned them, and his knees, his thighs, his hips and so on, up and up… 'Your neck, your chin, quite, quite without sensation, your muscles are loose. Let all tension go.'

He wasn't asleep, he was perfectly conscious, but he simply couldn't feel his body. It didn't belong to him. His head filled with air and Allsop's voice was just a fly's drone in his ears. Warm fingertips rested on his forehead.

'Listen to me, Archie. You may trust me completely. I will keep you safe. If you want to stop, just raise your right hand for me. Can you do that now?' He did so. 'There we are. So we're going to take you back to the end of that train journey, just before the crash.'

Archie felt as if he may have smiled, may have nodded his head, though he knew he hadn't. He believed the man implicitly. Of course he wasn't a villain.

'You are on the train, looking out of the window. Rain slashes diagonally across the glass and yet you, an artist with heightened levels of perception, can see past the trickling distortions to the embankment beyond. Tell me what you see.'

146

It came without effort. 'Shiny wet grass, silvering in the draught of air from the train, like the wind across water, a wooden fence, rough hewn and black with rain, trees, bushes…'

'What sort of bushes, Archie? You can see them clearly, remember. Slow yourself down so you can look at them properly. See them now? Tell me about them.'

'They're elderflower, creamy-white, almost fluffy.'

'More…'

'Tiny star-like flowers, buds, long stamens, dozens on a single stem.'

'Good. Let them go. The train is moving along really slowly now, almost imperceptibly. What else can you see?'

'A bird sitting on the fence, a magpie, black and white, iridescent blue on his wings, mad black eye.'

'More…'

'Drops of rain beading on his head. He is oblivious. He cocks his black beak at the train and flies off.'

'In which direction?'

'Oh, away to the right, to the woods beyond.' He thought he gestured with his hand, but was sure his hand didn't leave his lap. It didn't matter.

'Now we're coming to the tunnel, Archie, and we're still going slowly so that you, with your keen eyes, can see everything. Tell me about it, Archie…'

'A small furry mammal, a vole, is alarmed by the steam, the noise, and turns tail – not a vole, a mouse – and disappears down a hole in the embankment. Cow parsley shivers, shaking off water like a wet dog.'

'Slowly, slowly now…'

'Beside the track, about two yards from it, are four men – one sitting on the fence, another further back, and two standing in the grass, carelessly crushing kingcups, stitchwort and bladder campions. They're wearing muddy work boots, shabby trousers, dark and heavy winter coats. High-crowned bowler hats. Their expressions are grim; wet hair straggles with water. One in front has a beard, light-coloured.'

He struggles to see the face, but the beard and the hat pulled low make it difficult. Come back to him.

'Talk to me, Archie.'

'Yes, this one, slight build, aged about forty, wearing a black knitted scarf over his mouth, sallow skin, dark close-set eyes, dark shaggy eyebrows. The scarf blows back in the draught from the train, revealing a hard line of a mouth – no lips to speak of – and a thin pencil moustache. Pointed chin. Clean-shaven apart from the moustache. The one next to him is taller, perhaps a little younger, squarer-faced, fair complexion. This is the bearded one. His lower lip is thick and red, he has piggy blue eyes, and his hat brim hides his eyebrows. Behind the fence is an older man, paunchy, red face, baggy eyes, white hair and whiskers, sideburns, tweed hat, wearing a red-spotted neckerchief. His hat blows off in the gust of the train. He turns to get it.'

'The fourth?'

Not yet. Archie shut his eyes. Old man, old man, turn this way. No, he'd disappeared, off hunting for his hat.

'The fourth one, Archie?'

'Yes, the one on the fence is – is younger than the others, early twenties, I'd say, thickset, with dark greasy hair, dark skin, deep-set eyes, heavy eyebrows. Coat open, no buttons, leather waistcoat, collarless shirt, red neckerchief, floppy brown hat. High brown boots with buckles.'

'All right, Archie, that'll do. Let it go now. Take a deep breath. And another. In a moment I'm going to click my fingers and you will wake feeling refreshed and invigorated. You will forget—'

Before he could finish his sentence there came a sharp rat-a-tat on the door and Frank Tyrell poked his head in and said, 'Oh, sorry!'

Archie's eyes sprang wide.

Allsop cried, 'No-o!!' before the inspector could speak. 'Get out, you fool! Out!'

Archie said, 'Frank?'

'Sorry, sorry,' said Tyrell. 'I thought you must be finished.'

Allsop sucked angrily through his clenched teeth. 'Hell and damnation, man! Weren't you told not to disturb us? Don't you know the damage you could do?'

'It's all right,' said Archie. 'I'm fine.'

'Are you, though?' The hypnotist turned back to Frank and, with a little more decorum, said, 'Please go, Inspector. We must see what can be salvaged.' Frank retreated, wincing with embarrassment, and closed the door very quietly behind him.

'Stupid oaf,' muttered Allsop, through his teeth. We were so nearly there. Let's see. How much of the scene at the tunnel can you remember?'

Archie squeezed his eyes tight, as if dredging his subconscious for images. He shook his head. 'Rain, blurred shapes. Nothing at all,' he said. 'The train went too fast for me to see anything clearly.'

'Ah.' The hypnotist sighed, with relief or regret, it was hard to tell. 'Such a waste of my time and yours.'

'Do you want to try again?'

'No, no, that would be a mistake. Perhaps another time.'

Tyrell was waiting to help him back to his room. 'All right?'

'Think so. Quick, quick—' When the bedroom door was shut fast behind them, 'Paper, paper—' He grabbed his sketchbook and a pencil. 'It's all right, it's still here,' he said.

'I didn't hear him click his fingers like you said he would. I was afraid I was too late.'

But Archie had his eyes closed, and was breathing deeply, heading back towards the tunnel...

'Archie! Arch—' Tyrell's voice reached him from a long way off. 'Come to now, boyo, come back. You've done it.'

He took a deep breath and focussed on his friend. 'What?'

'Look.'

There on his lap was a drawing, a detailed close-up of a swarthy young man. Flipping over the page revealed an old man with white

149

hair. He was followed by a tall thickset figure with a beard, then a smaller weasel of a man, his scarf flying free. Then all four were there, staring straight ahead, their shoulders hunched, their eyes half closed against the teeming rain and the rush of air from the speeding train.

'That's them?' Tyrell had lit the lamp and drawn the curtains. Archie must have been 'out' longer than he realised.

'It is.'

'I'll click my fingers now, shall I?'

'Be on the safe side.' Tyrell's 'click' made no discernible difference, but Archie didn't want to be forever under Revilo's influence.

'There's more, you know. You started pages back.'

Slowly, with more than a little surprise, Archie leafed through the rest of his sketchbook, finding pictures he didn't remember drawing. There was the mouse he'd seen, and there the cow parsley shaking off water drops. A magpie flew off to the dark clouds, and there was a study of elderflower in close-up starry detail.

'Never seen nothing like it,' said Tyrell. 'Your pencil never left the paper, except when I turned the page for you. You're a what-d'you-call-it, boyo, a phenomenon. We could put you on the stage.'

'Not really, Frank. According to Freud, almost anyone's subconscious can be probed like this.'

'They can't all draw like you, though, Arch. Bloody brilliant.' He stroked his moustache. 'So, now all we gotta do is match the buggers to police records and haul them in. Tell you what, though, I reckon you was right not to trust old Revilo. He didn't want to try again, did he? Quite 'appy to let you go off thinking the consultation was a failure. Don't ever put 'im wise, is my advice. Did you hear him say, "*You will forget*—"? If I hadn't come in he was gonna wipe your mind clean, you mark my words. Someone's paying him to do that, else why bother?'

'I think I know who that is,' Archie said slowly and reminded the detective of the conversation across the auditorium the night before, whispers, wagging fingers, false smiles in their direction.

'You think Lord Beasley is behind this?'

'Well, someone wants to erase those faces from my memory.'

'I can't believe someone so grand would associate with that sort of riff-raff.'

'Unless they had something he wanted.'

'Like—?'

But neither could think of any common ground between the North and South poles of British society.

'He's good, though, say that for him.'

'Are you going to arrest him? For perverting the course of justice?'

'Need more proof, boyo. But if we keep an eye on him, we'll see if he leads us to someone. Tell you what, though, I will go and see if there's any more of that ginger cake. Almost as good as my Emma's.' He nodded at the sketchbook. 'Good job, Arch.'

When Tyrell had gone, Archie spent a long time in his armchair turning the pages, amazed at what could be achieved without drugs, and wondering why Oliver Allsop had wanted him to forget he'd seen these roughnecks.

There was a tentative knock on the door. 'A moment –' He put down the book.

It was Florence Anderson, his new friend. 'Just to say I've done those photos if you want to give them to Mr Tyrell. And— and I wondered how it went,' she said. 'I overheard your inspector telling the others how he'd barged in on your session. It's supposed to be dangerous, isn't it, to be woken suddenly from a trance?'

'I'm fine, thanks. Bit of a headache, but otherwise no ill-effects.' But she wasn't listening.

She was staring hard at his little fireside table: at Archie's sketchbook, lying open, at one of his recent drawings. She clutched one hand in the other, her knuckles standing proud.

'Archie—' she gulped, her eyes wide, the whites clear around the translucent irises. 'You must tell me – how do you know Lemmy King?'

151

Twenty-one

The weaselly little crook was one of her 'brother's' low-life acquaintances and one of his creditors – he'd been a persistent caller at the house in Hackney during Freddy's time in Pentonville. She eventually paid him off by working long hours in the studio, while her mother slept in her wheelchair, and by taking early-morning photos of Hackney, old and new, before anyone was about. They'd sold well, become collectors' pieces.

'What other pictures do you have? Oh dear, I – I shouldn't come into your room. Is there somewhere less compromising?'

The dining room was empty. The table was already laid for supper. She took the book over to the window for a better look and he followed, intrigued.

The pages quivered as she turned them. The old man with the white hair and the tall, bearded man were father and son, she said: Tuddy and Curly Skinner, the same Tuddy who had figured so large in Freddy's youth. He now ran a sleazy gaming club with his equally horrible son, Curly. They had both been regular poker players at the Porters' house, after her father's death, in games arranged by her brother. She didn't know the Romany.

'I'd steer clear of this crew, Archie, if I were you. They're evil.'

'I don't know them, Polly. These are the people I saw just before the train crashed.'

Her face blanked with horror. 'The train wreckers?' The breath went from her body. 'Oh! Archie, you know what this means?

That matchstick! That old Woodies' packet! It *was* my brother's. He was with them!'

'No, no, it doesn't mean that at all. I didn't see your brother, did I? I'd have known him. No, Tuddy and Co. wrecked the train to get someone else off the train, a convict…'

They stared at each other.

'What was his name, the convict?'

'Billy Maggs.'

The book fell to the floor. Polly staggered.

'Polly! Oh Lord, Miss er, Florence—'

She was distraught, beside herself – what were you supposed to do? Smelling salts? She groaned. He fetched a water jug and glass from the table. 'Here, drink some water, Polly. Careful. Small sips.'

'No, I need my wits about me.' She took a gulp, coughed and took another draught. 'You were saying?'

'What? Oh, about the convict on his way to Chelmsford Assizes, being sprung by the Skinner gang.'

'N-not B-Billy M-Maggs…' she managed to stutter. She drank more water and explained. Billy Maggs was a boy young Freddy used to bring home with him to 'play'. Neither of them knew the meaning of the word. She used to dread his visits. Between them, the boys made the little girl's life a misery. They'd tease her and make her do awful things like eat worms and beetles; they'd put glue in her hair, lock her in cupboards, sit her on the ground and poke her with sticks, make her cry. When her mother found out, she'd cry, too. Billy Maggs died young, got in the way of a runaway horse and carriage long, long ago. But yes, it stood to reason that Freddy would take the alias Billy Maggs to confuse the police. He was the only one who would.

'It *was* your brother!'

She scarcely heard him. 'And if they took him off the train j-just over the fields, on the other side of the woods, he could still be here, c-close by.'

153

'Not if he's any sense at all. There are policemen behind every tree looking for a runaway convict. He'll be far away by now.'

'I don't understand,' she said, 'why he was being taken to the Chelmsford Assizes in the first place?'

Better tell her. 'The police think your Freddy killed a man. They were taking him to the assizes to be tried for murder.'

'*Murder?* Oh, Freddy.' She buried her face in her hands. 'I knew it. I saw it in the newspaper. It was your drawing! And he really did it, did he? There's no doubt, no mistake? So that's why Tuddy wanted him off that train. He knew he'd be found guilty, that he'd hang. Another though occurred to her. The box! They said in the paper there was a rectangular object…' She shot a glance Archie's way. 'They'll go looking for it, and when they don't find it… Oh, God help me! All my running away was for nothing! *Nothing!*'

'Hush,' he said. 'Polly, hush, take it easy.' Her cries were becoming more frantic.

She ignored him. 'He's out there now, looking for me, and when he finds me he'll kill me this time, for sure! He has nothing to lose!' She rocked against the wall.

'Hey, stop, stop!' The last thing they needed was hysterics. 'Nobody wants to kill you, surely?'

Her hand flew to her mouth and she stared behind him.

Scratching his head, Frank Tyrell stood in the doorway. 'Oh, here you are! Sorry to interrupt, boyo, but I should be making tracks.'

'Frank, Frank, listen, the most amazing thing – Polly, em, yes, she's not – but she'll tell you. She can put names to them, the faces I remembered.' He offered her his hand to help her up. The poor girl looked as though she could have cheerfully flown away through the window on the Persian rug.

'Sorry, Polly, but we can't keep this from the police. Just tell Frank everything you've told me. He's the only one who can help you.'

The pale eyes became hard flints. If she could have killed him, she would have. 'No, no, I have nothing to say.'

'Look,' said Tyrell, coming into the room and scowling. 'Let's be clear, young lady. If you know something about the case, you'd better tell me. Withholding evidence is an offence, punishable by imprisonment. I suggest we clear a space at the table and do this properly. I'll fetch Beckett. Archie, I'll need you as a witness.'

In a few minutes he returned with a bemused constable. Archie and Polly, the latter white-lipped and drawn, had cleared four place settings and stacked them on the chiffonier in piles of napkins, cutlery and glasses, making room for four pairs of elbows, two notebooks and a sketchbook.

'Polly, eh? Would that be Polly Porter? They told me you'd copped it in the crash. They already buried you down home. You've got some explaining to do, my girl.'

As a weeping girl told the detectives why she had assumed a dead woman's identity, they browsed Archie's sketches of the Skinner gang. Meanwhile, he drew again, from memory, the bland, good-looking features of the man who had shot and trampled Jimmy Tomkins, and passed the sketch to the girl.

'Is this your brother?'

'Oh God. Yes, of course it is. You remember him from the market.'

'No, I remember him from a description given me by a policeman who was stabbed and almost trampled to death.'

Frowning, she shook her head as if trying to clear it. A shock would do that to you, he knew: confuse you, make you light-headed. 'Yes, of course, the picture in the *Guardian – The barefoot burglar…*'

Tyrell tapped the latest drawing, 'Also known as Billy Maggs. What's Freddy's surname?'

'Porter. Same as mine. My parents rescued him from the gutter as a child, and adopted him, though no papers were ever signed. He took the name Porter for want of another.'

'I see.' Tyrell nodded to Beckett who was making careful notes in his book, scoring heavily under several words.

'That day in the market, Mr Tyrell, the day I introduced myself to Archie, that was the first time I'd seen my brother in years. I thought he was still serving time in Pentonville for robbery with violence. He said he'd been looking for me. That day he – he gave me something to look after. I – I couldn't refuse.'

They waited.

Making grooves in the white starched tablecloth with a butter knife, she told them about a box he'd given her, a box she'd opened (she took a strengthening breath) to find hundreds of closely packed photographs – well, postcards.

'Postcards? What – views and that?'

'No.' With great difficulty, blushing madly, she blurted out, 'They were, you know, *indecent images.* Quite extreme, em, images.'

'All right, Miss,' Beckett said, with a frown, 'we get your meaning.'

Poor girl, thought Archie, this must be excruciating for her.

Tyrell looked up from his scribbles. 'So this box of mucky postcards – you didn't think to bring it to the police station?'

'I – I did, I was going to – but I thought you'd arrest me for receiving stolen goods. I suppose I wasn't thinking straight. I didn't know what to do, so I – I burned them.'

'You *burned* them!' exclaimed Beckett, his mouth agape. 'All of them?'

'You stupid little…' Tyrell was tearing what little hair he still possessed. 'They was evidence, they was! We could've traced the photographer, probably tracked down the entire vice ring and wiped it out!'

'Frank!'

'Archie, you don't realise what a chance—'

'Frank, hear her out.'

'But she's ruined—'

'Go on, Polly.'

She sighed. 'They were very old, antique, I should think. The photographer must be dead by now. He was a pioneer in photography, and it's such a pity he had to turn his hand to – to that. The thing is, Mr Tyrell, Freddy wanted my address so he'd know where to come for the box. But I – well, I didn't want him coming round, so I gave him a false address: 119 Church Street, in Stoke Newington – the post office!'

Archie snorted with laughter, much to Tyrell's disgust.

'Don't laugh, Archie, I was desperate.'

'I see,' said Tyrell, calmer now. 'So they'll go there for their box, find it's a fool's errand and…'

'And come back to the high street where he last saw me. Find my shop.'

'I *thought* I'd seen you before – next door to the Horse and Groom, right?'

At last.

Polly said, 'If he finds me he'll kill me for double-crossing him.'

'Not if we find him first. We'll keep an eye on the place for you, don't worry. Make a note, Stanley: the photo shop. We might strike lucky. Now then,' he said, eventually, 'I imagine this box of filth is what Freddy stole from Fitzell's house that night. You remember those parallel scrapes of blood across the desk, Stan? They'd fit the base of a box. How big was it, Miss?'

She described it by placing her hands on the table about eighteen inches apart and then twelve for the width and six for the depth. 'The empty box is still in my front room.'

'Aha! Make a note, Stanley.' Tyrell was stuffing his pipe with tobacco from a floppy leather pouch. 'D'you know, even to save his life Fitzell wouldn't part with that box. Just shows you the hold that sort of thing can have on a certain type of individual. *Erotica* they call it,' he explained to Polly. 'Don't suppose you'd know if your brother shared that interest?'

'He's taken dubious photographs, for money,' she admitted. 'Nasty enough, but not as evil as the ones this Fitzell had collected, the man he killed.'

'The man he is *said* to have killed,' he corrected her. She watched, fascinated, as he lit his pipe, sucking on the stem. She followed the flame being drawn again and again into the bowl, and when he wafted the match out and broke it with his thumbnail, she blinked in dismay. No, Archie told her silently, your brother isn't the only one to break spent matches. Tyrell went on, 'It's not yet proven, you see. Jeremiah Fitzell was found stabbed the morning after your brother was seen climbing back over his garden wall with a heavy sack, but that is not proof in itself. That's circumstantial. What we want is *irrefutable* evidence. Like if that box has Fitzell's blood on it.'

'You can tell a person's blood?' Archie asked.

'Blood group,' he said. 'We can tell if it's *not* his blood, or we can tell if it's likely – if someone has a rare blood group, say.'

'And did Fitzell? Have a rare blood group?'

'He did. A rhesus negative.'

'I see.' Polly rubbed her forehead, distractedly. 'Well, there is rust on the bottom of the box – whether it's blood, I couldn't say. But,' her face twisted in anguish, 'even if you have your *irrefutable* evidence, what good is it if you don't have Freddy?' Her voice rose. 'Shouldn't you be out there looking for him and the others, before he kills someone else – me, for instance?'

'Calm yourself, dear girl. We will, we will. Now we have names and faces it will help. Enormously.'

'Oh,' she suddenly remembered. 'The photographs I took yesterday…' She produced them from her handbag. 'You'd better have them.'

'You've done them already?'

'I was about to show them to Archie when…'

Tyrell spread them out on the table, black and white and matt.

There was the fence with the possibly incriminating clods of mud. Tyrell now had the packet of dried mud, containing sisal and sycamore bark, in his pocket, for scientists to examine. There were shots of the broken matchstick, the empty packet of Woodbines, the pugilist, all in situ, and there were the unshod

158

hoof prints. On the back of each photograph she had written the date, the location, and any measurements she had taken. There were those muddy footprints, clear as day, right and left feet, the tread worn on the outside edge of each. ('*Pointing towards the railway line,*' she had written, with arrows.)

'Curly is bow-legged,' she volunteered. 'He had rickets as a child.'

'What!' The three men drew their chairs closer. Beckett quickly wrote it down.

Tyrell blew a contemplative stream of smoke over the evidence. He examined the old man's print in the cowpat. ('*Pointing away from the railway line, ten yards in from the fence.*') 'Wonderful! Bloody wonderful,' he said.

'You say your brother went barefoot?' Beckett was scanning the montage of photos. There were no prints of bare feet.

'I was quoting the newspaper,' she said, and then sighed, 'but yes, he did. He found shoes constricting, but he was wearing them when I met him in the market.'

'He had shoes on when we had him in the clink. I took away his laces,' said Beckett.

'He preferred to have his feet bare when he was robbing houses.'

'Ah.'

'I used to follow him, sometimes, at night, without him seeing me. I couldn't believe his daring when I saw him climbing up house walls, fitting his fingers and toes onto the narrowest of ledges, holding on to nothing, it seemed to me, until he reached a window, which he'd open and slither in. I didn't wait around for him to come out again but hurried back home to bed. He always came home eventually, with a sack chinking with trinkets and money. It was always gone when I looked for it in his room the next day, and it was only later I learned that Freddy and the other children of the Roost turned over their hauls to Tuddy.'

So she'd known from an early age that Freddy was a thief. She'd kept this to herself until Pops died, when Mother had confessed that they, too, had known about Freddy's midnight jaunts. But they were powerless to stop him. They threatened him with the police, to send him away to school, to move to another part of the country, but to no avail. All he had to do was say he was returning to the streets for good and they would capitulate. 'They were afraid of losing him, you see,' she said.

'Why,' asked Archie, 'if he was such a bad lot?'

'Afraid of being seen to have failed,' said Tyrell. 'Afraid of what the neighbours would say.'

'Not really,' said Polly. 'They'd taken him off the streets to turn him into a good citizen and they had to keep trying, poor fools. But they couldn't compete with Tuddy.' In time, she told them, Tuddy Skinner, with money under his straw pallet, vacated the Roost, left it for the next generation of vagrants, and moved to the more salubrious climes of Whitechapel Road. But he remained a crook, running gaming houses and brothels. 'And Freddy followed where he led. He used Pops' cameras and equipment for Tuddy's own "sideline" and poor old Pops could do nothing about it.'

'Really?' said Beckett. 'This Tuddy was into mucky photos, too?'

'They ran it from the brothels.'

Tyrell patted her shoulder. 'Thank you, my dear,' he said, 'I know it's been hard for you, telling us all this, but you've helped this investigation along no end. These photos put the bastards at the scene of the crime, right where we want them. And these drawings, boyo, can we take them back with us? Get them etched up and printed for posters? We can even put names to 'em, thanks to you.' He drew on his pipe but it had gone out. 'We'll get to the bottom of it, won't we Stan? Mucky postcards, eh? It takes all sorts,' he said, shaking his head sadly over the evils of men. 'As for you, young lady, I'd keep that alias if I was you. They ain't gonna be looking for no Florence Anderson, your brother and his mates. And up in this neck of the woods you might be safer than down home. Yeah, you stop here for the time being.' He sounded

160

as if he was prescribing medicine. 'I'll square it with Mrs Gifford before I go. Right?'

'Ri-ight,' she echoed doubtfully. 'You're not going to tell the Giffords what I've told you?'

'No, no, my dear – you're Florence Anderson who has sold up back in what – Tottenham?'

'Lewisham.'

'And the job you was going to in Colchester has now been filled, so you're presently homeless. I'll say Mrs G will be doing you a favour putting you up for a bit longer, just till you get back on your feet, and I'll give the good lady a little something towards your keep, on the QT – no need to worry your little head about that.'

When they were alone and Tyrell was relighting his pipe, Archie tried to persuade him to stay on. 'Do you really have to get back tonight? That poor girl is frightened sick. We have to offer her some protection, don't we?'

'I couldn't agree more, Arch, but I'm afraid I can't hang about here when there's surveillance to organise – that post office in Stoke Newington, for one, and Miss Porter's shop. I need to be near a telephone. I may be too late, of course, but I'd really like to catch the buggers in the act. Plus – and it's a big plus – I need to get to the bottom of another little matter, like who the devil told the Skinners we were sending Billy Maggs to Chelmsford in the first place!'

'Oh Lord,' said Archie, running his palm across his chin. 'That's a nasty one, Frank. Someone's either been very careless or there's a rotten apple in the barrel.'

'It's got me beat, I can tell you. Trying to think who I told, apart from the escort, of course, and they're both beyond asking. There's been a bit of correspondence between me and the county court, of course, letters and telegrams, and to and from Springfield Prison, but that's all locked away safe in the file and everyone sworn to secrecy. Even Billy Maggs didn't know where he was headed.'

'Tough one.'

'I just wondered if Reggie let something slip. He mixed with some rum characters down at the wrestling booth, and if he'd been drinking…'

'Will we ever know, Frank?'

The detective was quiet for a few moments, taking a puff or two of his pipe. 'Think I'll send someone along there anyway. You never know.'

'I suppose I'd better stay on here for a while, too. I can't abandon the poor girl.'

'You could do worse, boyo. She's a nice-looking little thing.'

'Is she?'

'Oh, not to be compared to your Lizzie, but she has a pretty smile.' He took a moment to knock out his pipe on a side plate. 'Well,' he said, 'the Giffords are quite happy for you to stay. I put it to them you might do their picture. You're all kitted out now, aren't you, with canvas and that? Should keep you out of mischief.'

So there was method in the detective's generosity. 'You set it up, you crafty old devil!'

Of course he did. 'And there's Kitty Flanagan in Chelmsford for the season. You could borrow the pony and trap and be there in an hour.'

'Frank, behave yourself!'

'No, I mean you could paint her again. You used to say she was your muse, didn't you? Paint her singing on the stage. Truth to tell, Arch, you'd be helping me out no end if you hung around here for a while, kept an eye on the girl. As you say, she's vulnerable. Take *her* to the music hall, cheer the poor little creature up a bit. See, it ain't my patch, and the railway police are getting a bit shirty over me sticking my nose in, like. But those dirty blighters who killed Reggie are up to something round here, I feel it in my water. Why else would they stop the train out here in the sticks? No, there's some caper they've got planned, and that cat burglar, Freddy Porter, is mixed up in it somehow.'

'So you're leaving us up here like sitting ducks?'

'The Skinners have no idea where the girl is. They'll be looking for Polly Porter of Hackney, not Florence Anderson, house guest of a gentleman farmer in Little Nessing. She's safer here than anywhere else. I suppose I could lock her up in the high street cells for her own safety, but she might object to that. It won't be for long, I'm sure, and we'll have them buggers behind bars quicker 'n spit.'

The horses were in a lather, having been there and back in an afternoon. 'What you playing at, Freddy?' Onas shouted. They hadn't let Freddy go as it was too close to home. There were a few posters in Stoke Newington with his face on. '119's a fecking post office!'

'What!' Tuddy cried, eyes red as a rabid dog. 'Double-crossing bastard!' His right fist caught Freddy square on the jaw, knocking him to the ground. 'You dare!'

Freddy shook his head and slithered out of reach of Tuddy's swinging boot, holding up his hands for mercy. Tuddy in this mood was a killer. 'That's the number she gave me!' he pleaded.

Tuddy stood still, lip curled, piggy eyes screwed in thought. His boot, when it connected with Freddy's thigh, was restrained – one for luck. 'Yeah,' he sniffed, as Freddy struggled gratefully to his feet, 'that's the number you passed on. "Write this dahn," he says. "One-one-nine Church Street, Stoke Newington," he says. I lost the bit of paper, but I got it in 'ere.' The old man tapped his forehead. 'Wouldn't forget a fing like that.'

'Course not, Tuddy.'

'I mean, a bleeding post office? What, she's took lodgings under the counter, 'as she?'

'Your bitch sister's pulled a fast one, Fred!' Lemmy had a horrible sneer across his chops, his pencil moustache ready to take off like a happy little bird. He loved seeing Freddy hot and bothered.

'Not my Poll.' He rubbed his jaw. 'She wouldn't. She knows better'n to cross me.'

'Who else would it be, then, Freddy?'

That was true. He was mortified.

Onas wiped his horse's neck with a handful of hay and rolled his dark eyes at the sky. 'Jaisus,' he said, his gold tooth sparking in the firelight, 'sending us on a feckin' fool's errand, Freddy. You shoulda known better than to trust a feckin' woman…'

'Never did like that superior mare,' said Lemmy.

Freddy wasn't sure what he'd ever seen in her either. '*Superior mare*' was right, always looking down her nose at him, lips tight as a cat's arsehole. Stolen goods? She wouldn't dirty her hands on them. Sooner starve. Never once had she said, well done, Freddy boy, for bringing home the bacon. Yet again. Even Ma had been grateful. But not whiter-than-white Miss Goody Two Shoes. Not only had she got one over on him this time, showing him up to his mates, she'd shown him her true feelings. Playing hide and seek, for fuck's sake! 'I'll swing for you, Poll,' he swore and meant it.

'*I* would,' said the old man. 'Can't have no bitch taking you for a mug, Fred.'

'He'll have to find her first, Tuddy,' said Lemmy King. 'False address to put him off the scent, then legged it, I betcha. An' you thinking she was so bleeding fond o' you, eh?'

'Yeah, I did,' he said, feeling shameful tears welling up.

'Got any ideas, 'ave ya?' said Tuddy. 'Some bloke sniffing round? Some bird who mighta took her in or some old auntie you've forgot about?'

'She didn't have any. No mates, no aunties. Ma took all her time up, and now she's snuffed it Poll's on her own.' He cuffed his nose and thought hard. 'My guess is she'll flog those postcards, make a packet on the deal, and piss off to the sun.'

'Nah, a woman couldn't flog 'em.'

'Polly could.'

'Where did you see 'er that time?'

'Walthamstow market…'

'So what you doin' 'ere then? Get off down there and ask around.'

'I don't think…'

'Never mind thinking. We need that gear now. The geezer'll go off the boil if we don't get a wiggle on.'

'Tuddy, I daren't show my face down there; you know that, not after Fitzell.'

'Onas's bird'll make you over, eh, Onas? What d'you think? Tall, dark and handsome should do it, eh? They'll never know ya.' He sniggered. 'Tomorrer. Lemmy, you go wiv 'im.' He turned back to Freddy. 'Lemmy knows the place like the back of his hand – well, the wrestling booths, any old 'ow. S'where you bent that copper, were'n'it, the Standard? Good job he never lived to tell the tale, eh? Lemmy'll see you right, Freddy. He likes you. I don't ask why!'

Twenty-two

The Mackays were staying for supper and there was much to discuss, most notably the police, who'd only just departed, and the hypnotist who had 'cut across' to dine with his friend, the baronet.

Effie was less than thrilled with her experience of hypnotism. 'I don't know what I was expecting, but I feel "intruded upon", you know?' She put on a sonorous voice, *'There is something you are ashamed of, something close to your heart, that you cannot tell your parents, but you can tell me...* Well, I don't know what, if anything, I told him, but he shouldn't be able to access that sort of thing, surely?'

'Good God, Effie!' exclaimed her father.

'What sort of thing?' asked her stepmother, more mildly.

'I'm not telling you; that's the whole point. A girl must have some secrets.'

'Of course. He didn't, er, molest you?' He turned to his wife. 'You really should have gone in with her, Mabel.'

'I didn't know she was...'

'I was perfectly all right, Papa. I'm probably not a good subject, or whatever they call it. Doubting Thomas. I was perfectly aware, perfectly in control from start to finish. I slapped his face. He was still spluttering and protesting that I had the wrong idea about him as I slammed the door on my way out. No, he's just a dirty old man like his friend across the field, the very dishonourable Lord Beasley.'

'That bounder!' said her father, relaxing a little.

'Indeed.' She raised her eyebrows, exchanging a knowing glance with the doctor. Archie had the impression that the two were very close and probably had very few secrets from each other. 'You had a lucky escape, Florence.'

'So it seems. What's this about Lord Beasley?' Polly asked.

'Oh, this not really a subject for the dinner table, Effie,' said her father.

'She ought to be on her guard, Papa. Beasley is a lecher,' she said baldly. 'Beastly Beasley. You should see the pictures he has on his bedroom wall.'

Archie spluttered soup, nearly choking. The doctor explained that he and his daughter had had to attend his lordship during an attack of influenza. And yes, he wasn't betraying his Hippocratic oath to confirm that the man's idea of art was a little extreme – but each to his own.

'Well, I'm not bound by the oath, not yet, and I tell you, he's a horror. Papa was called up there the other day, to a burns case…'

'*Effie!*' Her father shook his head, but she tossed her curls, ignoring him.

'Unused to gas,' she told them all, 'a pretty young scullery maid had turned on the oven, delayed lighting it, and poof!' Her right hand made explosive movements.

'Oh my Lord,' said Archie. 'That's awful.'

'Poor Millie's face, chest and hands were burned. The girl was screaming with pain, so they sponged her with cold water and called for Papa, who dressed the burns as best he could. It looked quite serious, great watery blisters and singed hair. But when she came into the surgery last night so I could change her dressings, do you know what she said? "They *will* be permanent, won't they?" She meant the scars, Archie, almost as if she *wanted* to be disfigured. Of course, I tried to reassure the poor girl. I told her to come in regularly to have the dressings changed, and she could wear her hair differently to hide the worst, and Millie said, "Perhaps the old bugger will leave me alone now."'

167

'Language, Effie,' said her stepmother.

'Did she, by Jove?' Ice water trickled down Archie's spine. Some men were beasts, rotten to the core.

Florence lay down her spoon. 'I understand her reasoning.' She closed her eyes.

Archie held his breath. He knew what she was thinking, but she wouldn't say it, not here, surely?

She said, 'She was hoping to make herself repugnant in his eyes.'

'Oh, Florence, no one would go to such lengths,' said Lilian.

'You would if you were desperate enough. That girl, Millie, needs her job badly, and with the job goes the old – goes Lord Beasley.'

'Oh,' said Effie, 'Millie's not the first. He forced himself on a laundry maid a couple of years ago, got her in the family way. She left in a hurry and no one knows what became of her. And there was a parlour maid who lost her baby. She's still working up there. Then there was this young stable lad…'

'Effie, stop!'

'Dear Papa, you know what he's like. I have had to remove the noble hand from my own knee before now. He's one of the reasons for the revolver. You have no idea, Archie … minister … Richard,' she glanced around the table, 'what girls have to put up with.'

'I think I do,' said Archie. He pushed his plate away. 'My wife told me how women have to be constantly on their guard against stray hands, stray comments, unwanted attention. She said when women have the vote hopefully things will change.'

'Let us hope so,' said Norris.

'What about Lady Beardsley?' Lilian asked. 'Can't she put a stop to his carryings-on?'

'I don't think she has much to do with him,' said Effie. 'Her quarters are on the other side of the big house.'

'And hasn't anyone complained to the authorities?'

168

'What authorities?' said Florence, with some heat. 'The police? There aren't any laws to stop these "carryings-on" as you put it. Whom do you complain to? Slavery was supposed to have been abolished sixty years ago, but who needs a slave when you have a wife or a concubine or a maid afraid to lose her job?'

Archie sucked his teeth. This was true.

'Things will change,' said Norris, with some confidence. 'It's in the air, mark my words.'

Thomas and Maud brought in the next course. Everyone seemed to welcome the excuse to change the subject.

'Oh, Papa, while I remember, did that man come into surgery this morning, while I was in the dispensary? The one with the gunshot wound?'

'No? Waiting room was full, but there were no gunshot wounds.'

'I thought I might have missed him. I hope he's all right.' She turned, with a frown, to tell the other diners, 'Last night, when Papa was off on his rounds, I was in the dispensary making up the medicines, when a couple of strangers walked in. I mean not from round here – townies from the sound of them. Probably from the train.' She put on a deep, rough, totally exaggerated Cockney accent: '"'Ere, darlin', you're my last 'ope. Anyfink in your medical kit for my boy, 'ere? 'E's 'ad a nasty accident!" The patient had a stinky arm. I mean really stinky. Infected. The man with him said he'd been cleaning his gun a few days ago. It had gone off and he'd shot himself. Not that I believed him. Someone had chewed up some nettles or something and slapped that on, wrapped it up with rags, but it hadn't done any good. Some of the country remedies work, but many don't and this was one of them. The bullet had passed straight through, but it looked to me like septicemia. I said he ought to wait until Papa came home, for him to have a look. I've cleaned gunshot wounds before now, even dug bullets out with my bare hands, but this was all full of pus. Looked to me like the arm would have to come off. I'm not up to that, not on my own. I said I reckoned there was cotton in there somewhere, from his shirt, you know?'

Some of her listeners were green about the gills.

'Effie, dear,' pleaded her hostess, 'we're trying to eat…'

'Oh, sorry, I thought you'd be interested.'

'I am—' Archie and Florence spoke in unison.

'Anyway, I cleaned the man's wound as best I could with alcohol, put on a clean bandage, and made him a sling. It still stank like rotten fish. I charged him a shilling, and told him to come back this morning so you could have a look at it.'

'Well, he didn't come.'

Lilian looked worried. 'Oh Duncan, that's awful. Anyone can walk in off the streets – how can you leave the girl on her own like that, quite unprotected? And there are drugs, morphine, chloroform…'

'I'm not unprotected, Auntie Lilian. I have my revolver.'

Lilian's mouth set like a clamp.

'Archie,' Florence said, quietly, 'you don't have your sketchbook handy, do you?'

'I'll fetch it.' Scraping back his chair, he reached for his crutch.

Back at the table, he folded the book open at the sketch of the Skinner foursome and put it beside Effie's plate. 'The man with the bullet wound – was he one of these?'

'Yes, that's him.' Without hesitation, Effie jabbed a fork at the drawing of Curly Skinner. 'And this was the man who came in with him,' she said, pointing at Tuddy.

'So, they're still around,' he muttered.

Effie looked up. 'How is it you have their likenesses, Archie?'

'I saw them from the train,' he said. He compressed his lips. Of course, that wouldn't do. He looked over at the girl they knew as Florence with a question, and she swallowed hard and nodded. Yes, she gave him permission to tell them her part in the mess, if it came to it. As his host and hostess and their guests passed the sketchbook around, trying not to dip it in their gravy, he told

170

them how he had seen a blur of four men at the tunnel entrance before the train crashed.

'And you managed to draw them?' said Effie. 'The train must have been travelling at what – forty miles an hour!'

With the hypnotist's help, he told them, he had focused his mind on those men, seen their faces and drawn them. That was his job, back in Walthamstow: police artist. Inspector Tyrell had taken his sketches back to Chelmsford to print into posters to put around the town. These were copies. Soon everyone would be on their guard against the villains.

'According to Inspector Tyrell,' he went on, 'they used horses to pull that tree onto the line. Florence and I went to have a look yesterday and it's quite obvious. They engineered the crash.'

Lilian Gifford clasped her hands to her breast and smiled at her husband in relief. Their forestry management was not to blame.

'If you'll turn over the page, Lilian – that is Freddy Porter, a murderer. I drew him back in Walthamstow. He was travelling in the guard's van under police escort on his way to the Chelmsford Assizes, but clearly these men wanted him back. They stopped the train, stabbed the escorts and freed him.'

'I saw the van swimming in blood and – and the bodies, three of them,' Effie said, her face reflecting the pain of the event. 'I didn't realise. I thought the crash had somehow shattered a window or a mirror and that glass had somehow pierced their bodies.'

'Anyway,' he continued, 'that's how Curly Skinner got shot. It was no accident, Effie. One of the police managed to shoot him before dying of stab wounds.'

After the clamour that greeted this statement, he said it now looked certain that the men were still in the area. He didn't know why they were hanging around Little Nessing. As Effie said, they were real townies. They must hate it in the country. But they were armed with knives, at least, very dangerous, and should be given a wide berth.

'How do you know his name, Archie?'

Oh, Effie, thought Archie, *you'll cut yourself you're so sharp.* 'Sorry,' he said, looking somewhat thrown, 'I didn't…'

'You said the police escort shot Curly Skinner. How do you know his name?'

'I, um—' All eyes were on him. Avoiding looking at Florence, he lied for her. 'Tyrell told me. The Skinner gang – they're well known to the police. This older one, Curly's father, is Tuddy. This one is Lemmy King. Don't know this one,' he indicated the sallow-skinned fellow in front with the earring.

'I do,' said Lilian, unexpectedly. 'He helps out from time to time, digging potatoes, dousing the sheep. You know, dear,' she turned to Richard, 'the gypsy – Onas Something – Onas…' She squeezed her eyes. 'Hmm, did I ever know his other name?'

'Shipton!' Her husband thumped the table, making the spoons and crusts jump about. 'Lives down on Membury Common, by the river – the gypsy encampment. His wife, Lavinia, makes a nuisance of herself selling rabbits' feet and flowers round the doors.'

'I'd better send Tyrell a wire.'

'Too late, Archie. The post office is shut by now.'

'Surely the postmistress will open up in an emergency?'

'You don't know Harriet Manning…'

'What about the village bobby?' said Norris.

'Old Philpot? He's only used to poachers and scrumpers. He wouldn't stand a chance against five armed murderers.'

'I'll take the trap to Chelmsford,' said the doctor. 'Fetch the police.'

'I'll come with you,' said Effie. Her blue eyes were bright with excitement. 'That's where they are, your gang, Archie. Right here! With the gypsies down on Membury Common. No wonder the poor man's arm was festering if Lavinia Shipton's been treating it. Her love potions don't work either!' She giggled, with a sly look at Archie.

Polly was very quiet. Her dinner was pushed away, half eaten. She had gone as white as the tablecloth, her eyes dark smudges.

'They're here,' she murmured, 'half a mile up the road...'

'Nearer two miles,' Richard put her right. 'There are woods in between.'

But that didn't make any difference to Polly. She was casting about, her eyes darting here and there. 'I must pack. I can't stay here. I...'

'Why would they come here, Florence?' Lilian reasoned. 'We have nothing for them.'

'I – I must – must get away.'

'Inspector Tyrell was most insistent you stay here...'

She calmed down eventually, and the dinner guests left, all agog, while Richard and Lilian went about the house, barring the windows and doors, and gathering shotguns and pistols to oil and prime.

'Archie – I've had an idea.'

They were in the drawing room with Norris, a sleeping chaperone. Archie looked up from his book, smiling. He'd been laying bets that she would be the first to speak.

'What we need is an actual *photograph* of Freddy with the gypsies – and of the others, of course, but Freddy's the one who murdered that man in Walthamstow, he's the one the police were sending to the assizes. The wanted picture appeared in the paper weeks ago, but people will remember it, I'm sure, and if they can see the likeness between that drawing and a photograph of him with the gypsies, they'll know where he is and who helped him.'

'How are you going to take a photo without them seeing you?'

'No, no, you – you're right, of course.' Poor girl, she was still frightened out of her wits. She'd been dropping cotton reels all over the place, sticking herself with sewing needles. He'd had to thread her needle for her. She stood up, gathering her mending. 'No. It's a waste of time thinking about it. Of course, it's impossible. They know me. You're – like you are.'

173

'What do you mean?' he laughed.

'You couldn't run fast enough. How could we possibly do it?'

'We?' he demanded. 'I see. No,' he said, as she started to go, 'I think you're onto something. Wait a minute, Polly. Sit down, sit down. I think I know a way.'

Twenty-three

Lavinia cut and dyed his hair and eyebrows, shaved off his mutton chops, and lent him her father's shiny old wedding suit and shoes. 'There,' she said, 'now the specs. Oh, what a fine gen'lman you are, Freddy!'

'You don't have a couple of hatpins, do you, darlin'? The filth took away my tools in clink, and I've a feeling I'm going to need something.'

'Ye even talk posh,' she observed. 'How d'you ever get mixed up wi' this crew?'

'Oh, I'm one of them, duckie, make no mistake, cut from the same cloth. Tuddy's been like a father to me all my life. Who else would've rescued me from the gallows? Only Tuddy.'

'He'm no good.'

'He saved my life.'

'So now you owe'n. 'E'm got ee where 'e wants ee. In Beasley's pocket.'

'And you're not? Fuck, if I were Onas, I'd up sticks and move on. Supposed to be a traveller, isn't he? But he just sits here in Little Nessing and takes it, bloody cuckold. Lets Beasley bed his wife whenever the fancy takes him.'

'Don't, Archie. Onas takes it very 'ard. Beasley can do what 'e likes round 'ere, you know that.'

'Move on. Go while you're all still in one piece. He'll ruin your lives.'

'T'ain't so bad. 'E turns a blind eye to us poachin'.'

'Oh, Lavinia! Go and find me some hatpins, for goodness' sake.' The old letch could do what he liked with Lavinia and if Onas complained, Beasley would get Tuddy to top him, without a qualm. Tuddy was not sentimental. The only person he cared for was Curly, his son by some tart in the dim and distant past. He must have had other progeny, but they weren't left on his doorstep – well, on the tiles – for him to take care of.

Lavinia's hat was a black bowler handed down through the men of her family, and it stayed on in the fiercest gale, so she didn't need hatpins, but she asked around and came back with a fine specimen, gold-topped and bejewelled. Lovey Watkins' granny had worn it for her wedding.

'Nah, too fancy,' he said, rejecting it.

Off she went again, knocking on caravan doors. Came back with two, one with a silver crescent moon, the other, a jet bird with spread wings. 'All I could find,' she said. 'They wants 'em back.'

'They'll do,' he said, poking them into his lapel.

'No,' she said, 'not like that – too flashy.' She fastened them, one each side, under each lapel so they didn't show.

You could see what Beasley saw in her. Under her greasy black hair, she was a good-looker was Lavinia. See her sitting on the caravan steps, peeling spuds, smoking her pipe, or skinning a rabbit round the fire, laughing with her cousins, showing her fine white teeth, a man might dream of wild nights and wicked sex. But Beasley had claimed her, and you didn't go against his lordship. Freddy had no doubt Tuddy would kill him, too, just as easily. As for Onas, well, who gave a tinker's for Onas? Only Lavinia, and she would come to her senses one of these days.

He felt rough; he hadn't slept a wink. Quite apart from Curly tossing and turning, filling the caravan with the stink of his rotting arm and his hollering, the terrible, shameful moment when they discovered Polly had made fools of them had been playing over and over in his mind.

*

It didn't take them five minutes to find out where she lived. There were no stalls out this afternoon: early closing on Wednesday. So all the shops were shut, everything, except a pub near the top of the main street. They left the horses round the back hitched to a rail.

'Polly Porter, you say? Oo's asking, if I might make so bold?' The old girl pulling pints was acting cagey. Strange, Freddy thought.

When he said he was her brother, he was expecting the usual flirty, 'Plain to see who got the looks in *your* family, darling,' but instead her flabby face puckered like an old deflating balloon. 'Her brother! 'Course, I remember you from – ooh, must be a week or so back. You come along while I was getting me picture done. You won't have heard, then? Oh dearie, dearie me, you best sit down, son.'

When he heard that Polly was a casualty of the Chelmsford train crash and that Mrs Reeves had been one of the few mourners at her graveside, 'just last Saturday, up Saint Mary's', he and Lemmy both sat down hard on a bench against the wall, the news a knife thrust under the ribs.

'Bugger me!' said Lemmy. 'Poor old Poll.'

'*She* was *on the fucking train!*' Freddy buried his head in his hands. 'No-o-o,' he moaned. She had cared. She'd been on the train, going to the Assizes to see him tried, as he'd thought. It wasn't fair! All his dreams of domestic bliss drifted out of the pub door like an old man's pipe smoke. They could have made a go of it, him and Poll. He'd have won her round. Who could he blame? 'You and your train crash killed my fucking *sister*!' he growled, jabbing his finger at Lemmy.

A hissed, 'Shut the fuck up!' changed swiftly to a more appropriate, 'Freddy, old mate, I'm so sorry,' as the landlady came within earshot, bearing three whiskies on a tray, one for herself.

'On the 'ouse, boys,' she said. 'Condolences, condolences.'

'Yeah, right,' said Lemmy, into his handkerchief.

'Yeah, poor little mite, and on'y just moved in next door! See the photo she done?' She pointed to an enlargement on the wall over the bar. 'Them's all our reg'lars lined up outside. That's me and *Mr* Reeves. *That's* me, an' all,' she simpered, pointing to a pencil drawing. 'You see 'im doin' it, didn't you? Done it lovely, ain't he?' They grunted their admiration, while marshalling their scrambled thoughts. 'Goin' on 'er 'olidays, she was, up Yarmouth for the cure. Asked me to stop 'er milk and papers and keep an eye on the place. And she goes and gets herself topped, poor little mare.' She polished her pudgy red nose, sniffed back her tears. 'Well, I s'pose yore be takin' over the shop, now, won't ya?'

Not likely. Bleeding millstone round your neck, bricks and mortar. Though she'd said it was rented. Still, he could sell the cameras and that. They should have come to him anyway – Mr and Mrs Porter's beloved son. Fetch a bit, those cameras. That was why Polly had been stringing him all that guff. Never wanted him to find her and take what was rightfully his, lying bitch. Wonder her tongue hadn't fallen out. Well, it probably had by now.

Stoke Newington, be damned, Polly's shop was just a few steps along from where he'd left her that day. Newly painted, waiting for the sign to go up. Nice little place, as it happened. Curtains upstairs and everything. But it was all locked up tighter than a witch's whatsit, and the missus eyeballing every move they made.

'You best nip over the police station,' said the old girl when they'd downed their drinks and gone outside. 'Tell them who you are and they'll let you in. They got them skellington keys.'

But the clink was the last place they could go. The cops'd think it was Christmas.

How were they going to get in? Ten to one that's where the stash was: in a cellar or up a chimney or under the floorboards. Polly was always hiding stuff from him in Hackney – money, food, Ma's laudanum. He found himself swallowing an unexpected lump in his throat. Poor old Addie. Gone at last. And Polly. He was the last of the Porters.

Lemmy shaded his eyes to see past his reflection in the window. Inside, a pot of whitewash stood on the floor. 'Now I'm thinking—' he whispered. 'There used to be a way underground. I'm wond'rin' if them putting in the sewers fucked it up.' He sucked his bottom lip thoughtfully, making a kissing sound. 'Well, there's one way to find out, Freddy, on'y one way. We're gonna need candles and that.' He turned to where Old Beady Eyes was propped against the wall at a polite distance, but watching their every move. 'If we might impose on you again, my dear –'

Back they went to the Horse and Groom, on the pretext of using the privy out the back. In and out and half a dozen candle stubs the richer, they took their leave of the landlady.

'Best go and break the news to the family—'

Off they went, down the road, passing pubs and shops and houses. They eventually came to hoardings where a skull and crossbones made clear this was a deserted building site. *Danger Keep Out!* A small enamelled notice said it was private land. Yeah, right. Some geezer, Percival Reeves, was going to build the Walthamstow Palace of Varieties on this spot.

Lemmy jerked his head. 'Down here, mate.'

No 'mate' of yours, thought Freddy. There was no love lost. His own fault, bungling the Culpepper job. He'd gone to jail owing Tuddy and the boys money. Polly had settled it, but Lemmy hadn't visited him in Pentonville. Tuddy said Lemmy liked him, but it wasn't true. They'd worked well together in the past and that was it. All the same, he followed Lemmy down an alleyway to a roughly boarded door in the fence locked by a padlock.

'Got your gear?' Lemmy stopped to get out a tobacco pouch and roll himself a fag before passing the pouch to Freddy. He hunched in the door to light up against the wind. 'Get going, Freddy,' he said.

Looking around, Freddy drew out his 'knife and fork', the hatpins from his lapels, one in each hand. These clever little darlings poked inside the tiny lock. Come on, come on – he'd done this a hundred times. The bad news about Polly was making him all fingers and thumbs, that and Lemmy breathing down his neck. Gotcha! He felt the mechanism release.

Lemmy pushed Freddy through the open door and closed it behind them, kicking a loose brick into place to hold it shut. They looked around. Nothing. Foundations had been laid for the new building and then work had stopped.

'Down there,' said Lemmy.

They climbed down brick footings for about eight feet to a dirt floor full of puddles. 'This was where the basement was,' he said. 'There should be a tunnel going under the street.' There was – via a dusty old door in the wall – without a handle, but Lavinia's hatpins made short work of that.

It opened onto a dark dirt tunnel and they lit a candle each.

'Sewers musta gone in over the top,' said Lemmy, 'that's good.'

Jesus, it was creepy. They had underground passages like this over in the Old Nicol, with pit props keeping the ceiling from falling in and spiders' webs hanging like curtains. Some of Bethnal Green's derelicts lived down there, strays and addicts, but Tuddy's boys had preferred the Roost, and fresh air. Gawd, the stink down here was chronic.

'Don't mind rats, do ya?'

He shook his head. This stench was more than rats. Human rats had been pissing down here – and worse. 'Is it safe?' he asked. A draught caught his candle and nearly blew it out. He cupped his hand more securely round the flame.

'Yeah, course. Been here 'undreds a years. Used to duck down here meself when the cops was after us and things was tight. They only found out about the tunnel a few years back. Been talking about closing it, but they ain't, so that's all right. Hear that?' He stopped and cocked his ear. There was a faint rumble as a heavy cart went along overhead. No earth shook loose. They couldn't hear the horses' hooves. 'Safe as 'ouses,' said Lemmy.

The next door was unlocked and led into a more substantial-looking tunnel with a brick wall to one side. Tree roots poked through the mud and the floor was pocked with footprints. A placard on a door read 'Doll's Hospital'.

'Their basement,' Lemmy explained. 'There's cellars and storerooms all along here. It's the underground route, if you like.'

Sure enough they passed by the Chequers pub, stinking of booze, an oil merchant's, and the Sally Army, though their entrance had been bricked up – many moons ago, it looked like. Above here was the tea shop where he and Polly had had that drink. A baker's shop, a shoe shop, a fish shop, though none of these were labelled. You could tell by the smell what they sold. And here was the boozer they'd just come from.

'Now then,' said Lemmy as they breathed in a faint cheesy smell. 'This'll be it. Used to be Higson's cheesemongery before your Polly took it on. Grew their own Cheddar down here, if I'm not mistaken.' He stopped at a door with the number 339 chalked on it.

'Take the candle, Lemmy.' Freddy bent to examine the keyhole. 'Closer. Let the dog see the rabbit.'

A fiddle and a poke, a sharp twist o' the wrist, and they were in. Jesus, he was good.

The acrid smell of lye made Lemmy's rat eyes glint and his thin whiskers twitch. He looked down at the gleaming floor tiles. 'She was a grafter, your sister. Woulda made someone a good wife.'

'Yeah – me,' he muttered bitterly.

'Don't give us that, Fred. You never give a stuff for that dowdy little drab. She was 'andy and that was about it.'

'Nah!' he protested, but yeah, he thought, Lemmy could be right. He'd felt more affection for his mates on the street than for the family who had taken him in. The boys had accepted him for what he was. At Maybank Road it had always been 'Must try harder'. He was a disappointment.

There was a brick washtub up against the wall, soap and grater, jar of soda, blue bag, scrubbing board and brush lined up neatly on the draining board and, behind the little fire door, paper and kindling laid ready for the next washday. An empty ashcan told its own story. Broom, mop and bucket stood to attention. He parked his candle on the copper lid.

'So, d'you reckon they'll be down here, Fred, them photos o' Fitzell's?'

'Soon see,' he shrugged. 'It's a tin box. There's crates over here – boxes. Mind the coal heap…'

Lemmy started tugging at lids, using a fire iron he found as a jemmy. There was a grinding of glass, and a cracking sound.

'Go easy, Lem. Them's glass plates. Negatives.' He took out a slide and peered at it in the candlelight. Kids playing round a lamp post. Had to be hers or the old man's. Not his, certainly. He slotted it back carefully and took another. Some old beggarwoman on the street. What was that for? No one would buy that. Nevertheless he replaced it gently. These were his now she had snuffed it, and you never knew, they might be worth a bob or two in time.

Here were boxes that were older, dustier. He prised one open. As he held a negative up to the candlelight, his heart leapt. Well, well, who'da thunk it? She hadn't checked through these. Blimey, that was a long time ago. He couldn't have been very old. Youngest cameraman on the block. They'd sold. The magazine – what was it called, *Gentleman's Relish*? Yeah, like the pickle, very spicy. They had taken the lot and paid him for them. Those were the days. If necessary – if they couldn't find Fitzell's stash – these might have to do.

'Come on, Freddy.'

These negs hadn't seen the light of day in, oh, years and years. Taking off his shoe, he used the heel to tap the nails back into their holes. 'Lemmy, if we can't find the Voss prints, we'll use these negatives to make our own smut and hope to God Beasley doesn't twig. I'm no Dutch master and these've been used already, so

182

strictly speaking, they're seconds. But keep looking for the real ones. We don't wanna make unnecessary work for ourselves.'

He lifted the lid of the washtub to see his dark, candlelit face reflected in a dribble of clear water in the rounded bottom. 'Nah, they won't be down here. Too steamy for postcards.'

The plank ceiling went across the top of the cellar steps, but you could see the outline of a trapdoor. One good shove and it opened upwards, falling back against a scullery floor, except it wasn't a scullery any more: it was a pitch-black darkroom, with the windows blinded. Developed photos hung like washing pegged on the line: pictures of a butcher's shop, a second-hand clothes stall, old women knitting outside their front doors. Everything else was tidied away: the chemicals in packets and jars on the shelves; the baths for developer, stop and fixer empty. The enlarger's lens peered down at an empty space. If they couldn't find Voss's prints he was going to need all this.

Lemmy looked through all the drawers and cupboards, but there weren't any tin boxes containing ancient smutty pictures. What had she done with them?

Through they went into the studio, where the cheese shop must have been. And couldn't you tell? Cheese still lingered, all mixed up with whitewash and carbolic, sepia and ammonia and acetic acid. You could hardly breathe. Streuth!

They found chairs, some with fancy arms, a plush chaise longue, and a small carved table with a decorative planter, to pose the customers, make out they had a few bob. Not much different from the studio in Hackney. Same props: same old fur rug for the baby pictures, a few ostrich feather fans, a doll, a kiddies' hoop. There was her filing cabinet. Nothing doing there, either. Where were they? Had she taken them with her? Were they among the rubble of the train?

He flung open the door of Pops' big cupboard. High up were two shelves: lenses, screens, neck clamps, lanterns and blank slides. On the floor were carboys of made-up pyro-soda developer, more of sepia toner. Facing him were packets of chemicals to make the fixer – sodium hyposulphite, one pound to be mixed with one ounce of potassium metabisulphite and forty ounces of water. 'Wash for one hour before drying.' It all came back to him.

And there it was, wedged between the packets. The tin box.

Empty.

Inside the door a note was pinned:

Freddy. Knew you'd come by sooner or later. Don't waste your time pulling up my floorboards. Look in the fireplace. You'll see I've burnt all your filthy photographs, every single one. They are gone, Freddy. You and the world are better for it. Polly.

'You what! Fuck, look at this!'

The fireplace surround was layered with smoke and soot, up as far as the mantelpiece. The ceiling was brown with it. In the sooty grate and raked out onto the hearth was a great fluttering heap of black photographic ash. Spreading across the floor, a dirty trail of soot and ash led to the window. On the sill was a dead bird, black and festering, stinking, its feathers ruffled by maggots, its tiny beak open on a death rattle.

Twenty-four

When Archie suggested borrowing the chaise to go out looking for subjects to draw, Richard was taken aback. Surely there were enough animals on the farm to provide material for hundreds of paintings, without the need to go gallivanting about? Archie agreed, and he had sketchbooks full of inspiring stuff, but he needed people. People were his stock in trade; paintings of people sold. If Richard and Lilian wouldn't sit still for five minutes he would have to go elsewhere.

He assured the farmer he was well used to driving a mule cart around Walthamstow, wouldn't go far and would stay out of trouble. He felt like a schoolboy making promises to his mother with his fingers crossed behind his back, and felt the same glow of triumph tinged with guilt when his wishes were granted.

Polly helped him prepare but was happy to stay behind – anything to avoid running into her brother. She trusted Archie to do what he had to.

It felt so good to be out driving again, even if it was only a mile through Membury Woods. Too soon he smelled smoke from the gypsy fires and came out onto the common. Half a dozen caravans and make-shift huts stood about, horses were grazing, and men and women were going about their business, or restraining dogs that sprang up growling at the stranger.

'Whoa, Bonnie.' He reined the pony in close by gorse bushes. The yellow blooms and thorns were covered with wet shirts and sheets.

'Good day to you!' Archie called to a fellow sitting on a caravan's steps, making a snare from sticks and cord. He hoped he sounded more composed than he felt. 'Might I have a word?' He clambered down awkwardly. He'd left his sticks, splints and crutches behind. His leg felt pretty good this morning, but he didn't want to put all his weight on it. When he turned back to the man, the poaching equipment had disappeared.

'I'll come straight to the point, sir. I'm staying at Gifford's farm down the road, recovering from the train crash. I'm an artist and I'm looking for some local colour to draw – wondered if I might spend an hour or two sketching around your camp? I can show you some of my stuff, if you're interested.' He opened the book at sketches he'd done in Walthamstow and hadn't sold for one reason or another. Before long, heads were popping out from caravan doors and women were abandoning cooking pots and washing. It must have been a great source of curiosity, a townie peddling to gypsies.

'What you chargin', then?'

'Oh, a few pence, that's all. Cross my palm with silver,' he joked, 'just to help me pay my way at the farmhouse. What about you, sir, you've an interesting face?' he said to a barefoot young fellow with a floppy felt hat and an alarming moustache. 'You could give it to your sweetheart to pin on the wall, what do you say? I could draw you standing against your 'van, with your dog or your pony, or sitting on the steps, if you'd prefer.'

Soon he had several takers, jostling to be first. He unfolded his stool and set down his bag on the grass, and produced an empty cigar box with a slot cut into it to receive any cash.

The Romanies were a handsome breed, with bones honed by their hard outdoor life. His chosen medium, Conté sticks, came in graphite, white and sanguine, which he used for their burnished skin. He liked the square cross section of the clay-based crayon, the sharp corners of which were useful for fine lines.

The gypsies tended to favour bright primary colours: scarves round necks, heads and waists, gold earrings and teeth, colourful bangles round wrists and ankles, necklaces. Archie sorted through his bag, came up with a yellow crayon for a lad's neckerchief and gold earring, and that touch of colour among the black, white and brownish-red was all it took to make a distinctive picture. Curiosity soon won out over diffidence, and people wandered over to see what was going on, attracted like wasps to jam. Used to the crowds of the street market, Archie was soon perfectly at ease, talking and joking with them, while his hand flicked over the sugar paper, making a likeness appear as if by magic.

As he finished each one, he signed it Archie Price, and the sitter gave him a silver sixpence or thruppence, whatever he had, and both buyer and seller were well pleased with the transaction. Time and again Archie delved into his bag for a new sheet of paper and fresh crayons.

There were grandfathers with cheekbones like Sioux Indians, young bucks, dark-eyed beauties, and one Onas Shipton, who came up with his lovely wife, Lavinia, wanting to be drawn with their arms linked. He charged them sixpence.

'I've seen you before, haven't I,' a slightly more educated voice demanded, 'drawing pictures in Walthamstow market?' Archie didn't recognise him at first, this pale young man emerging from a primitive, leafy hut. It reminded him of pictures he'd seen of Iron Age dwellings. 'You were chatting up my sister?' he reminded him. 'Polly Porter?'

Lord, it was the man himself. But his hair was black, as was his eye, and his hands were blue. Like his sister's. What was *he* doing with developing fluid?

'Oh, of course. Sorry, I didn't recognise you. Were you on the train, too?'

'No, no – thank God!' The assurance came so pat you'd never believe it was a lie. 'Up 'ere working.'

'Well, it's a small world, Mr – em – Porter? Do you want your portrait done?'

'No, you're all right.'

'Do me, if you like,' piped up another, coarser voice.

So Archie got to draw Freddy's partner, the weaselly Lemmy King, in his tall bowler hat and sitting at a small table before two rows of dominoes. Freddy took a seat across from him and they played as Archie drew. There was nothing pleasant about Lemmy's face, and Archie's heart was beating like a drum as he took up his carpet bag to find a sharp black Conté stick to shade in one of the domino pieces.

Freddy spoke again. He must have been studying him. 'She's dead, you know.'

'I beg your pardon?'

'My sister, Polly. Had a shop down Walthamstow. Bought it in the crash.'

For a silly moment he thought he meant that Polly had acquired the shop in some sort of run on the bank. He stopped drawing. 'What? Your sister! No!' So the lie had reached him. Tyrell must have spread the news, and Freddy Porter must have been down to Walthamstow very recently to hear it. 'She was on that train, too? I didn't know. Oh my Lord, that's awful. She was so young, and – and enterprising. I am so sorry.'

Lemmy said, 'They buried her yesterday fortnight.'

Polly's bereaved brother, Freddy, jerked his chin and tapped his domino twice on the table. 'Go, Lemmy.'

As Archie put his name to King's portrait, a stringy, white-haired old man stuck his head out of a caravan door and yelled, 'What you playing at, Fred? You ain't got no time for bleeding dominoes. Oo's the geezer?'

'S'alright, Tuddy. Bloke I met in Walthamstow.'

'What – yesterday?'

'No, weeks back.'

Archie swung round to face the 'father' of the gang. Heart in mouth, he blurted out, 'Draw your likeness, sir, for a tanner?' He put his bag on the table to search for new crayons.

188

The old man spat juicy contempt and turned his attention to his protégé, lowering his voice. 'How's it going in there?' He nodded towards Freddy's hut.

Polly's brother waggled his head back and forth, 'So-so, Tud. Working up a bit of a fug.' Archie had noticed the fishy smell seeping from the hut. 'Came out for a breather.'

'You *are* gonna get 'em done in time?' he glared.

'Told you, didn't I?'

'How many so far?' It was a challenge, his scowling face creaking into a criss-cross of angry lines.

'Hundred – hundred and twenty. But I'll have to fetch that other box from Walthamstow today. *And* I've run out of developer.'

'Listen up, Freddy—' the man was spitting flecks of fury. 'I've told you, he wants it yesterday! We can't keep 'im 'anging about.'

'Couldn't carry it all in one go, Tud, not on two horses. Paper weighs a ton, and the ink. Plus there're all the chemicals. And a box of negatives, too. Now, if we had a wagon... No, all right. Don't want to draw attention. Don't you worry none, we'll manage. There's a bed upstairs. Thought we could stop up all night, do them there, bring them back tomorrow.'

The face lost some of its anxiety. 'You do it right or you're for it, you know that. Last bleeding chance. I don't want no more a your cock-ups, Fred. Got a lot riding on this one.'

'Give us an hour here and we'll take the negs back, out of your way. And we'll stop down there 'til it's done. They're not antique, but he maybe won't mind too much. We have the original box, that's the important thing.'

'It's a start. You just make sure it's full when he comes a-calling. And clean it up. Bleeding rusty ol' thing!'

Archie almost sprang off his seat. No, don't, he wanted to yell, that's important evidence. Unwisely, he raised his head.

'What you looking at?' Tuddy barked.

'Me? Nothing. My sitter...' He gestured to the man in the chair with a small dog on his lap. Bending again to his task, he dared to pull his bag towards him, ostensibly to look for a small knife.

'What you doin' 'ere anyways, snoopin' around? Di'n't I say, Fred, no strangers on the site, no one at all?'

'He's only drawing pictures, Tuddy. He's doing no harm.'

'Don't know so much about that. What's 'e got in that bag of 'is? Eh? Have a look, Freddy. Could have a gun for all we know.'

Freddy pulled the bag open and Archie leaned back helpfully, the picture of innocence.

'It's just – just my drawing things.'

The gangster ran blue-dyed fingers through the mess and rattle of pencils and crayons and squeezed tubes of paint. 'What's in these boxes?'

'Have a look.' Archie mentally crossed his fingers and willed them not to shake as he took the lid off a cardboard box to display fat tubes of paint in rows.

'Tud!' Lemmy's warning wasn't directed at Archie, whose heart was in his mouth, but at something on the road. It had an alien sound, a continuous roar, one Archie recognised. Back in Walthamstow, Frederick Bremer had built a petrol-driven automobile and driven the wretched contraption around the streets, frightening the horses.

The old crook came down the steps and lowered his tone to match. 'Blimey, it's Beasley, come early. Get back in that hut, quick, yous two.' He was finding it difficult to speak through the grimace of welcome he put on for meeting nobility. Archie allowed his heart to travel back to its proper home as Freddy left the bag and did as he was told.

The motor car stopped with a spurt of mud and stones. The be-goggled driver called across, ignoring the old man with his hat in his hands, 'Aha! Mr Price, the very man, I have run you to earth!'

The peer of the realm stepped out, fastidiously avoiding a muddy patch, and picked his way across the grass between dirty cooking pots, odd pieces of furniture and piles of horse dung.

'You want *me*?' Archie rose from his stool to take the man's outstretched hand. He wondered if he was expected to bend the knee.

'I do indeed. I understand you are the author (does one call you an author?) of my little *Songbirds.*'

'I'm sorry?' What was he talking about, this stringy aristo? Up close, the man's complexion had a chalky texture, one of his Conté portraits come to life. His curled hair and moustache were from the 'darker' end of the palette, or bottle perhaps, liberally smeared with pomade. His lips were thin and his teeth stained, but his clothes were handsome: country tweeds with the trousers tucked into his boots, a red silk cravat and an elaborate flat cap.

'Sorry? Sorry? Hah-hah-ha-a-ah!' Such strange laughter – considered and practised. Not at all natural. 'No need to be sorry, my dear sir. It's a beautiful painting.' Archie realised his lordship was referring to the double portrait he'd done of Kitty and her old singing partner, Mary Quinn, some years before. Kitty said he had bought it from her.

'Saw you at the Playhouse the other night,' Beasley said. 'Meant to come over and have a word, but you'd already gone. When the delectable Kitty told me your sorry story, I tootled round to the Lodge, in the hope of persuading you to paint *my* portrait before you depart. Lilian Gifford was kind enough to show me your latest works, the, uh, oils on wood. It's what they call "pure painting", isn't it? Somewhat avant-garde. Is the world ready for you, Mr Price? That's what we have to ask ourselves. But you know as well as I that it's a question of exposure. Show them something enough times and they'll begin to think they like it. Hah!' He laughed again, amused at some witticism he felt he was making.

'I suppose... But you like them?'

'I have to say I do. No market just yet, as I say, but, doubtless, their time will come. I might be interested in acquiring them, if you've a mind to sell.' He nodded.

Archie was too stunned to speak. The man might be a lecher and, if Tuddy's deal with him went through, a grubby voyeur of pornography, but he could be Archie's meal ticket. What was he to do? He had come across his sort before and had lived to regret selling to them or being in any way indebted to them.

'Treasure these drawings you've bought,' his lordship told the gypsies. 'Get them framed. Pictures signed by Archibald Price will be worth something in a few years' time, if I'm any judge.' Quietly he said, 'So, no more of this, Mr Price. This will do you no good. Pearls before swine, pearls before swine.' Raising his voice, he invited Archie to attend him at the hall the next day at noon. 'Bring the pictures with you. It will be to your advantage, I assure you. You might be interested to see a rather nice bronze I've just acquired by Monsieur Gauguin – one of his Tahitian fillies.'

Lord, the man had money to throw around. Horseless carriages and works of art – no wonder Tuddy Skinner was wringing his hat and grinning like an ape. At last, Beasley deigned to notice the old crook.

'Ah yes, that little piece of business we spoke of, Skinner, shall we say tomorrow evening? At the hall? Otherwise the deal is off.' Without waiting for an answer, he turned his back on the fawning throng, wound up his car with a starting handle, jumped inside and roared off.

Archie watched him out of sight. So, Freddy had found the tin box and was bringing it back to Beasley tomorrow, filled with photographs of his own? He must tell Tyrell. As for his paintings, he was definitely flattered. It would be wonderful to have someone of influence buying his work, giving him commissions. But not this man, please. Not only was he offensive by reputation, he presumed too much. What right had he to go poking around in his room in his absence? Lilian should not have allowed it. But everyone seemed to be at this man's beck and call. 'I should be getting back,' he told the man whose dog he was drawing. He put the finishing touches to the creature, an intelligent glint in its eye, a wag in its tail, and the customer, well pleased, posted his sixpence in the box. Archie began packing up.

'Pearls before swine, eh?' Tuddy snarled. So his hearing was not impaired. 'Likes of us ain't good enough for you now you got the big man interested.'

'Uh?' Archie half laughed at this unexpected sneer. 'Those were his words, not mine. I'm going because I want my dinner. But I have time to draw your picture if you like or anyone else's…'

'Nah. Piss off! We don't want no arty-farties round 'ere. On yer way, nancy boy.'

Archie raised his hand in acknowledgement, as though expecting such dismissal, shouldered his bag, and climbed back in the trap. 'Sorry, folks,' he said to the queue of disappointed customers. 'Now's not the time.'

'What! I been waiting ages.'

'That ain't fair!'

'Take no notice of the Lunnoner!'

All the way back to Gifford Lodge he kept glancing over his shoulder, amazed at what he had just got away with.

They had kept his dinner warm and he ate it in the kitchen.

Someone in the parlour was practising the piano. A rousing Sousa march came to an end – 'Liberty Bell', if he remembered correctly. The door opened. 'Was he there?' Polly asked, slipping into the seat beside him. Their hosts had gone to plant potatoes. The preacher had gone to his room to prepare his Good Friday sermon. Mrs Fowler and her scullery maid were outside plucking chickens for supper and the kitchen door was shut against the flying feathers. They were alone.

He nodded with commiseration. 'Freddy? Large as life. *And* all the others.'

'Oh, Archie…'

193

'Don't worry, he thinks you're dead.'

'He does?' Her hand flew to her mouth. 'How did he find out? He must have been to Walthamstow.'

'I think they went yesterday. They knew all about your, em, funeral a week or so back. Also, Polly—' There was no easy way to tell her. 'I think they may have broken into your shop.'

'Oh?' She didn't seem surprised or shocked. She gave a slight, tight-lipped nod. 'What makes you think so?'

'Looks to me like he's printing out negative plates, and he must have acquired the chemicals and paper from somewhere.'

'Yes. Yes, of course.'

'He's rigged up one of the gypsies' huts as a darkroom. It stinks of chemicals. Almost fishy?'

'That'll be cuttlefish ink – for printing in sepia. I suppose he's trying to make the prints look authentic. He'll have found the carboy in my darkroom. Ho-o-oh,' she breathed, her slim shoulders sagging, 'so I destroyed those wretched postcards for nothing. Now he's printing up his own!' Her face paled as realisation of another sort dawned, and she put her hands to her head, whispering, '*His own! Oh God, his own…*'

'He must have had some negatives stashed away.'

She stared at him, not seeing him. She had gone very pale. 'No, I – I did. I found them when I moved house, in the cellar in Maybank Road. I was in two minds whether to hang on to them, in case he found me and wanted them back, or to expose them, destroy his – his horrible images and maybe use the plates again, you know – *waste not, want not* – but I – I couldn't decide!' she wailed. 'And now he's found them in my cellar and – and…'

'They're selling them to Lord Beasley.'

'Worse and worse!' She seemed frantic.

'What is it? What's the matter, Polly?'

She shook her head, attempting a small smile, 'Nothing, nothing…' She changed the subject. 'Beasley was here, this morning, tooting his horn and making his engine roar, choking everyone with the smoke. Loathsome man.' She shuddered. 'Lilian showed him your paintings.'

'I know. He came by the gypsy camp. He's talking about buying them.'

'Oh no, Archie! Please, please, don't be beholden to him. He'll ruin you.' She sneaked a look at him. He had the feeling she meant 'ruin' in more ways than one. *Corrupt,* perhaps. 'You should have seen him this morning. Ogling, leering, making innuendos. Sickening. When you think how that man takes his pleasure – and Freddy is feeding his obsession... Oh, Freddy, you evil toad!' Her voice was muffled as tears dripped through her fingers.

'Don't, don't, Polly. He's not worth it.'

'You don't understand,' she sighed. Small muscles moved in her jaw. Whatever it was he failed to understand, she didn't enlighten him. 'Oh God, I knew it was a mistake, pretending to be dead. This is my punishment.'

'Don't be ridiculous. This isn't divine judgement. Besides, I think our plan worked.' She'd forgotten, hadn't she? 'Busking?' he prompted her.

'Oh yes, of course. How did you get on?'

He opened his carpet bag, took up his knife and cut the strings that had kept the box in place. As he brought it out, a shower of coloured crayons rained onto the table. 'Such an untidy creature!' He held up his hands and put on affected voice. 'Everything loose in the bottom of my bag. It's a wonder I can find anything!'

Polly gave a watery smile, recognising herself and almost every other woman with a handbag. She took the package from him. Wrapped in cardboard, it looked no different from his boxes of paint tubes. She took it into the old pantry and, having lit the lamp in its red shade and turned the wick down low, beckoned him to come in. There wasn't a lot of room with the door closed, but this was the moment of truth and she wanted him to share it with her.

She removed the cardboard, took out his small black Kodak camera, and unclipped its back. 'Good,' she said. 'Looks like you took about a dozen photos.'

'It wasn't easy,' he said. 'I was all fingers and thumbs. I was sure everyone would notice the viewfinder peeping through the hole in the bag and hear me winding the film on. I suppose the paint rags muffled the sound pretty well. You sure you can develop them?'

'Pretty sure, yes. People have brought me these cameras before, rather than sending them off to Eastman's for development. It's not difficult.'

'I'll leave you to it then. There's somewhere else I have to be.'

'Oh.' She sounded disappointed. 'Don't you want to see the fruits of your labours?'

'I'll see them later. This is important.'

Skylarks rhapsodised high above his head as he walked down the lane to the village, minding the potholes – jarring his ankle wouldn't be sensible. Over the hedge a team of horses was turning the soil ready for spring planting, and, as he walked past the cottages bordering the lane, a sweet scent of wallflowers made him reel with nostalgia for Wales. Such carefree days. No thugs, no pornography, no risks beyond apple scrumping and kissing Bronwen Pugh behind the haystack.

The post office nestled between a modest Georgian house and a smithy. He couldn't hear a hammer striking an anvil or hissing steam without his mind flying back to the day they found shreds of Jimmy Tomkins' uniform in the shoe of Freddy Porter's horse. And they had let the bugger escape! He'd hardly been able to speak civilly to the man this morning – carrying on without a care in the world. Never mind that he was Polly's brother, the sooner he was brought to justice the better.

Proprietor Harriet Manning, licensed to sell strong liquor was written above the door. *Ping* went the bell and, ducking through

196

the low doorway, he nearly tripped over a sack of animal feed and collided with a roll of chicken wire hanging from the ceiling. It was an obstacle course, but, eventually, he made it to the counter where, between a basket of eggs and a long loaf of carbolic soap, he found a cloud of cigarette smoke and a dried-out husk of a shopkeeper. Silver sixpences and thruppenny bits jingled in his pockets. He hoped he'd brought enough.

'Mr Price, the painter, ennit,' she rasped, 'up at the Lodge these past few weeks?'

'You're well informed.'

She ignored him. 'A telegram, you say? Name and address?'

'Mine? You seem to know it.'

'Where's it going, clever clogs?' She licked her copying pencil, leaving purple 'indelible' dye on her yellow tongue. 'Swan Hotel, Chelmsford?' She looked it up. 'So that'll be fourpence a word, my dear.' She gave him paper so that he could work out what he wanted to say in the shortest and cheapest way. He used his own pencil.

'SUSPECTS WHEREABOUTS KNOWN STOP PHOTO-GRAPHIC PROOF STOP NEED YOU ARREST URGENTLY STOP ARCHIE' told Tyrell the gist of his concerns. Four and thruppence. Lord, it soon mounted up.

'Have they got their own telegraph machine at the Swan?'

'They have. Won't tek a minute to send'n. You'm best wait.'

While she dotted and dashed the message through the wires, he picked up a newspaper, yesterday's *Chelmsford Chronicle*. There was nothing about the crash, though he looked all through it. There *was* a notice of a suffragettes' meeting in Chelmsford on Saturday. Perhaps that would interest Polly.

'You 'avin' that, my dear?' the shopkeeper asked. 'See that Marquis of Macaroni's will be movin' into Hall Street presently.' (The name was Marconi, Archie noted from the paper, not Macaroni.) 'The silk factory.' She pointed to a photograph of the same smooth-faced foreigner who had been sitting with Beasley at the music hall the other night. 'Rich as Croesus an' clever with it,' she said. 'Telegrams without cables, if ee don' mind. They say he'm puttin' up poles all over, trying to catch sounds in the air. D'you ever hear such nonsense? Believe it when I see it.'

Archie waggled his eyebrows in agreement, hastily refolded the paper and put it back in the pile. He headed for the door.

'Whyn't you wait fer the reply? Save the boy bringin' it up to the Lodge. I'll pour us a cuppa. Come through and rest your legs.'

He followed her, like a lamb, into the back room, where a brown enamel teapot steamed on a kitchen range. The air was thick with a mix of tea and cigarette smoke. Added to the heady stew of the shop – the paraffin, bacon and chicken manure – he could hardly breathe.

The tea was very strong, the condensed milk making little difference to its muddy colour. He stirred it well.

'You with the police, my dear, them as were round here asking questions t'other day?'

'Not with them exactly, no – but I need to get a message to him.'

'About the train crash?' Lord, she was sharp! 'They'm saying as some scallywags done it for a purpose.'

'Really?' The old gossip was getting nothing from him. It would be round the village in seconds and the Skinner gang would disappear like smoke.

'What for, I'd like to know? You don' wreck a train, kill all them poor innocents for nothing, my dear. You see 'em all laid out up the church? A dozen or more, kiddies an' all.'

'No, I…'

'Poor souls never knew what fate 'ad in store when they got aboard that train.' She nodded to her own newspaper on the table. '*Chronicle* been a bit quiet on the subject lately. 'Spec' they'm all muzzled.'

There was a thought. 'Who would muzzle them, Mrs Manning?'

'High-ups – them who can use blackmail and back'anders to get what they want.'

'Ah.' Disappointing. He'd thought for a wild moment that she might actually know something.

'Namin' no names, and you never 'eard it from me, my dear, but there's some, not a million mile from 'ere, who has their fingers in all sorts o' rotten pies and macaroni puddings.'

Archie had heard Lord Beasley mentioned too often now. 'Perhaps you ought to take your suspicions to the police, Mrs Manning.'

She shook her head in firm refusal. 'And I'm Miss. Not missed the boat. Not missed me chance. I'm Miss because I choose to be. I en't lettin' no 'an'some bugger get 'is 'ands on my little shop.'

'Good for you.'

'I've 'ad me chances, don't mistake me.' Her eyes creased with the sting of smoke.

'I don't doubt it.'

'But I chose not.'

'But the law's changed, Miss Manning,' he said, though perhaps too late for this old girl, whose chances of marriage had probably slipped away before the Women's Property Act came into being.

''En't changed that much,' she grumbled. She might have said more, but there was a *ping* announcing a customer and off she bustled to serve them. In the meantime, the ticker-tick-tick of the telegraph machine heralded Tyrell's reply.

It read: 'KEEP A LID ON IT BOYO STOP BE WITH YOU SOONEST STOP'.

No sooner had Archie sat down in the scullery to take off his boots than the front doorbell rang.

'Oh, Lavinia, Lovey, hello! I was just going out!' Lilian was speaking in an unusually carrying voice. 'Frost on the way? Do you think so? But it's almost April! You know – there *is* a nip in the air – and I've just put my carrot seeds in. Isn't that always the way?'

Another woman spoke, too quietly for Archie to catch what she said.

'Who? Archie Price? I – I, em, I'm not sure he's in.'

Dammit. He'd brought the gypsy hordes down on their heads.

'Looking for me?' He was aware of looming over his little guardian as she made room for him on the front step. She had her hat on. It looked as though she really was going out. "Fraid you've caught me on the hop, rather,' he said, indicating his feet, one boot off and one on.

The women hadn't come alone. Onas was there and the man they called Dukey. They all smiled, flashes of gold among the white.

'What can I do for you?'

A commission. They wanted him to come back to Membury Common and paint proper portraits. In oils. Three, at least. Money no object.

Lord, the turns of fate.

Lilian was a-twitch. 'You went over to Membury Common, drumming up custom, Archie? That was *unexpected*, wasn't it?' She smiled a lips-only smile and shut the door firmly, with him and the gypsies on the outside. A moment later, it swung open again. This time she was wrapped in a thick shawl, as well as the hat. 'Sorry, I didn't want to let the cold air in. Why don't you take your friends round to the back door? There's a warm fire in the scullery. If you'll just go round!' she called out loudly, then, for his ears alone, she hissed, 'I just have to run a message for Richard – it's the servants' afternoon off. Keep an eye on them, Archie, for heavens' sake.'

Oh. So now he'd upset Lilian. Dammit. Dammit.

Bringing them into the kitchen was a mistake. His work bag was still on the table, with Conté sticks, pastels and chalks spilling out among a litter of string, charcoal and bits of torn cardboard. Hastily he swept them all back into the bag, hoping no one could smell deception in the action. The women sat down in the chairs he and Polly had occupied only hours before, while the two men stood looking around furtively. No one spoke.

Archie slipped off his other boot and stroked his chin. 'Well, I, em, I suppose we'll have to work out some dates or something.'

The pantry door opened and Polly stepped into the light.

'Oh,' she said, blinking, 'oh, sorry, Archie, I heard your voice and thought—' She broke off, her eyes showing their whites as she stared at the back door, which was now open, letting in the cold air and...

'*Tuddy!*' she gasped. He closed the door behind him.

'So, missy...' said the old gangmaster, his nasty smile revealing any remaining shit-coloured teeth. 'What a turn-up, eh? So you ain't dead after all. Come in, come in, by all means join us. Lovey, give the lady a seat, why don't ye?'

Neither woman moved.

Sweat crept between the hairs on Archie's back.

'A little bird tells me you bin grassing us up to the cops, Mr Price. Some story about us watching the trains go by?'

'No!' Oh God, how did they know that? 'How could I have seen—? I mean that's plain ridiculous!'

Tuddy snarled. 'And we'll have that camera, now, if you will, Mr Price.'

'Camera?'

The one you 'ad 'idden in your colouring bag, when you come a-callin' earlier on? Freddy reckons, the way you kep' fiddle-faddlin' about in that bag, 'e's guessin' a grass might've 'ad somefink in one of 'is pretty boxes. Now if it was a camera lens peekin' froo this 'ere 'ole in your bag, Mr Price, I'm gonna slit your gizzard!'

'Sorry, I don't know what you're talking about. All I have in my bag is – well, you can see, just my drawing thi—'

The rest of the word was splattered over his face as a fist connected with his teeth. Somewhere, far off, he heard Polly scream. He fell back against the dresser, sending china crashing to the floor just before *he* did. He should have stayed on his feet, he realised, as a heavy boot connected with his stomach. Excruciating pain shot through him.

'Camera!' demanded Tuddy, raising his foot to stamp on his face.

'I'll get it!' cried Polly, and dashed back into the pantry. The boot hovered, changed its mind and kicked him in the balls.

He doubled up as white-hot pain knifed through his innards. God Jesus!

Vaguely he heard the pantry door open and voices exclaiming over the contents. Didn't they realise that exposed to the light the photos would... And they mustn't find...

Too late.

'Sure, and that's a nice little photy of you and me, Lavinia.'

'There's your Freddy, playing dominoes, Tuddy. Good job he had his wits about him, eh? Secret cameras, whatever next?'

In his pain, Archie was just able to sift through the words. Of course, Freddy was as much a photographer as Polly. He'd know all about detective cameras. As for 'grassing', how else would Tuddy have heard that Archie had talked to the police, other than from the hypnotist? Allsop was in cahoots with Beasley, he knew: he'd seen them together. Was there any other reason the gang needed Allsop's special skills?

'Well, lookee 'ere! Is this a camera or is this a camera? Gotcha, Price!' There was a crunch as the heel of a boot demolished Lizzie's wedding gift. 'Fuck, you even got one of me on the caravan steps! Give these to the cops, and they'll know exactly where to come looking? Eh? Eh?' Each 'Eh?' was accompanied by a kick.

'No, you're wrong.' Polly's voice was plaintive. 'He's a painter. Think about it, Tuddy. He was going to *paint* the gypsies from the photographs.'

'So what 'e want to take the Lunnoners for?' demanded Dukey. 'An' Lavinia chatting up Lord B, and Onas givin' 'im the evil eye? No, missy, you'm a liar. Your bastard townie wants us all in a row wi' our necks stretched.'

At least now they were letting him die quietly, too busy breaking the slides. Polly brought him a wet tea towel to bathe his wounds: his lip was already swelling and there was blood in his mouth. But Tuddy pulled her away, picked up him up by his hair and punched him again.

When he came to, he was alone.

They'd taken her! They'd taken her to her hateful brother. Oh Lord, her worst nightmare! He had to go and find her before they – what? Don't even think of it. He had to go. Oh God, could he move? There was a smell, an acrid smell. The floor was awash with chemicals, water and piss. His piss. His breeches were wet with it. Lilian would have a fit. But he didn't have time to mop it up. He'd let the mess speak for itself.

He staggered to his feet. His balls were on fire. Crippling. He hurt just about everywhere. It was like the train crash all over again. But at least he was walking. Just. He shuffled to his room, carefully, gingerly removed his soggy breeches and sponged his bruises, those he could reach, and his ballooning, blackening nether regions. No skin was broken, thank God, except his lip and a bloody tooth. That hurt too! Putting on fresh clothes was agony.

He needed a weapon. Where would he find one? Richard had brought them all down to be cleaned the other night. Shotguns, pistols, revolvers. Where had he put them? Sideboard drawer, desk drawer, chiffonier? Ah, top of the bookcase? Nope.

He found them all eventually in an oak chest in the hallway, under the hats and coats, with ammunition: bullets for the pistols and cartridges for the shotguns. He had never fired a gun in his life, but the murderers didn't need to know that. He took the smaller firearms and distributed them about his pockets.

Her cloak was hanging up. He'd take that, in case she was cold. Back in the scullery he emptied his work bag and stuffed it with food, and money from his morning's work: sixpences, shillings and thrupenny bits. Slung it over his shoulder. His wallet was in his inside pocket, containing very little but enough, perhaps, to hire a horse or two, or a room for the night.

He left a note: *Send police to gypsy camp,* and struggled to put his walking boots on again. In the state he was in, he couldn't ride a horse. Even sitting to drive the chaise would be killing.

Twenty-five

'Well, lil Miss Bu"er-won'-melt. What we gonna do wiv you, then?'

He was right, neither butter nor anything else could find room in her mouth to melt, stuffed as it was with her balled-up handkerchief. And – she was only too aware – he could do anything he damn well pleased. Her hands were tied; her dress and stockings were muddy and torn – she'd tripped over twice in the woods; her hair had come loose and was straggling down her back; she'd broken her heel and was sweating and dirty from being pushed and shoved between trees and bushes. Tuddy tipped up her chin and she stared into those merciless gimlet eyes, her heart racing.

'A detective camera!' Tuddy nodded. ''Oo's idea was that then, eh? Very tricksy. 'Course you'd know all about cameras and that, wouldn't ya, darlin'? But so does your lovely bruvver. Forgot about that, din'cha?' She glanced around, expecting to see Freddy leering at her. 'No, 'e ain't 'ere, missy. An' 'e wouldn't 'elp you none if 'e was. Right upset 'e was about that box 'o snaps you burnt. Cheeky lil cow, en't ya? Put us to a lot a trouble you 'ave. An' your mate back there. Grassed us up good, ain't ya? 'Spect they'll be along 'ere, shortly, sortin' us out.' He delved inside his grubby shirt for a sheaf of photos. 'Onas, bring that lantern a bit closer, boy. Stand back, the rest o' yous, let the dog see the rabbit. Fuck me,' he said, riffling through them, 'you *as* been a busy little camera-girlie, aintcha?'

She struggled with the gag and Onas whipped off the dirty neckerchief and winkled the sodden rag from her mouth. 'No, Tuddy,' she croaked, struggling without saliva, trying to believe the lie with all her heart to make it more convincing. 'You've got it all wrong. Yes, it was my idea to hide the camera, but Mr Price wanted the photos to paint from. He wanted unposed photographs.'

'What d'ya fink, I'm light or summink?' he demanded, shoving the handkerchief back in, tying the gag hard, pinching her skin. 'Eh? Eh?' He gave her a prod and, with one heel lower than the other, she staggered, losing her balance. Onas pushed her upright again. 'No, Polly, mate, I don't believe you. Never 'ave done. Your the one shopped pore old Freddy last time, wa'n't ya? Six years' bird 'e done for yous. An' the dying crap. Properly upset the boy that did. But, o' course, you was trying to 'ide from us, wasn't ya? Bleedin' burnt my box o' porn? What was that for? Eh? Didn't like to be reminded, di'n't ya? Too good now to 'andle a bit of how's your father? Gaw', I recall a time, my gel, when you give as good as you got, if you take my meaning.' He spun her around once and back to face him. 'Well, well, well, what we gonna do with you, eh? In all your fine clothes 'n' that? I fink you need a good seeing to, meself. What d'you fink, Onas?'

'I – if you say so, Tuddy…'

'What'ya say, Onas, cut the little gel's froat, shall we?'

'Oh, I don't know…'

'No, you wouldn't. You always was a bleedin' milksop. I know my Freddy would wanna do it hisself. 'E 'ates grasses. An' what's 'e gonna say, missing all the fun? Eh, Onas? That ain't fair. And Beasley? He's partial to a bit of the other. In fact, I got me an idea… Real tasty. Right, so we'll keep 'er on the boil 'til Freddy gets back. Let 'im decide how to finish 'er off. Now where shall we put you where ya won't get up to no mischief? Let's tie you up, nice and tight, and park you somewhere out of 'arm's way. Though strictly speaking, there's 'arm and there's *'arm*.' He waggled his whiskery old head from side to side as if considering her for the pot, plump and ready or too scrawny and tough. 'Oh, I dunno, Onas, we'll let Freddy 'ave the last bite, save 'im a slice, but we can all 'ave a little nibble first, eh?'

When he cackled, it was the very same cackle as the one she'd heard way, way back, when he was egging on Freddy and the other boy burglars to have their fun at a little girl's expense.

She knocked her head as they threw her on the ground and must have passed out. She came to as the first 'nibble' was being taken, by Tuddy himself, the few brown teeth he had gnawing at her neck, while his sweaty hand scrabbled around under her skirts. His fingers stung. Her own hands were tied. There was a rope fastening her arms to her sides. And – and she couldn't move her legs. She looked down and found her ankles tied to pegs in the prickly ground! She was spatchcocked! Close by, she heard the bushes move. They were not alone. Someone was watching. Waiting their turn? As the old man lay atop her she could only buck and squirm and protest helplessly through her gag. Losing patience, he reared up and cracked her across the jaw to make her lie still, while he made himself at home. Her throat ached, her face hurt, her heart was pummelling in her chest, but he took no notice. She was an unexpected gift for an old man and he was determined to enjoy it.

She tried to concentrate on *breathing*. Her nose was stuffed with tears. Only if she stretched her mouth to its widest could she pull a little air in through her gag to relieve her bursting lungs. Out of her fervid brain came an image of her poor mother, desperate to die, begging for the pillow over her face. And in the end, Polly had given in, pressing down, leaning with all her weight, smothering, suffocating until it was over. She still hadn't forgiven herself.

She must have lost consciousness again. Some time later, out of the utter darkness, someone lifted her head. They took the gag from her mouth and clamped their hand swiftly across it. Oh

God, she prayed, let it not be another rapist. But her head was propped on someone's knees, and someone else, squatting beside her, allowed her to fill her deflated lungs. A woman? She could smell smoky fires and cooking stew. They prized her lips apart and something hard was inserted, which chinked against her teeth. Too narrow for a bottle neck, and it was a chink not a clink: glazed pottery not glass. Her tongue explored the intrusion. A spout of some sort. Good grief, a teapot! But it was cold, and it was cool water dropping onto her tongue. Wet, wonderful water! A stream of it gurgled down her parched throat, and she coughed once with swallowing too fast. Someone, some people with pity, had come to her aid.

'Thank you,' she whispered. 'Lavinia? Onas?' It *was* them. Dear, kind people.

Immediately and roughly, her gag was replaced, and the back of her head let go with a thump onto the needle-sharp ground. Two shadows merged into the darkness and whispered away.

Well, that was kind of them. But it was just prolonging the agony. In the morning, she knew, Freddy would come. And then she would surely die.

Twenty-six

In the dead of night, a large shadow crept through the dark woods beside Membury Common, without a lantern and with suppressed oaths and cries of pain as it tripped over tree roots and brambles. All was quiet on the gypsy encampment; even the owls were asleep. Not a squeal, not a bark. Not a candle flickered. Doors and windows were closed tight on the sleepers within. With a gun in either hand, Archie stepped around cooking pots and kettles glinting in the moonlight, climbing steps, peering in dark windows, expecting, at any moment, a knife to fly out of the night and skewer him.

Where was she? They wouldn't have killed her, surely, not Freddy's sister? What if she were tucked up in bed with him, sleeping peacefully? Though wasn't Freddy in her shop in Walthamstow tonight? Despite the frosty air – the caravans were rimed with white and he'd creaked across frozen puddles a few times – he thought he could have curled up under a bush, wrapped in Polly's cloak, and slept for a week.

Everywhere hurt as he crunched through fallen holly leaves. His face smarted. He stopped. Wasn't that a moan?

There she was, trussed like a chicken among the spiky leaves. He stifled a groan of his own. Oh, Polly! As he fell to his knees to untie her gag, her eyes widened in recognition. She turned her head away. 'Don't speak,' he whispered, 'don't say a word.' He turned her head back and took the slippery ball of rags from her mouth.

But she did; she took a gasping breath and exhaled, 'Go away, Archie, go away! Leave me alone!'

Ignoring her, he worked at her bonds, numb fingers fumbling at knots, pulling at ropes and the pegs that held her feet apart. Poor, poor girl!

At last, she was free and he helped her to her feet, but when he tried to put the cloak around her shoulders she sagged and would have fallen. 'All right, all right, I've got you!' He picked her up, trying not to mind the shooting pains between his legs. Their closeness would warm her, he thought, give her a chance to become human again, so he staggered away with her into the bushes.

His instincts told him to take her home, back to the farm, where she could bathe and rest, but the gang knew where to find them now. The farmhouse was the first place they'd look, and if they found Polly they'd kill her, not to mention the rest of the household. So at the crossroads, he turned right instead of left. He'd take her to Chelmsford, where he'd find Tyrell and get him to put an end to the gang, to this whole horrible business, once and for all. How many miles? Five? Ten? At this pace? Could they do it in a night? Would the gang find them before morning and finish them off?

'Keep still, Polly, I'm doing my best here. I'm hurting, too.' At that, she stopped struggling and put her arms around his neck, trying to help, allowing him to carry her through the woods.

'I'll get over it, Archie. I always do,' he thought he heard her whisper. 'It's not as if it's the first time…' There was a pause as he pushed through clinging blackberry prickles. 'At least he didn't use cameras.'

'Sorry – what? I didn't catch…'

'Nothing, nothing – it doesn't matter.'

He let it go. He'd always suspected that she hadn't told him everything, that Freddy had been intimate with her, probably since she was a little girl. It wasn't her fault. She was a ready-made victim. And he'd let others use her, too, Tuddy. Yet she'd come through. As she said, she got over it.

When the trees began to thin, he glanced down in the moonlight to find her gazing at him.

'Your poor face,' she murmured. She gently touched his sore lip. Now *he* turned away.

'It wasn't such a good idea, was it, Archie?'

'What?'

'Taking photos of the Skinner gang,' she said.

Laughter was the furthest thing from their minds, but the wildness of her comment triggered a quiver, almost a giggle, a mad lifting of the spirits. They were going downhill now, towards the gleaming railway line. He put her down. 'Can you walk?'

'Yes – well, I'll have to break the other heel off.' She did so.

'Bit warmer now?'

'Yes.'

Hand in hand, helping each other over dark stiles and streams, creeping along, repeatedly looking back for anyone behind them, they stumbled through the night. Although it was slower going, they kept to the trees. With the railway line to their right they headed north by the Pole Star, the Plough their signpost.

Coming out onto a bare heath, they felt the rabbit-riddled ground begin to reverberate beneath them. Hooves. Although the night was only just glimmering to grey, she had been missed. Several horses were coming. Unharnessed, unshod. Dogs, too. They could hear them.

There was no way, at their pace, they could reach the next stand of trees in time. They would have to go back.

Quickly, they ducked back through the woods, to a tall fence marking the boundary between public and private land. In their present state it would be impossible to climb. They found a fallen tree and, driven by fear and adrenalin, they balanced on the trunk. With her foot in Archie's cupped hands, Polly scrambled over, and he followed.

On the other side, civilisation. A narrow band of cultivated trees led down to a swiftly flowing stream. There was nothing for it but to throw themselves down the muddy bank, take off their shoes and wade in, up to their calves, through the shock of icy water. He had reached the other bank and was crawling out when he realised Polly wasn't with him. She was bending down, midstream, one arm holding her skirts as high as she could, and splashing water frantically between her legs. Rags and tatters trailed away downstream, like weeds.

'Come on!' he whispered, 'we don't have time!' But, of course, it mattered dreadfully to her. He waited with his back to her, then turned, grabbed her hand, and pulled her out of the water. Her face was wet. 'Shh, shh, it's all right,' he murmured, with an arm around her, knowing it wasn't. It never had been; it never would be again.

Tall, moth-eaten bulrushes screened them from anyone peering over the fence, and then there were willow trees, bushes and flower beds. A recently mown lawn, crisply silver, led up to a large house, glowering sternly against the stars. Footprints would show on the frosted ground, so back they crept, along the water's edge, to an ornate bridge, under which they crouched, trying to stop their teeth chattering and giving them away, as half a dozen ponies and their riders trotted by on the other side of the fence. Dark heads bobbed along, breathing steam into the air, their keen hunters' eyes searching the dawn for their prey.

The fugitives waited, listening to the water and their own breathing, and, in less than ten minutes, they heard horses and riders riding back, defeated. The virgin heath had shown no sign of footprints and the gypsies' hearts weren't in it, anyway. Their mongrel dogs were miserable too, whining their frustration at losing the scent.

When the gypsies had gone back, Archie and Polly found a gardener's shed, unlocked. Inside, after only a moment's indecision, they stripped off their clothes, wet with river water and sweat, draped them over the workbenches, lawnmower and roller, lit a Primus stove with shaking fingers and matches they found, and lay down, shivering, on the floor, among seed packets and dried compost, beetles and spiders, too exhausted to care. They lay spoon-fashion, their freezing legs intertwined for warmth, covering themselves with empty sacks and fruit netting.

He had only been asleep for minutes, he thought, but the sun was up and a boot was nudging him awake. 'Oi!'

Opening a bleary eye, he found a ruddy-faced man, in worn sweater and overalls, staring at them rudely. 'What 'you playin' at then, yous two? I'll 'ave the law on you, I will.'

'Oh, please do,' he said, pulling the rudimentary covers up over Polly's shoulders. The Primus stove had gone out. 'That would save me a job.' He explained that they had had a narrow escape from a gang of crooks, after going 'through hell and high water' (he gestured at their drying clothes), and that they were on their way to tell the police in Chelmsford. 'Though, if your employer possesses a telephone? Oh well. If you wouldn't mind stepping outside for a few moments, my – the lady and I will get dressed and then we'll be on our way.'

'Ain't letting you outa my sight, mate!' said the gardener.

'Do you think I'm going to make off with a lawnmower or a sack of potatoes?'

'You can get dressed, but I'm stopping here.'

Archie, pushed to extremes, produced a gun from his jacket and said, 'Out!'

They splashed their faces at the gardener's hand pump and Polly twisted her chestnut locks into some scrappy sort of order. The rips and tears in her bodice Archie fixed with garden twine and his cravat pin. Then they were off, through a door in the fence that the gardener gladly unlocked. Their clothes were still damp around the hems, but they would soon dry in the heat of the day.

The heath was swathed in mist, perfect fugitive weather, and steam rose from the trees. They decided to chance the open ground beside the railway line, it being the quickest route. An hour later, the stopping train to Margaretting, pulling out from the sidings, saw two walkers taking their morning constitutional along the embankment, too immersed in their own problems to respond to the driver's cheery wave.

The posters were up. Every other telegraph pole, it seemed, bore a named image either of Tuddy, Lemmy, Curly or Onas. 'Oh dear,' Polly mourned, 'not Onas, too. He didn't want to be mixed up in any of this.' She told him of the Shiptons' kindness the night before. 'If Tuddy had known, he'd have flayed them alive.'

'WANTED DEAD OR ALIVE' each poster declared, 'for the wanton destruction of a train and the deaths of 11 passengers. £100 REWARD.'

'So that's four hundred pounds if you get them all,' Archie said. 'I wonder who's putting up the money – not the police, you can be sure.'

'Someone related to a dead passenger, I expect. Or maybe they're clubbing together. I see the reward for Freddy is £500.'

'That'll be the Fitzells,' Archie told her. 'Ida said they were going to.'

'So much money! You'd think it would have encouraged people to have tracked them down by now – bounty hunters, people like that.'

'Or information leading to the arrest of…' Archie read.

'Well, that's us – we have information.'

'Not me,' he said. 'Strictly speaking I'm police, so I don't count, but you could put in a claim.'

'No.' She made a face. 'I'll shop Tuddy, quick as a shot, but I can't do that to Freddy. Not again. In a way, he's a victim.'

'What?' He was shocked. 'The things he's done to you! He's killed Fitzell, maimed Jimmy Tomkins. He's raped, lied, cheated and stolen all his life. How on earth is he a victim?'

'He had no choice, Archie. Tuddy made him what he is. And it was society put him on the streets as a tiny child. He really isn't to blame for what he's become.'

Archie took a huge breath of disbelief. 'Lord help us, Polly…'

'I hope so,' she said.

Arriving at last at the Swan Hotel, they found Frank Tyrell and Stanley Beckett already out and about their duties. They sank into plush seats in the entrance hall, too tired to go on to the police station, prepared to wait – forever, if needs be – for them to return. The receptionist telephoned the police station and left a message.

Panting from a struggle with the hotel's double doors, half an hour later, a shapely blonde straightened up from her bulky perambulator in surprise. What was Archie Price, of all people, doing asleep on the studded sofa, with a woman's head on his shoulder?

'My darlin' boy!' she squealed, waking them both.

'What the—?' he said, half-opening one eye. 'Kitty?' he blinked. 'You're here?'

'Sure an' we're up on the second floor, me and Charlie. Don't we always stop here when we play the Variety? Here…' She held her face to him, pointing to her painted cheek. 'Kiss, kiss…'

He did, breathing in delicious fresh outdoor scents on her skin, before introducing Polly as a fellow convalescent from Walthamstow and explaining that they were waiting for Frank Tyrell.

'A social call, I hope,' she joked, jiggling the pram to lull the infant. 'Oh,' she said, her pretty face falling into a frown. 'Oh dear. Perhaps I shouldn't ask.' But she did, all the same. 'Sump'n to do with your session with Oliver, was it? Only I heard them talking, him and Peregrine Beasley, in the bar the other night, and your name was mentioned.'

'Really?' No surprise there. He described how the hypnotist had tried to wipe his memories of the people he had seen from the train.

'The devil he did? Archie, I'm so sorry. It was my fault – I thought you could trust him, so I did.' She looked so woebegone

214

he had to put her mind at rest. 'So he failed? Well, it's not often you'll get one over on that one. Those people you saw were probably known to him, and to Peregrine too. In his pay, mebbes? That Olly – he's a two-faced shag-bag, so he is.'

He blinked at her language and found himself relishing, for a split second, a plump cleavage prettily displayed by striped silk ruffles. Quickly he brought his eyes to her face – sparkling eyes, rosy cheeks, artful make-up. Motherhood suited her. Suited many women. Lizzie had never looked better than in the last days of her pregnancy.

He sighed. 'Oh, I don't trust the man and nor does Tyrell. The police are taking their time, though,' he said with some regret. 'Waiting to catch them all red-handed or something.'

'You're all right, though, no ill effects?'

'*I* am, yes.' He couldn't help stealing a glance at Polly, which Kitty pretended not to notice. Polly had sat grim-faced, hardly saying a word, throughout the meeting.

'But, if ye don't mind me sayin', I've seen you lookin' better. Been in the wars, ain't you? What have you been up to, me darlin'? Are yez in trouble?'

'Well, I—' He looked with a frown at the receptionist who was leaning on her hand, absorbed in their conversation. 'Perhaps not here…'

'Come upstairs, the both o' yez, and I'll have a look at that lip for ye.'

'Won't Charlie mind?'

'Not at all. He's off playing football with his pals, and I'm glad. He gets like a caged lion, shut up all day wi' me and the babby. Come along, we'll leave the pram down here. If you could just bring that shopping…'

Upstairs, in a room redolent of babies, greasepaint and cigarette smoke, they made themselves comfortable on the unmade bed while Kitty put away her purchases one-handed, the plump baby in her other arm grizzling.

Finally, having sorted out some glasses and uncorked a bottle, she was ready to listen. The baby sat on her lap, a dummy in its mouth, fascinated by Polly's deadpan face. Her eyes, Archie thought, it had to be her eyes, large and luminous in a pallid face.

He poured out their story over a warming tot of gin, glossing as lightly as he could over Tuddy Skinner's part in Polly's present state of collapse. Kitty turned to him with, 'Here, hold the child,' and without ceremony dumped her mewling offspring on his lap. 'I'm going to run a bath for Polly. No arguments, now. Come, darlin', there's towels and soap for ye, sweetheart, and a change of clothes. I said "no arguments", did I not? Now you come along with me and take as long as you like.'

By the time she'd returned with Polly's dirty, torn rags, which she fed into a rubbish chute, Archie had got the little boy to sleep by walking him up and down and crooning lullabies.

'Oh, I was going to feed him, but I'll not look a gift horse in the mouth.' She removed the child from Archie's broad shoulder and laid him in his cot. 'You have the knack, Archie – you can come again.' Then, pulling the cot covers straight, as if continuing an earlier conversation, she said, 'Well, darlin', your friend looked as if a hot bath wouldn't come amiss, and the rest of the gin, too, if I'm not mistaken. I don't know what's she's been through, but if I know Tuddy Skinner, it's nothing nice.'

'You know him?'

'By reputation. Dirty old man – used to bother the chorus girls at the Hackney Empire, back in the day. You know he's palled up with Beastly Beasley and Olly Allsop? Three of a kind, to be sure. I don't know what's goin' on, but they're all as thick as thieves. Olly gets them complimentary tickets for the front table at the show and they all sit together getting pie-eyed and frisky wi' the girls.'

Archie didn't mention Polly's connection with Freddy, just that she had fallen foul of Tuddy by destroying something belonging to him, something that Beasley wanted.

'I knew sump'n had gone awry with their plans, 'cause Tuddy

216

was gettin' short shrift of it. Peregrine was wavin' his arms about, telling him to clear off and go to hell.'

'When was this?'

'The other night, T'orsday, was it?'

'Well, they were fine yesterday morning. I saw them both at the gypsy camp.' Lord, was it only yesterday?

'They must have come to some other arrangement, for weren't they all smiles again when I left the bar.'

Yes, thought Archie, because Freddy was developing another set of pictures for the old lecher. Tuddy was keeping his master sweet.

Thirty minutes later, Polly emerged from her ablutions, pink as a shrimp and perspiring in a dress that was slightly too big but decent, not Kitty's usual style at all. Her hair was wet and wound in a towel. She may have looked serene but Archie knew she was in misery. Her eyes were cloudy, her mouth grimly set. She had been foully used and, since then, had been in fear for her life, soaked and bitterly cold, and forced to sleep on a shed floor with a man she hardly knew in order to keep warm. Not that anything had happened, or could have happened, the state they were in.

While Kitty rubbed Polly's hair dry, and plied her with more tea and biscuits, Archie made quick use of the bathwater, adding a jug or two of cold before he found it comfortable. (The gin bottle, beside the bath, was still half full.) Both were ready and waiting when Tyrell and Beckett came to the door, the inspector looking distinctly unhappy.

They took their leave of Kitty, leaving her to feed the baby, and went downstairs.

'The bastards!' raged the inspector, on hearing their story. 'I'll swing for the buggers, I will!' Archie had never seen him so distressed.

It turned out he'd just been speaking on the telephone to his wife Emma. She'd been searching through Reggie's wardrobe to find a uniform that wasn't covered in blood, one that he could wear in his coffin – the funeral was on Saturday. She had found in his jacket pocket a notebook with the entry: *119, Church Street, Stoke Newington. Tell Tuddy.*

'No-o-o!' he'd cried, his heart breaking. 'My God, Em, he was the one. He was b-bent! You're sure it says, *Tell Tuddy?*'

'I am. Is it important?'

'Emma, don't bother with the uniform.' He had sniffed, in control now. 'Civvies will do for that bugger. And tell them no guard of honour, right? No guard of honour!'

The sun was up when the two plain-clothes men and a dozen uniformed specials from Chelmsford and railway squads descended on Membury Common, setting the dogs barking. Curious heads poked out of doors and windows, and gypsies rose from their chores. Guns and truncheons in hand, the lawmen swarmed through the camp, blowing their whistles and shouting and banging on doors. Dogs and horses and roosters joined in. The racket could have been heard in the next village.

The caravans were emptied and their occupants rounded up in the middle of the camp. No one on the site escaped. But of Tuddy and his boys, there was not a sign. Even Onas and Lavinia had disappeared, and no one knew where.

'What Lunnoners? No, they never 'ad no Lunnoners stopping there. Never seed 'ide nor 'air o' no train wreckers. Nothing to do with them.' As for darkrooms, negative plates and boxes of postcards, they didn't know what the inspector was talking about. That whiff of fish? The inspector was free to examine the remains of the large pike they had shared last night.

It was clear a caravan had recently been driven off the site and a hut had been dismantled and removed, leaving a patch of yellow grass where the sun hadn't shone. But where they had gone was anyone's guess. The trail left by wheels and hooves petered out in the woods. The gypsies claimed they had simply moved caravans around, to prevent the grass being permanently damaged.

When Tyrell and Beckett returned to the Swan later that

morning, in foul tempers, Archie and Polly were drinking coffee in the hotel bar. Archie's heart sank. He had expected triumphant smiles.

'The raid was a washout – the birds have flown.'

'You didn't get them!' he cried.

'They're still on the *loose*?' Polly's cup hit the saucer with a clunk.

The gangsters must have realised that the game was up and quickly packed up and moved off. But where? The woods were empty.

'They could be anywhere,' said a dejected inspector. 'Anywhere! We've lost them.'

'They won't have gone far,' Archie said. 'They've got a date tonight with Beasley and a lot riding on it. Freddy and Lemmy intended working all night in Polly's shop, printing up a crate of Freddy's negatives, stuff he developed years ago. They're hoping to fob Beasley off with them.'

'What, him in the big house? He has something to do with this?'

'Everything,' said Archie. 'He's up to his skinny neck. He may even be behind the Fitzell burglary. He's desperate to get his hands on obscene material.'

Polly sat back in her chair, her fists tight in her lap. It looked to Archie as though she were trying hard not to lose her grip. 'So,' she tried to clear her throat, 'what do we do now?' Her voice seemed to move over grit.

'Well, we can't stay here,' Archie said, 'we've no money. We can't go back to the farmhouse…'

'I think we must, Archie,' she said. 'Everything I have in the world is there: my camera equipment, my – my trunk. Apart from a rented shop, I have nothing else.'

Tyrell thought for a moment, scratching his ear. 'No, that's not safe – you can't go back to Walthamstow. Listen, what if I collect your things and bring them back here? I'll find you lodgings, both of you…'

'No, Mr Tyrell,' she said firmly. 'I'll collect my things and hire a carriage to take me back to Walthamstow. I have money.'

'Your brother's there,' Tyrell protested.

'No,' Archie explained, 'he's coming back here today, and Lemmy, with the rest of the prints.'

'Then we'll catch him red-handed at the handover.'

'They're *his* prints.'

'It's not his box. That box links them all to Fitzell's burglary. Whether Beasley had a hand in the murder remains to be seen. So the deadline is tonight?'

'That's what I gathered from what they were saying yesterday. Look,' he went on, 'I have an idea. I'm supposed to go over to Elmscott Place this morning with those pictures I did of the crash. He wants to buy them.'

'Really?' The look of disbelief on Tyrell's face was not flattering.

'I might have a chance to look around. I wouldn't be surprised if that's where you'll find Tuddy and Son.'

'What time's the appointment?'

'Twelve.'

It was nearly eleven already. Tyrell offered to give them a lift to Little Nessing, for Archie to collect his paintings and for Polly to begin her packing, if she felt she had to. He would leave Beckett as Polly's bodyguard, if he could square it with the Giffords.

On foot, it had taken Archie nearly all night to walk from Gifford Lodge to Chelmsford, with stops off in between, and he must have covered a full eight miles. A carriage ride, at a gallop, would take about half an hour. 'Just time for you to have a shave, boyo.'

Archie's heart was heavy as he pushed the squeaky handcart of paintings up the avenue of poplars leading to Elmscott Place. Although his leg had stood up well to all that capering around last night, it was as much as he could do now to put one foot in front of the other. He felt he was about to enter the gates of hell. This man he was going to see was evil. He could never be a policeman, he thought, and do this for a living. Tyrell sometimes asked him to go 'undercover', but he was always afraid that it would be all too easy to become tainted with criminals' easy attitudes to vice and wrongdoing. He could understand, he thought, how Reggie had succumbed to temptation.

In a way, too, he understood Freddy Porter, who could not shake off his early influences. Nature versus nurture – were you responsible for what either made of you? Polly seemed able to come back from abuse more or less unscathed – but she was strong, brave, tough as old boots.

He had left her at the house, packing. She was not looking forward to going back to her shop in Walthamstow, which she felt had been contaminated by Freddy, but she was going to reclaim her belongings at least, before she decided where to go next, now her time as Florence was over.

Elmscott Place was a mansion, a stone edifice, like a crown on a velvet cushion of lawns and gardens, fringed by trees. Symmetrical wings led off from the centre, with a semi-circle of steps leading up to the grand front door, guarded by pillars. As he mounted them, he couldn't help wondering which wing housed the baronet and which his estranged wife. According to Effie, the two did not get on.

He was expected. People clearly did not let his lordship down.

'If you'll follow me, sir…' The butler showed him into a barn of a room that must once have been a banqueting hall with panelled walls and an ornately plastered ceiling. It had been brought up to date with modern furnishings: a grand piano, tastefully placed chests of drawers, chiffoniers and ormolus, glass-fronted display cabinets, occasional tables, comfortable seating around a roaring coal fire. The butler directed him to one of these armchairs, stuffed to bursting, before leaving to announce his arrival.

It was impossible to remain seated: there was too much to see. Gold-framed paintings on the walls called out to him, enormous portraits, one of which could have been a Rubens, complete with fat cherubs and a rosy, flimsily dressed young woman. Wasn't that a Joshua Reynolds, that pale young man in the wig? One of Beasley's predecessors presumably – there was a definite family likeness. And this woman with the powdered hair – 'Lady Lorraine Beasley, 1766' was inscribed on the frame – had his lordship's pinched nose, the same set to the eyes, and was painted by Gainsborough, no less! Good Lord. The man was well connected, in every sense.

He spotted a van Dyck, one from Goya's 'dark' period, poor man, and that, surely, was a Rossetti, his sitter Morris's wife Jane, she of the full lips and unmistakable mane of black curls. He was admiring a Rembrandt, the incredible brushwork in a study of hands, when he became aware of someone behind him, a voice murmuring, 'The colours: the blues and the greens he gets into the skin. So lifelike. Truly marvellous!'

Archie swallowed. This dreadful man – 'Beastly Beasley' Kitty had called him – who molested kitchen maids, had such bloody good taste when it came to art. And he wanted to buy two Archie Prices? Maybe commission a portrait? He would be made!

They sat on a settee, and Archie opened his notebooks at sketches he'd done of the Giffords ('Maybe, one day, I'll paint them, if I can get them to sit still for long enough!'); of Polly at the piano, which seemed to entrance his lordship ('Ah, yes, Miss Anderson'); of Thomas and Maud. The baronet recognised them all with triumph. Minister Norris he did not know, but he whooped at Kitty Flanagan, and seemed to appreciate the beggars and prostitutes that crowded Archie's pages. So then… Affecting a casual manner he did not feel, the artist turned to the gypsies and their guests, the Skinner gang. What did his lordship make of these?

'Well, I see you have captured the entire rats' nest – Dukey Watkins, Onas Shipton, Jezekiah Gray,' said Beasley, as he stabbed each with a long, manicured finger. 'I wondered whether you had kept any drawings from yesterday?'

'Yes, I drew these for my own amusement. I intend painting them when I get back to Walthamstow.'

Affronted hazel eyes stared at him. 'Why on earth would you want to paint these – these scavengers?'

'I find them fascinating,' he confessed. 'A colourful people, with a long tradition and the courage to be true to it.'

'These, too?' He pointed at the Skinner gang.

'They have interesting faces.'

'I beg to differ, Mr Price. I find these faces very bland, almost featureless. Indeed, if I were you – an artist about to be offered a sizeable commission – I would erase these three from your book and your memory forthwith.'

'Fair enough.' His lordship wanted a veil cast over his dealings with the Skinners. He didn't know that once Archie saw a face, he never forgot it. If he tore these drawings out of the book, ripped them into a dozen pieces and consigned them to the fire, as he did now, to his lordship's satisfaction, he could easily draw them again a day, a week, a year later, and in greater detail.

'The gypsies are different, I give you that,' said Beasley, his thin mouth twisting. 'They are a handsome people, but parasites. Human vermin. Poaching, stealing, littering up the place with their scabby animals, their filthy children! You look shocked, Mr Price, but you haven't tried getting them off your land.'

'I thought it was common land?'

'It's common if I say it's common! It is part of the Beasley estate, always has been. My soft-hearted great-grandfather made the mistake of permitting his tenants to graze their animals on Membury Common, it being unsuitable for arable farming. But my tenants have allowed gypsies to camp there and haven't the strength of will to turn them off. So I am taking it back. And if I choose to sell my own land that is nobody's business but my own. Don't you agree, Mr Price?'

Archie murmured something non-committal and hoped his disapproval didn't show. 'With regard to your own portrait, sir, I wondered whether you would prefer to be painted outside, say against a background of Elmscott Place, or inside with some of your favourite possessions, to show your interests, your passions...'

The noble lord tugged at his dyed sideburns thinking, then summoned his valet and asked him to lay out his 'writing' jacket for 'Price's' preparatory sketches. 'Indoors, I think. I see myself with quill in hand, Price. I write poetry, don't ye know?'

Archie blinked. He might have guessed.

'Yes, I have penned several little ditties over the years. You may care to cast your eye over them – to inform your painting, you understand.'

'Goodness,' he said. 'Yes, absolutely. Great help…' He managed a smile. 'Well, my lord,' he had to clear his throat again, 'if you're happy for me to paint you indoors, I won't take up any more of your valuable time, but perhaps you could lend me someone to show me around, so I can get a feel for a possible location? We need to consider natural lighting and composition and suchlike.'

He couldn't get away from the man soon enough. In any other circumstances this tall, whey-faced man with his superior height and attitude would have made a librarian or gallery guide, but because of some quirk of history, some battle won in some war that made some king somewhat richer, this part of England had been carved out and presented to this man's ancestor as a reward. Forever after there had been Beasleys in Elmscott Place lording it over the surrounding countryfolk.

Upstairs, on the large four-poster bed, lay a white silk shirt with an open collar, a black velvet dressing gown and breeches, a red embroidered waistcoat and matching slippers, and oriental turban-style headgear. Did the fool fancy himself as Lord Byron?

There was more artwork up here, though of a different kind entirely. Shelves lined the walls, filled with three-dimensional erotica: statuettes, of all sorts and sizes and positions. On the walls were paintings and photographs. Even the chairs, hand-turned to perfection, had arms that ended in highly polished phalluses, and their cushions were woven with titillating designs. No wonder Lady Beasley slept elsewhere. She'd never have a moment's peace in a room like this. But the chambermaids had to clean the room, dust the picture frames, polish the woodwork; they must feel defiled. What a heartless, selfish pig their master was, obsessed with self-gratification almost to the point of madness.

There were other shelves of well-thumbed books on art and art history, on ancient Greece and Rome, on literature and poetry. The man was clearly cultured, high-minded in one respect. Nearest the bed were piles of specialist magazines – *The Oyster*, *Playbirds*, *The Boudoir*, *Temptation* – in contrast to Milton and Gerard Manley Hopkins.

Archie couldn't resist a peek at the young ladies with their spread legs and come-hither glances. They reminded him of his early drawings, that had found homes very quickly among his friends. Aren't all adolescent boys obsessed with sex? There were erotic novels, piled one on the other, with titles such as *Older Men and Younger Women* and plain brown envelopes. Curiosity led him to open one, and he sat down heavily on the bed, his breath punched away with shock. There were half a dozen images of the baronet himself in the envelope, naked and in flagrante delicto: various poses, various victims (for they *were* victims, no doubt about it; none looked willing; most looked drugged – or hypnotised). Archie could hardly breathe. Perhaps this was the basis for Revilo's friendship with the Beast. He cast his spell over a victim and they became powerless to resist his lordship's sexual demands.

How utterly foul! Beasley sat in the House of Lords, making laws for Britain! Lord help us all!

In desperation he opened the window. Drank in the clean fresh air. God Jesus.

And there it was, large as life: a green-and-red painted caravan among the distant trees. A curling plume of smoke disappeared into the blue sky. You probably couldn't see it from ground level. He could just about see a dark figure moving about, but he couldn't make out whether it was bent from age or sickness, or whether the hair was white or brown. He ducked back into the bedroom as the manservant reappeared, summoning him.

His 'Nightmare' paintings, that were presently laid flat on a massive dining table – would Archie sell them to him? Two hundred pounds each? Beasley said he prided himself on his ability to spot trends in painting. There were gifted young artists on the continent, who, like Archie, were breaking away from traditional representation and experimenting with very different ways of painting. In ten, twenty years' time, their work would fetch top prices. 'Keep your ears open for these…' He mentioned some names: French, Belgian, German, some of whom Archie had heard of but whose paintings he had never seen. 'And there's a Dutchman I'm in two minds about, post-impressionist, died a few years ago, but his work is different, very different.'

'May I get back to you about mine?' he asked. 'Because they're on wood, they're still wet, as you can see. I brought them in the handcart so that I wouldn't smudge them, and I'd rather they were left to dry for a month or two before I let them go.' A lacewing had managed to attach itself to the paint on the way over. Archie picked it off with his fingernails and smoothed the paint even again with the ball of his thumb.

'About the portrait, I don't know that I'll be in Little Nessing for much longer, so it would be helpful if I could come over tonight to make the preliminary sketches. This afternoon I'll prepare the canvas – I thought a life-sized image would be about right, yes? Good. And then we can get started.'

'Not tonight, I'll be up to my ears. Tomorrow should be all right. About noon. See the butler and he'll book you in.'

God, thought Archie, as he left the building, and allowed his face to drop the ingratiating smile he had been forced to wear, what an awful man. He had no intention of spending the afternoon framing canvas or preparing it. With a bit of luck the baronet would be behind bars inside a week. So what if Archie never sold him any damn paintings, never had the man's patronage? At least he'd have the satisfaction of knowing that one more evil bastard had met his just desserts.

Twenty-seven

As the clock on the drawing-room mantelpiece chimed the half hour, Archie watched through the dining-room window as Geoffrey Norris mounted some wooden steps onto the farm-wagon and clambered awkwardly onto the bench. *Missionary Travels* sprang to mind, and stick insects. The old man's trousers were sponged clean of dinner spots; his black shirt was freshly washed and ironed, the dog collar bleached and starched, and a large Quaker-looking hat fitted over his sparse grey locks. Lilian Gifford was fussing over him. Would he like another rug for his legs, a bottle of tea? Did he have everything he needed: gloves, handkerchief, Bible, sermon? It must have bothered her conscience, as it did Archie's, that the poor old soul was venturing out alone, with one blind eye and one good, and no protection save the manservant. 'Do you need another lantern, Thomas? Be sure to drive carefully.'

She'd taken hold of the tailgate to fasten him in securely when Archie leaned out of the window, driven to desperation. 'Hang on,' he cried. 'I'm coming, too. Wait for me.'

Grabbing his coat and hat from the hallstand, he burst through the half-open front door.

'Budge up,' he said to the old man, as he hopped up the steps. Lilian waved and gave the order to Thomas to walk on. A click of the tongue was all it took. Cartwheels scrunched on gravel and they were off.

By the time they reached Boxstead, some three miles down the lane, in the opposite direction from the common, the poor old man was raw with cold, his lips and nose magenta and his eyes red-rimmed and watery. Luckily they were early and he had time to warm up in the vestry where a small fire was burning.

Being Good Friday, the chapel was stripped of any decoration. There were no flowers and the cross on the altar was draped with a black cloth. Several large candles had been placed in sconces along the walls but, even so, it was dark. The pews were already starting to fill, as Archie and Thomas took their seats at the back of the tiny hall.

Although it was supposed to be the saddest day in the Christian calendar, the day Jesus was put to death, it was a lively meeting with plenty of 'Praise the Lords' and 'Hallelujahs' and 'Amens' coming from the congregation. As one hymn finished, someone struck up the last verse again and it was sung with great gusto.

Then it was the minister's turn to speak.

'A week or two ago,' he began, peering through the dim light at the congregation. 'A week or two ago,' he repeated, 'I was one of the passengers on the eight twenty-nine to Colchester which crashed. I was in the derailed carriage, having the breath punched out of me, as the carriage rolled over and over down the embankment. Completely helpless, I was thrown about, banging painfully into the walls, the floor, the ceiling. Other passengers flew past, some alive, some not. As we fell against a wall, everything else fell too – bags and umbrellas, books, hats, loose change, thumping us about the head, winding us, if we still had any wind. Suitcases spilled. The cries of the hurt, of the dying, of children for their mamas assailed our ears…'

As he described the experience, Archie went through it all again, realising that the minister, the funny old Methodist preacher man, with his knack of forgetting names, his partiality to sweeties, his sister in Colchester, had suffered just as he had, as Polly had, as thirty others had, a dozen of whom were now dead.

The old man compared their experience to Jesus on the cross.

'It was a nightmare for us. It must have been a worse nightmare for Him. A nightmare from which He *knew* He would not wake up. We had hope; He did not. "Why hast Thou forsaken me?" He cried towards the end. Jesus had been scourged with whips and mockingly crowned with thorns, now He was tortured, with nails driven into His hands and feet, pinning Him to a wooden cross which was then raised and hammered into the ground, leaving Him to die. He was in excruciating pain, physically and mentally. He was exhausted, abandoned by His friends, humiliated, forsaken by God, and yet… And yet He gasped for a last breath and gathered all His strength for one final cry. "Father, into Thy Hands I commend my spirit."

'Why would He choose to speak so close to the end? Why would He use the last energy He had to cry out? Couldn't God have *heard* His thoughts? Unless God wasn't the only one intended to hear. Unless His voice was pitched loud so that we too might hear this final dedication of His soul. A dedication made despite the pain, despite the derision, despite the agony, despite the horrible aloneness He felt. A dedication made to God before the resurrection, before the victory of the kingdom, before any assurance other than faith. Jesus entrusted His spirit, His life and all that had given it meaning to God in faith. Even at the point of His own abandonment, when the good seemed so very far away, He proclaimed His faith in God. The darkness could not overcome it. "Father, into Thy hands, I commend my spirit."'

Archie was sure he was not the only one to feel tears gathering at the back of his nose, for Jesus, yes, but also for the good old man, up there, whose faith was such he could actually say, 'I count myself lucky to have gone through that dreadful experience, with the loss of an eye, to realise, in small part, what Jesus suffered – for me and for you.'

His voice went on, surprisingly strong, as he stepped from the pulpit and proceeded to snuff out the candles around the church, repeating other words Jesus had spoken from the cross. 'Forgive them, Father, for they know not what they do,' followed by the words of comfort to the criminal hanging beside Him, more to his weeping mother and John, then the desperate cry to God: 'I thirst.' Another candle was extinguished. 'It is finished...' And finally, as the preacher neared the pulpit again, he repeated, 'Father into Thy hands I commend my spirit,' and pitched the chapel into total darkness.

And utter silence.

An image came into Archie's mind: Polly, as he had seen her last night, tied up in the moonlight for any man to use. That must have been a death of sorts. And she had come back. She had always come back. From her brother's abuse, from the train crash, from this.

He recalled how she had looked after her bath this morning. Pink from hot water, but her eyes were lifeless. No, she had *not* come back this time. She had a strong spirit, but it was too much to expect that much resilience. Poor, poor girl. She would go under, unless...

Oh Lord, thought Archie, what happens now? He began to fidget. This was too much, too dramatic. Too much was being asked of him. In a darkened church with a hundred strangers whom he couldn't see.

There was movement. Norris's voice again, praying for the congregation to remember why Jesus had to die, and asking them to thank Him for his sacrifice.

They did.

Voices came from the dark, giving thanks to the Lord for sending Minister Norris to Boxstead, for saving him from the train crash, for his eyesight. There were prayers for every injured train passenger billeted with them, some of whom were here, under this roof. There were prayers for healing, and thanks for providing the congregation with this opportunity for service. There were some strange prayers, too: prayers for sick animals, requests to bless the newly sown seed potatoes and save them from slugs, frost and blight, concerns that too many youngsters were leaving home to work in the towns. 'Lead them not into temptation and deliver them from evil.' Lastly, there was a heartfelt prayer that Lord Beasley would see the error of his ways before it was too late. Really?

And Archie prayed silently for Polly, that she might recover mentally and spiritually from her ordeal. Prayed for himself, too, that he might do the right thing and support her. He didn't pray for Freddy. Unlike Polly, he didn't believe the man was blameless. Yes, he had had a bad start in life, but he'd had good people to love him and teach him right from wrong. He could have gone straight if he'd wanted to. He had had a choice. His prayer for Freddy would be that he'd be brought to justice quickly, along with his foul friends.

A few lanterns were lit at the end of the service to light their way out. And as they shuffled along the pew his neighbour, a burly farmer, spoke to him.

'Haven't seen you here before?'

'No, I'm just visiting – I was on the train, too.'

'You have my sympathy, son. God send you a speedy recovery.'

At the chapel door, Minister Norris stood to shake everybody by the hand, and Archie went outside to wait for him. He watched, almost enviously, as everyone thanked the old man for the sermon. His words had meant the world to them, it seemed. How comforting, Archie thought, to have the church habit and a faith.

'God saved you from the disaster to speak to us,' he heard one woman say.

What, he wondered, had *he* been saved for?

Far from being warmed by the success of his sermon, the preacher shivered and shook as they helped him into the wagon.

'Good sermon, minister,' said Archie.

'It wasn't t-t-too m-much about me, do you think?'

Both Archie and Thomas assured him that his testimony of pain and confusion had touched everyone. They would remember

231

that Good Friday sermon for a long time. Then, of one mind, both men took off their overcoats and wrapped the old man up so snugly that, within minutes, he had fallen asleep.

Sitting up with the driver, Archie asked Thomas about some of the other final prayers. 'I know Beasley's an old lecher,' he said, 'and has a few unsavoury tastes, but there seemed to be something else that was bothering the congregation directly.'

Thomas explained that his lordship was 'feeling the pinch'. Elmscott Place needed extensive repairs – the attics were flooded every time it rained, the plumbing wasn't fit for purpose, and draughts whistled down the corridors. The only way his lordship could stop his ancient pile falling into ruins was to sell off part of the estate. First to go would be the tenancies: the farms, including Gifford Lodge, and labourers' cottages, and the commons and woods – if he could get away with it. That was what the prayers were about.

'But Beasley has plenty of money. He only has to sell some of his treasures…'

''Tis to buy more treasures he wants money.'

Good Lord. Get your priorities right, Lord Peregrine.

'I thought Gifford owned the Lodge.'

'No, Master Richard is a tenant farmer be'olden to his lordship.'

'But can't your master appeal to someone, the Land Registry or the Lord Chancellor?'

Thomas chuckled. Clearly he thought Archie was joking. 'I'm serious, Thomas, this is important. Hasn't *anyone* stood up to him? Told him that he has no right to do this? Good Lord, man, this is daylight robbery. He'll be flung into prison if the police ever hear of it.'

'Old PC Philpot *do* know. He'm paid to turn a blind eye, like Nelson, afeared to do else.'

'So you're going to stand by and let it happen?'

'Nothing *I* can do, Mester Price, sir, nor nobody else neither. When old Peregrine sets his mind to a thing 'e generally gets it.'

232

'Can't you get up a petition, or write to the newspaper, the *Chronicle,* or alert your MP? Miss, em, Florence could take a photograph…'

'Nobody'd take no notice o' working men, sir, no matter 'ow many we got be'ind us. They'm get the troops out arter us. Maybe an 'igh-up, someone wi' the vote, a property owner or somesuch might fare better, but they en't affected by the taking away of our rights.'

'No, no, quite so.' He was silent for a moment or two, listening to the regular clip-clop of the horse. 'Speak to Mr Marconi, explain the situation. I'm sure he doesn't want to lay himself open to accusations of illegal land-grabbing.'

''E'm a furriner, sir. ''E woul'n't unnerstand a word any of us said to 'im.'

Archie frowned. It looked as if they were going to let Beasley ride roughshod over them all. And, as if to illustrate this thought, a pair of horses came galloping towards them now, foam-flecked, manes streaming, eyes white and wild in the moonlight, spooking poor Bonnie. She reared up in the shafts, whinnying with fright, but Thomas managed to pull the wagon over. The riders had no intention of slowing down or stopping. Sooner mow you down.

'Get out the way!' shouted the front runner, thundering past.

'Where's the fire?' shouted Archie, shaking his fist, while Thomas concentrated on keeping a tight rein and crooning to Bonnie.

Too late, he'd recognised the murderer, Freddy Porter, and his sidekick, Lemmy King, lately come from Walthamstow, he guessed, from the shop. They'd be rushing back to the gypsy camp with freshly printed postcards, and Fitzell's precious tin box, desperate to meet Beasley's deadline. He reached into his pocket for a pistol but, by the time he'd pulled it out, cocked it and taken aim, they'd vanished into the darkness. Too slow, too slow, Price, he berated himself. This won't do.

Twenty-eight

Freddy and Lemmy had finished the job and filled the box, so it looked like new. Old, rather. Well thumbed. He'd strapped it on his saddle and they'd raced back to Membury Common, stopping for nobody and nothing, only to find that Tuddy and Curly had cleared off.

Onas came clattering out of his caravan to greet them. 'Sure, an' weren't you the lucky ones to be outa the way? We've had the polis here, lookin' for the both o' yez.'

Onas told him Tuddy had decided to check up on the artist, Archie Price, to see if he'd had a detective camera in his bag, as Freddy had thought. He'd found not only that Freddy was spot on, but that the person developing the photographs was none other than Freddy's sister Polly, right there at Gifford Farm.

'Polly?' His heart lurched. How could that be?

'She ent dead at all. Sure, she was in the train crash, but she took someone else's name.'

'Why? Why would she do that? Didn't she care that I'd be looking for her?'

'Don't look like it.'

He was right, the bitch! He lit a cigarette, broke the match. Inhaled for calm. 'So where is she now?'

'Nobody rightly knows. He brought her here, last night, did Tuddy, an' I have to say, Freddy, he didn't treat her proper. Tied her up and – well, you know what Tuddy's like, the old goat. But she got away somehow, and she musta went straight to the polis and grassed us up. Came here this morning, they did, making us out to be train wreckers.' He sounded quite indignant. 'We just got away in time.'

'You and Lavinia?'

'They know our faces, Freddy. All of us that got you off the train. That mind reader got them out of the painter, who went straightway to the polis. Our mugs are plastered all over Chelmsford, wi' a reward on 'em, Beasley says. Names and all.'

'Names? How did he get our *names*? I thought Beasley told him to wipe the geezer's mind. Pack 'im off to the loony bin, if needs be, but make sure he couldn't identify us. Jesus, now they know who they're looking for, and where to find us too, I shouldn't wonder. The sooner this job's finished and we're out of here the better.'

Onas shrugged. Onas and Lavinia would move on, no doubt, to the next bit of waste ground, and go back to poaching and selling pegs and lucky white heather.

He drew hard on his Woodie. 'How did you know to leg it in time?'

'Your sister escaped. Stands to reason she'd go directly to the polis and blab.'

'Good thinking. So where's Tuddy?'

'Took the caravan over to Elmscott. They're round the back among the trees, out of sight, out of mind. Curly's in a bad way, Lavinia says; on his last legs. Tuddy reckons he'll see him out, take his cut and go. Retire. Not tonight, o' course. They're waiting for you to get there with the photos.'

'So it's still on?'

''Course! They're waiting for you now.'

'You coming?'

His face was regretful. 'Give this one a miss, Fred. Lavinia's not—' He gestured indoors and shrugged.

'Yeah, yeah.' He understood. Lavinia had put her foot down for once. Dirty postcards and Lavinia didn't mix. 'Lem! Time to go.'

*

'What the hell are these!' Beasley cried, holding up a fistful of Freddy's best shots. 'These aren't Hans Voss!' The old perve kept scrabbling through the box, like a dog at a locked door.

'That's what it says on the lid,' said Tuddy, acting his evil heart out.

'Come off it, you old fraud, these aren't what you got from Fitzell!' The strained voice squawked like a startled chicken. 'Fitzell was a connoisseur. He wouldn't have given these houseroom! This is dross – tawdry rubbish! You stopped a train for these?'

Shrugging, they did their utmost to convince him that this was indeed the box that Freddy had stolen from Fitzell.

'I don't believe it. Yes, the box is authentic – there's dried blood on the bottom.' (Tuddy glared at Freddy, mouthing, *I bloody told you to clean it up!*) 'But the contents…' The ashy face was fiery with disappointment. 'What did you do with the originals?'

'Nothing,' Tuddy insisted. 'These are what we found in the box.'

'I'll grant you they might fool some people. The edges are burred to look aged and worn, the sepia print, all very cleverly done. But the images. They're far too late. And Voss was Dutch. These are – these subjects are English, aren't they? I mean, look at this…'

'Either,' said Freddy, seeing the picture Beasley had in his hand and digging deep for something to distract the geezer, 'Fitzell got one over on us, or someone else got one over on Fitzell – though, as you say, that's unlikely.' With his big brown eyes, his angelic face, attributes that had charmed people from his earliest years, he managed to persuade the baronet that Fitzell himself had switched the contents, suspecting that someone would try and steal his precious Voss collection, as they did. 'The originals are probably still around the house, in a safe or something. I'll go have a look-see if you like.' He was conscious of the others staring at him, open-mouthed. Seeing his famed mendacity in action was something to behold.

236

'Well, you can say goodbye to any payment. These pictures are not what I asked for.'

'You don't want them at all?'

'They're not worth the paper they're printed on.' His thin wrist flicked away, preparing to toss the image from his hand, but he paused mid-action.

Everyone held their breath.

'Surely,' he said slowly, 'I know this face, this little girl. Those eyes. She's, she's…' He nodded. 'All grown up. Of course she is.' Cunning lit his eyes. 'Oho,' he said. 'I see what you've done. That tart I saw you with last night, Tuddy! Lovely.'

Polly? Onas had said Tuddy had had her – and this geezer had watched? A voyeur. Well, he supposed, it took all sorts. Or perhaps it had been too cold for him last night, too uncomfortable? Perhaps he preferred to do it in comfort? Freddy felt a small stab of – pain? Resentment? Jealousy? Only a small stab. Mostly he felt worry. Were they all for the chop?

'I'll tell you what I'll do, my friends, and we'll forget all about your ridiculous attempt at deception – I'll have her tonight, that one.' As he looked around, seeing oil lamps and candles, something changed his mind. 'Second thoughts, tomorrow – tomorrow morning – the light will be better.'

The light? Freddie had a sudden inkling of the man's plan.

'I'll want you all here, ten o'clock sharp, and I'll telephone Allsop, get him over. And you,' he narrowed his gaze at Freddy, 'this *is* your work, I take it? Yes, yes, of course it is. Very good. Not such dross, perhaps. Not Hans Voss but, in time…' You could see the ideas teeming behind those clever little eyes. 'Your name, boy, remind me—' He clicked his fingers.

Freddy looked around for help. Tuddy was frowning; they all looked puzzled. How did he know Freddy had done the work? He looked down at his hands. He'd scrubbed them well, but around the nail edges, the telltale blue of chemicals. Fuck.

'Freddy,' he muttered. No use denying it.

'Ah yes, Freddy *Porter*. Seen your face on the posters. You're famous, boy.' His smile was a snake's. He had him where he wanted him. 'So you, dear boy, shall be our cameraman. Your very best work, if you please – a nice record of my performance with that young tart and I might forgive you. *Freddy Porter*. And Mr Skinner shall have his money, after all.'

'You want to keep the photos then?' Tuddy dared to ask, unable to believe his luck.

'Oh yes, this collection will increase in value as time goes on. I'll make sure of it.'

There would be three cameras arranged around the bed, he said. Glass slides for the best results. Probably wouldn't need a flash if the weather was fine. Freddy nodded. He hadn't done any photography in years, but he certainly knew how. He was to go from one camera to the other, taking photographs from every angle as he saw fit. He shook his head. This geezer was full of surprises. He would even have the hypnotist standing by to make sure the victim was compliant with Beasley's every foul whim. Nothing was left to chance, only…

'The girl?' he asked. 'Polly?'

'Is that her name?' As he stared at the photograph, his eyes took on a dreamy look. 'Well, that's your job.'

'Mine?'

'Go fetch her, Freddy Porter.'

Twenty-nine

It was late when she came upstairs, the candle throwing vast, foreboding shadows.

Archie had told her, 'The very slightest thing – I'll be in the room below yours, ears flapping. Just bang on the floor and I'll come running.' She'd smiled. His leg was better, but she didn't think he was up to running upstairs just yet. 'Watch me,' he'd said.

Should she lock the door? Would she have time to unlock it in an emergency? Could she bear to keep it unlocked, knowing Freddy might come in? Oh God, she felt so tired, so lightheaded, her mind flitting about like a moth around a lamp. After last night, no sleep, the pain and the fear and the degradation, and everything going wrong with the police raid this morning, she was a bag of nerves.

She locked the door behind her, after all, and jammed the dressing table chair under the handle. Yes, that was safest. At least if he came for her that way, she'd have some warning.

Constable Beckett had stationed himself by the back door, Inspector Tyrell by the front, and everyone had guns, including her. She undressed to her shift and brushed her hair, then climbed into bed and placed the loaded revolver under her pillow. She lay down with a book: Mark Twain's *Huckleberry Finn*, but her eyes danced over the words. Why hadn't the Walthamstow police picked them up at the shop? Archie had told Tyrell where they'd be. But the detective had made some excuse about his squad being two men down since the train crash, and stretched to the limit. The real reason, she knew, was he wanted to wait for Freddy and Lemmy to get back here so that he could kill all the birds with one stone and reap the glory. Never mind that *she* might well be killed in the process. She'd already been raped, why not just finish her off?

Whatever deal they had with Beasley would be made tonight or never. The gang *had* to get out now that their faces were plastered all over town.

She put down her book and got out of bed to close the sash window. She'd left a gap at the top, hoping fresh air would chase away her headache, but no: that was madness. It was the way he would come, she was sure of it. She scanned the outside walls, the empty farmyard, the dark fields and woods beyond, and slid the catch across to lock the window tight before closing the shutters. The bedside candle flickered in the draught under the door. She read for a while then blew out the flame.

Something woke her. The house was very quiet. Moonlight silvered the room. But surely she had closed the shutters?

Her heart nearly burst through her ribs as his hand clamped across her mouth. Screaming was impossible. Her mouth, her jaw, her head were held in his iron grip, the thumb pressing under her cheekbone. A cat burglar's hands. The full length of his body pinned her to the bed, and though she writhed and bucked, he held her fast, his knees drawn up to her sides, his shins trapping her arms. Her shoulder, that had given her no trouble for days, really, really hurt. Oh, please God, don't let it slip out of its socket again. He was in shirt, jacket and britches, his burgling gear. She knew his feet would be bare.

'Poll,' he whispered, 'you cost me dear, bitch – why'd you go and burn those postcards? You really fucked me over.'

She couldn't see his face, but she could see the glint of a knife. A clock ticked somewhere, its beat out of time with her heart, which was galloping crazily.

'Those pics were special. They were worth a bleeding fortune. Irre – bloody – placeable. I tried – I tried,' her stepbrother said through his teeth. 'Got some of my old negs from your cellar. Just as spicy, and they printed out perfectly, but he knew they weren't right! Wrong period. Dead giveaway.'

Fashions change. Freddy should have known that. The styles of ten years ago were different from 1840; men's, too. Underwear, hairstyles would show their age. She wasn't surprised he was found out.

She remembered those photos, when they were taken. And how. She moaned.

'Shut it, Poll, you'll wake the house. Oh Gawd, we were so nearly there. That old perv down the road was going to pay us half a grand, half a bleeding grand! We'd have been made. And we worked so hard, me and Lemmy. You should've seen us last night, freezing our nuts off down your shop to get them all printed and dried and packed away, and for what? "This isn't Voss," he goes, straight off, "this is dross!" I tell you, Poll, I'd have slit his gizzard if he hadn't offered us a way out.'

So things hadn't gone well for the Skinner gang…

'Lucky he's taken a shine to you, after last night.'

Last night? Had Beasley been there, too?

'Tuddy let him watch. You're really something, you know. He wants you over there in the morning, with cameras. I'm meant to fetch you, take the photos. It'll be like the old days.' The knife glittered. She recoiled into the pillow.

He took his hand from her mouth. Now was her chance to scream, if she was going to. That blade, glinting in the moonlight – she could almost feel it slicing through her windpipe. She could picture a line of blood growing, soaking the sheets red and stinking of iron. One false move and she'd be dead, she knew it. Never mind what Beasley wanted. She knew Freddy.

She dared to wheedle, 'You – you don't have to do what they tell you, Freddy. Ever again. I can give you money, lots of it. I have a bank account now. You can set up shop somewhere nice, take photos—'

The knife hovered. Glint. Glint. It was thinking. Money?

'You'd do that for me? You actually care, then?'

'Of course. What did you think?'

'Oh, Poll, if only I could believe that...' He lowered the knife into shadow. 'You were on that train, gave out you were dead, like you didn't want me to find you.'

'Freddy, Freddy,' she whispered, and drew her breath through her teeth, 'I was coming to your trial. I had to take on an assumed name or they'd have stopped me. I was going to speak up for you. I knew you couldn't help it, any of it. Um, could you get off my arm, dear? My shoulder was injured in the crash.'

Obediently, he shifted. The terrible pressure eased and she lay still, thinking fast, no longer confused, no longer woolly brained. She'd known he would come. Why hadn't she smeared the windowsill with butter, sprinkled some of Archie's drawing pins about? But now, what could she do? Could she hope that someone in the house could hear their hoarse whispers? Where was Archie? Should she drop something on the floor to wake him? A book? Play for time, play for time, Polly. Think.

She cleared her throat. 'I didn't know until afterwards that you'd been on the train, too. The police told me you were missing. I – I didn't know where to find you. The painter thought you might have taken refuge with the gypsies. He went up yesterday to look.'

'The hidden camera?'

'Exactly. He brought the film back for me to develop. It was only then that I knew you were there. But Tuddy came. And well, I suppose you know what happened then?'

He pocketed his knife. She let him stroke her hair, her face. Then his smoky lips covered hers; his lying tongue pushed against her teeth, his arms went round her, pulling her into him. 'C'mon, Poll, girl...' There was just a split-second chance, if she was quick... Her right hand was caught under him, but her weaker left hand, still aching where his knee had been, with pins and needles pricking and numbing, travelled up the bed and under the pillow. Closed around solid metal.

242

'Get off me!' she hissed. 'Get off me, *gutter slime,* or I'll shoot you dead.'

'Eh?' He realised what it was digging into his neck. He leaned away to check her face in the moonlight and what he saw – hatred oozing from every pore – must have left him in no doubt that she meant to kill him.

Oh, the power surging through her, the singing joy of knowing that with just one twitch of her finger she could end this menace.

But could she? Could she kill him? Perhaps she wouldn't need to. 'Get off me,' she repeated. 'Off the bed. Off.' She almost smiled as he obeyed. What a wonderful thing was a gun, that was able to make the whites of his eyes gleam with fright. 'Keep your hands where I can see them! Up!' The floor creaked. Not loud enough.

'Turn around.' He did. The floorboards creaked again. *Wake up, Archie!* Would he hear her silent scream?

She transferred the gun to her right hand and jabbed it in his back while with her left she swept books and candlestick, a glass of water, off the night table. The noise was startling. The candlestick rolled down the sloping floor, hit the wall. *Now! Wake up, Archie!*

'Take your knife out of your pocket, slowly, slowly, and throw it out of the window.' Her finger on the trigger squeezed. They could both hear the click-click of the ratchet, the spring mechanism moving. She would beat him to any draw.

'Don't, Poll,' he wheedled, with a nervous little laugh, 'this is me, your Freddy, you don't wanna do...'

'*Throw your knife out of the window!*' Both her feet were planted squarely behind him, both her hands were on the gun. She was in control. Archie was taking too long. She would have to deal with this by herself. 'Now!' she said.

'Come on, Poll, we both know you ain't got it in you.'

'Oh, I have, Freddy,' she said to his back. 'More than anyone. Forged by fire, me, and you the smithy. I killed Ma, you know – put a pillow over her face.' She didn't say how it had taken her all her tears and strength, worn down, at last, by Ma's non-stop pleading. *Put me out of my misery, Polly. I cannot bear it. I want to die.* 'And I can kill *you* if I have to and say good riddance – so be a good boy, get rid of the knife, and we'll see.' Her voice rose to a screech. '*Throw it!*'

He threw it through the window and she heard a faraway clink as it landed on stones. Good.

At last there was Archie at the door. 'Polly, Polly, are you all right?' But, of course, she'd locked it. The key was this side and she couldn't move. There was a thump as he charged it and the impact reverberated through the ancient timber bones of the room.

'He'll batter it down, Freddy. You'd better go now.'

'You're letting me go?'

Shards of dark glass lay on the sill and on the floor, where he had broken the window to switch the catch. It might occur to him to stab her with them if he saw them.

'Turn and face me, Freddy.' He did so. His face was in darkness. Unreadable. 'Go and tell your masters that I decline their invitation, thanks all the same.'

The door shook as Archie charged it with his shoulder. The ceiling shook down flakes of whitewash, the window rattled, a picture fell off the wall.

'Back up, back up to the window. Go! Go!' she repeated. 'Never mind the glass.'

Feet first, Freddy couldn't move fast enough. Knees, then snaky hips, slid through the gap, fingers gripping the window frame while he found his footing. He must have done this a thousand times.

The door burst open with splintering wood, the chair buckled, and Archie hurtled into the room. The heavy window dropped onto Freddy's fingertips and sent him, screaming, to his death.

She dropped the gun as if it was molten metal and Archie held her tight until she stopped shaking.

Everyone believed her when she said the sound of breaking glass had woken her. That when she saw a burglar standing on the window ledge, she had leapt out of bed, knocking into the bedside table, sending everything flying. That had alerted Archie, who scooted up the stairs.

How very brave of her, they said, to draw her gun and see him off. He would still be alive if Archie hadn't battered the door open. The reverberations through the ancient timber frame had loosened the sash and brought the window crashing down, severing his finger ends.

'What *about* my door?' mourned Richard. 'My window?'

'What about poor little Miss Anderson?' said the preacher. 'What a terrible experience.'

'Thank goodness she didn't actually fire her gun,' said Lilian. 'She needn't have his death on her conscience.'

Terrible accident, they all agreed.

They were all gathered round his body on the path, their lanterns alight, like children singing Christmas carols. Huddled into dressing gowns and blankets, shivering, they stared at her brother's face, unnaturally pale against the dyed black hair, and the blood seeping into the daffodil bed from his fingers.

'All they that take the sword shall perish with the sword,' quoted the minister.

'Poetic justice,' agreed Tyrell.

'Yon's the bugger's knife,' said Thomas, with his arm around a whimpering Maud. No, it was hardly a sword, but just as deadly, and it lay on the path, the blade sharpening to razor thinness as the clouds cleared from the mocking face of the moon.

If he'd been quicker, thought Polly, he'd have got away. But he's gone. Gone. Why wasn't she glad?

'Lucky he never got to you, Miss, em, Anderson,' said Beckett. *Mmm*, she thought bitterly, *no thanks to you*.

'*Incredibly* lucky,' murmured Archie, with *his* arm around *her*.

Even his nightclothes smelled of oil paint and turps. Weak with weeping, she didn't struggle. Whether her tears were from relief or regret or exhaustion she couldn't have said.

Archie reminded the others where they had seen the burglar's face before. That drawing he'd shown them the other day? A badly injured policeman's description of his attacker? He'd knifed the young constable then trampled him. This was the same Freddy Porter who had been on his way to stand trial for killing another man when the Skinner gang had crashed the train. He was very dangerous indeed.

'But he has such a nice face,' said Lilian.

Her husband regarded her with scorn, Polly with tears in her eyes, the rest with pity. Surprisingly the minister had no biblical quotation to hand this time.

'I wonder you didn't hear the breaking glass, constable,' said Lilian, bristling. 'You were stationed at the back of the house.'

Beckett squirmed. He must have been asleep.

Tyrell said quickly, 'The ladies are getting cold. Why don't you take them inside, Gifford?'

'We can't leave him lying here all night,' said Richard. 'The rats and foxes will get him.'

'Good,' said Archie.

'Cover him with a tarpaulin,' said Beckett, all efficiency now. 'If you have a handcart I could borrow, I'll wheel him down to PC Philpot. Time he earned his keep. He can put him in the lock-up for the night.'

'Good idea, Stanley,' said Tyrell, with the kindness and patience due to an underling, 'but first I think we should take measurements and proper notes, so there's no question of how he met his death. If I might impose on you a moment longer, Polly, I'd like to borrow your camera for a moment or two to take a few photographs?'

'*Florence*,' Archie corrected him.

'I'll fetch it. You may need some help. In fact, it would probably save a lot of trouble if I took them myself.'

'You sure you're up to it?' said Archie.

'I think so.' As she was leaving, Tyrell thanked her. 'That's solved that one, I think!' he said in her ear. What he meant, she couldn't be sure.

Thirty

He watched as she pulled the cloth over her head. It looked as if she couldn't get the subject into focus: she moved the camera an inch or two. What was she looking for – the knife, the spread arms, the growing pool of blood at his head where the skull was cracked, that thatch of dyed black hair? Ah, of course – her brother's dead face. She twiddled a knob and then another. He followed her gaze to stare at eyes that were once fine and sharp, at the Grecian nose soon to be picked clean by maggots, and the lips, the perfect Cupid's bow.

Her hand shook.

'You don't have to do this, Polly.'

He peeled back the black-out cloth like skin from a blister, exposing her to his scrutiny.

'*Don't!*' she said.

He took her by her shoulders and turned her towards him. Slowly, unwillingly, she met his eyes. Her face was blotched, her nose streaming, her mouth an ugly worm of grief.

'Don't cry,' he said, and took her in his arms. 'He's not worth it.'

'But I killed him, Archie, I took his life.'

'No, it was an accident.' In fact, if anyone had caused the burglar's demise, he had, running in. Ruefully, he rubbed his shoulder.

'You poor thing,' she said, glad of an excuse to change the subject. 'I shouldn't have locked the door. I could probably have managed without getting you out of bed – and you were so tired, too. Once he'd thrown the knife out…'

'Did he – did he hurt you?'

She shook her head. 'He was going to. Then he was going to take me to Beasley. Apparently I was to be the booby prize, making up for the loss of the Hans Voss prints.'

'Your own brother would do that to you?'

'I don't think he had any choice.'

'He hasn't now. Good Lord, Polly. It doesn't bear thinking of.'

'What will happen to him?' Polly said.

'They'll get Doctor MacKay to issue a death certificate, and then they'll need a coroner's report. They'll write up their files and then release him to you for burial, as his nearest and dearest. And then they'll draw a line under it.'

'Oh, dear God. I don't want to be his nearest and dearest. Suppose I continue to be Florence Anderson. It's not illegal, is it?'

He frowned. 'I'm sure it is, but you'd better ask Frank. Taking money under false pretences. I mean you have her bank book, don't you? That is illegal.'

'I – I feel very guilty.'

'About being Florence?'

'About Freddy.'

'He was ready to kill you, Polly. No one will blame you. Pulling that knife…' He gestured to Beckett, measuring its distance from the body. 'He brought it on himself – he deserved everything he got.'

'Did he?' She blinked, almost believing him. 'Didn't Tuddy have something to do with it?'

'Stop it, Polly. He was a responsible adult. He had a choice. Now blow your nose.' He handed her a handkerchief from his dressing gown pocket, crumpled but clean enough.

'Archie, I can't do this.' He thought she meant the handkerchief, but it was the photography she couldn't face. Perfectly understandable. As it turned out, it wasn't just that the subject was her dead brother – there was something else, something she didn't tell him until later.

'Let me, then. You light the flash.'

When photographs had been taken from every angle, including close-ups of the head and the bloody fingertips, and a line of chalk drawn, recording how the body had fallen, Archie helped the detectives heave Freddy's corpse into the Giffords' handcart. They set off down the lane to the village, and he heard the sounds of their voices and the rumbling of the wheels gradually dying away, the wheel that squeaked growing fainter and fainter.

He helped her collapse the tripod and pack away the camera. They were about to go in when Polly held up her hand, signalling for quiet. Yes, he had heard it, too: crunching gravel. It was too soon for the policemen's return. He followed her round the side of the house.

'It's Onas Shipton! He must have been with Freddy. He'll have seen everything.' Her whisper was anxious.

'No, he's carrying something – a dead bird or a rabbit. I expect he was out poaching and saw the flash of light. Came to see what was up.'

'Mmm.' She sounded doubtful.

They watched him creeping away across the lawn.

'Hey, you!' There was Gifford on the front step, menacing the gypsy with a shotgun. 'What are you up to, you filthy—?'

There, too, was Lilian, with a lantern. 'Richard, leave him,' she begged. 'No more upsets tonight, please.'

Archie and Polly reached the door and saw Richard lining up his shotgun, with Onas in his sights. 'Stop or I'll shoot!'

He didn't stop and Richard pulled the trigger. A loud report shattered the night. Birds flapped out of the bushes and trees, dogs began barking. Pale faces appeared in most of the windows.

'No, Richard, no,' wailed Lilian, hanging onto his arm. He shook her off and reloaded. That last shot had been a warning only.

'This time…'

Onas got the message and blundered off into the bushes.

'Bloody pest,' said Richard, running to the front gate and firing a shot up the lane.

'Did you get him?' Lilian joined him and the rest of the household straggled out into the turning circle.

'No. Bloody fool. He'll live to tell the tale. Go back inside, everyone; you'll catch your death out here.'

At the door, Polly caught Archie's arm. 'Beasley will wonder where Freddy is…and me. Freddy came to fetch me for a special thing he's got planned – some sort of camera shoot…'

'Camera?' he said, stupidly. 'What do you—?' Suddenly light dawned. Beasley wanted her for his sick collection of egomaniacal photographs. Presumably he'd been counting on Freddy taking them, which was even sicker if he knew that Freddy was Polly's stepbrother. 'Of all the twisted…' he spluttered.

'No, Archie, listen. What if, in the morning, I take myself over to Elmscott Hall, on a plate, as it were?' She gave a shudder, her eyes blinking with the enormity of what she was suggesting. 'With you and the police as backup, of course. They'll all be there, Archie. Tyrell can scoop the entire gang red-handed.'

She was proposing to set herself up as bait! 'Never!' He glared at her. 'Don't even think about it, Polly. Lord, I never heard of anything so *stupid*! I won't let you.'

'Archie, I know you mean well – but – but you're not my keeper.' That stung. She turned to go in. 'I have to. This has to end.'

He could see that. He rubbed his chin. It was a plan, but it was so bloody dangerous. 'Polly!' he pleaded.

'I'm going. I'll wait up for the police and tell them what's happening.'

Was she brave or just plain stupid? Perhaps she had a death wish. After all she'd been through, she was looking for a way out. Whatever her motive, the police were keen to have her try it, much to Archie's dismay. He wanted the villains caught, but not at any price.

They said that Archie should go first, to keep his sketching appointment, and then, when Polly came calling, make it seem as though he had left. Then he must find somewhere to hide, so that he could let them in at an appropriate moment.

'I can't just abandon her, Frank. They're terrible men.'

'You're both armed? Then leave her to play along. She's a sensible girl.'

His sketchbook was full in no time. Beasley kept insisting on adopting some pose, like a ham actor, affecting to be the proud master of Elmscott, with a hand on his hip, chin in the air, looking down at his estate from the window. Next he was the soulful poet, *The Thinker* made flesh, elbow on knee, seeking inspiration from the dancing flames in the large fireplace of the banqueting hall. He leant against the fireplace with his sheaf of poems in one hand, his quill pen in the other, declaiming (and, Lord, were those poems dire!). He lay on his couch trying in vain for a 'vacant or pensive mood', unsure what it meant. They were both exhausted by the time the butler knocked on the door to ask his master to come and sort out a commotion in the entrance hall.

'Stop here, Price, I'll see to this.' He left the door ajar and the butler to keep an eye on him.

Archie recognised the earthy voices: Tuddy, Lemmy, Onas, excited and high-pitched, their words tumbling over each other.

'Burglarising … fell orf … dollop o' dead meat…'

'What the hell was he thinking, bloody young fool?' Surely those were the hypnotist's heavy tones?

'Couldn't leave her be, could 'e? Shouldn't never a told 'im she was stopping at Gifford's.'

'So now we have no cameraman and no tart either?'

'Oh my,' said the butler, and walked out. Archie followed him to the door. 'If you'll just excuse me, sir…' The door was shut firmly in his face.

It was difficult to hear through the thick oak, but, despite the bad news, Archie made out some laughter. Never say die, apparently.

Footsteps approached the door. He backed off, pretending to examine the workmanship in an ancient wall hanging: a bloody hunting scene, aptly enough. Who would be the unlucky victim now? Beasley came back in.

A little later, as their interview was coming to an end, they were interrupted again. This time it was a young woman at the door, a Miss Florence Anderson, wretched and tear-stained, they were told. Beasley's noble mask dropped for a second, and although the brows lifted in surprise, Archie caught a gleam of greed and lust in his jaded eye. Beasley ordered the butler to show her into the 'small reception room', the merest hint of a suggestive undertone in his voice. Archie immediately took his leave, assuring his host that he could see himself out.

Thirty-one

So Beasley was the man in the shadows, the man who had so enjoyed watching Tuddy rape her last night; he couldn't wait to do the same. For all his wealth and standing, for all his fine manners and good taste in material things, he was titillated and aroused by a woman brought very low. She should run a mile from such a monster, yet here she was now, in his house. Was she mad?

She stuck to the truth as far as possible, describing how she was a photographer stranded in Little Nessing by the derailment, who was now looking for work in order to pay her way at Gifford Lodge. She sniffed and explained that her dear brother had called on her last night with news of a job at Elmscott Hall. At this point she resorted again to her handkerchief.

'Dear lady,' said the old hypocrite, his thin face abject with sympathy, 'please don't distress yourself. Whatever is the matter?'

She told him that her poor brother, being something of a gymnast, had scaled the wall to her window, as was his custom late at night, to avoid disturbing the rest of the house. After he had given her the message, he was returning the way he had come when the heavy sash window dropped on his poor fingers and he had fallen to his death. So, here she was, complete with camera, in accordance with his last wishes.

'I see,' he said. 'Yes, I do see.' After a moment's further thought he summoned the butler. 'And your brother is—?'

'Freddy Porter, sir. I – I have assumed the name Anderson for professional reasons. I believe you knew him.'

'I did, I did. And you say dear Freddy suffered a fatal accident? How dreadful! He was so young, too, so, um, good-looking, with such a future ahead of him. Why, we were discussing it only last night.'

'So I understand.'

He ordered the butler to bring him a whisky. 'For shock,' he explained. 'Will you take a glass, my dear? It is a great restorative of spirits.'

'I won't, thank you, sir, em, your lordship,' she sniffed, dabbing at her nose with her handkerchief. 'I like to keep a clear head. If you would just tell me what it is you wish me to record, and how much you are paying?'

'Better than that, my dear, I'll show you. But perhaps you would excuse me for just one moment.'

'Of course.'

If only her hands would stop sweating. She had wiped them on her skirts before she realised what she was doing, smearing the silky material. This was the most glamorous outfit in Florence's trunk. The sound of its rustle usually made her feel wildly sophisticated, but today her temples throbbed beneath the gleaming swathes of hair Maud had taken so much trouble over and a vein in her neck beat far too quickly. She was sure she'd be found out – as what? As a lamb to the slaughter or as a police plant?

She wondered where Archie was hiding. She had heard the front door slam, advertising his exit, but there'd been no sound of footsteps on the gravel. So he was still here and not too far away, she hoped, with his pistols in his pockets. Perhaps he had gone up to the bedroom already. She touched her reticule for reassurance. Yes, her gun was still there. But could she shoot a baronet or an earl or whatever he was? Or anyone? Not yet, anyway. Red-handed, Tyrell had said. Soon, but not yet.

She could hardly breathe; her stays were too tight and the room was airless, gaslit and heated. There seemed to be no windows at

255

all. Perhaps they had been blocked up years ago for tax purposes, or perhaps more recently to block off a means of escape. She swallowed a great lump of fear that rose in her throat. No, God, not now. She mustn't be sick.

She gazed around the room, trying to breathe normally, noting that the understated green of the big stuffed armchairs, one on either side of the hearth, matched the flock wallpaper which bore the same fleur-de-lys design as those on the brass fender. The gas lamps were turned down as low as they would go without snuffing out; the fire was gas, too, and burned in pretty blue columns with a steady hiss. She yawned and rubbed her eyes.

'You're looking very comfortable, my dear.'

Good God, who was this? She hadn't heard him come in.

'Please, don't get up. I don't believe we have been formally introduced. I know who *you* are, Miss Anderson, or should I say Miss Porter? How would you like to be known?'

She knew him now – the hypnotist. She whispered a name.

'Miss Anderson. May I call you Florence? How do you do? I am Oliver Allsop.' He extended a hand, but she was clinging so hard to the arms of the chair she couldn't take it. 'I understand you have suffered a bereavement – your poor brother – my sincerest condolences, my dear – and yet you have come here anyway…'

'I – I have come about a j-job, em, a photographic opportunity.'

'But you seem agitated. Are you sure your hands won't shake and spoil any photograph you take?' He didn't wait for an answer. 'Let me put you at your ease, my dear.'

Oh God, here it comes, she thought. The influence. Harden up, Polly. You will not go under, you will not. Nursery rhymes, they're the thing. She remembered her mother singing to her.

Little Polly Flinders…

'Listen to my voice.'

'Your voice?' Mother's, you mean. Mother's voice will keep me awake.

Sat among the cinders…

'Trust me now, Florence.'

How the name jarred, alerting her to its incongruity, its wrongness. She was confident that every time she heard it she would be startled. She wouldn't relax.

Little Polly, pretty Polly…

No, what was it?

Polly put the kettle on…

No, that's not it.

Flinders! Cinders! Ashes and cinders! Her mother came and caught her…

'You are warm enough?'

Warm? Warming her pretty little toes.

'That's good. Let me assure you that you are quite safe. You are in no danger. You can safely relax. Re-la-a-ax… Allow your hands to go limp, your fingers, your feet, your toes. Your limbs are heavy, and your eyelids. You are sinking, sinking into a sweet and dreamless sleep. You are so very sleepy, my dear. Breathe in, and out…'

Her mother came in, her mother came…

'With every breath out, you sink deeper into sleep. Can you still hear my voice, Florence?'

'I hear you.'

Warming her pretty little toes…

'You will do exactly as I say no matter what is asked of you.'

'I will.'

And spanked her little daughter…

'Breathe deeply, my dear, in … and out … in … and out… You will sleep, Florence, sleep. And yet your eyes will remain open. You will wake only when I tell you to, and when you do you will feel refreshed and happy and remember nothing of what has passed.'

'I'll remember nothing,' she said.

And spoiled her little daughter…

257

'Good, very good. Now, Florence, unpin your hair.'

She began removing her pins, lining them up neatly on the arm of the chair.

Naughty Freddy Porter…Spoiled her little daughter…

He crossed the room. Her hair was loose about her shoulders. He twisted a lock of hair about his fist and gave it a sharp jerk.

She continued smiling serenely.

Thirty-two

He saw them leading her up the stairs and opening the door to the bedroom, where Beasley's guests had already made themselves comfortable. They were smoking some substance he didn't recognise, and the pungent smoke drifted out along the landing.

Allsop led her by the hand, as though she were a tame animal on a leash. Her hair was down around her shoulders. Her feet made no sound on the thick carpet, but he heard the rustle of silk as she passed his hiding place, caught the fragrance of Lily of the Valley. She seemed quite collected and calm, though her skin was glistening with perspiration. She stared fixedly ahead. Oh Lord, she was either in a trance or acting impeccably.

'Good girl,' came Beasley's thin voice. 'Put your things on the chair.'

''Ello, Poll, last night not enough for ya?' he heard Tuddy greeting her, and she didn't cry out or react in any way. 'Come, sit aside me, duck, and I'll 'elp you wiv your fastenings. Lem, leave 'er be – you'll get your chance later. Get back be'ind that camera, tha's your job!'

It was warm in the linen cupboard even with the door ajar and sweat trickled between his shoulder blades. He should do it now. If only they would shut the bedroom door he could go down and let the police in. The servants were probably all in some other part of the house. Or maybe they had been given the day off. He hadn't seen anybody but the butler, who had long since made himself scarce, and who could blame him?

He heard Allsop's weighty, 'Now step out of your dress, Florence, there's a good girl. And we'll just unlace those stays...'

'Lovely,' said Tuddy, breathlessly, as he watched silk slither to the floor. 'Ready, Lem? The camera, fuckwit!'

'No, we'll have one of her on her knees first. Come, my dear.'

He couldn't see the cameraman or the flash boy – Allsop presumably. Tuddy was sitting on the bed, pinkly naked, his old man's veins standing out on his arms. Beasley was still fully dressed apart from his cheeky backside, which was just visible beneath his shirt tail; he was looking down at Polly, who was out of sight, just beyond the door frame.

It was up to him – only him – blundering Archie Price. It was too late to go downstairs. They would never make it back up here in time. Shit, shit, shit!

Guns ready. Better make it look convincing. Deep breath. Now!

'On the bed, you swine! All of you!' He was in the room in two strides and kicking the camera to the floor before Allsop and King knew what was happening. Seeing the firearms they leapt aside. 'Beasley, you, too. *Polly, wake up!*'

'Fuck!'

'Don't you—!'

'Polly, come out of it. Now!'

'He ain't gonna use that thing, Lemmy. Get him!'

But unfortunately for Lemmy, Archie, no gunman, was wildly trigger-happy, and as he whirled round, the gun in his left hand went off and Lemmy's legs went from under him. He screamed as he fell, and Allsop threw himself under the bed, taking with him a closed tin box. Archie's other gun was levelled at Beasley, but he saw Tuddy bending, reaching for his britches, presumably for his knives. Dammit, he needed to reload – he couldn't cover both men with one pistol.

Tuddy's gnarled old fingers stretched and stretched, but never reached what they were looking for. Out of nowhere, came a loud gunshot. Tuddy folded over, a black bullet hole in his wrinkled forehead.

Polly was no longer smiling: her lips were tightly compressed, her eyes fierce. She had recovered her senses and her gun, and dealt summarily with her tormentor.

Beasley threw himself at her, hoping to wrest the revolver from her grasp, but without even thinking about it, Archie shot him in the back.

'Oh, God no! Polly, Polly, are you all right?'

She wasn't moving. It struck him what he'd done. His bullet must have passed through Beasley's scrawny body into Polly's. He'd killed her!

'No-o-o-o!' Allsop may have been crawling from the other side of the bed, but he had to let him go. Polly needed him. Over Lemmy King's groaning, he was sure he heard another shot fired some distance away. The police must be having trouble outside.

Much closer, deafeningly close, another shot, barely inches away, whizzed past his ear – and there was Polly's bare arm, her hand clutching her revolver, her finger still on the trigger. She'd been using Beasley's back to steady her aim. She looked as though she were cuddling him. From under his lordship's dark, dyed mop, her determined little face appeared, eyes dark with relief and satisfaction at the sight of Allsop clutching his shoulder and reeling against the wall. An erotic painting crashed to the floor as he spattered the wall with his blood.

Any exit the showman might have hoped to make was blocked by a stout tweed stomach. Tyrell arrived, red in the face from the stairs, having heard the first shots and blasted the front door lock. Beckett was behind him, pistols drawn, ready to do battle, but battle was unnecessary; he only needed to handcuff Allsop and Lemmy King and his job was done. They prodded their injured prisoners downstairs to the Black Maria.

Archie helped Polly extricate herself from Beasley's corpse, and then rang for a terrified maid, who had been cowering upstairs, to help dress the young woman, while another servant went to fetch Doctor Mackay for the formal death certificates.

The next day, Easter Sunday, was a day for giving thanks; Monday one of departures: Geoffrey Norris set out for the sanity of his sister's home in Colchester. The inspector and his sergeant gave Archie a lift home to Walthamstow in their carriage. He would return later for his paintings, which were still too tacky to move.

Richard took Polly to Chelmsford, to hand in Florence Anderson's trunk and bank book at the police station and to claim the reward for being instrumental in the deaths of at least two members of the Skinner gang and helping to bring the others to justice. All except Curly Skinner, who had died of his wounds on Good Friday. She recovered her own suitcase from the left luggage office at the railway station, but consigned it to the dustbin in disgust, seeing how blood and the dirt of the guard's van had stained the contents.

When she returned to Walthamstow to pack up the shop, she brought good news. She had secured a job on the *Chronicle* as a news photographer, after her picture of the train crash. Bartholomew Spratt had identified the photographer as Florence Anderson, but made it clear that she had asked to be known, henceforward, as Polly Porter, now lodging at Beehive Lane, Great Baddow, Chelmsford. As she travelled about with her new horse and buggy, and her name became known, she explained to anyone who asked that there had been a mix-up after the crash – a case of mistaken identity. Accordingly, her headstone in St Mary's churchyard was replaced with one reading *Florence Anderson, 1872 – 1897*.

The high street gossips had a field day when they saw how close the two erstwhile neighbours had become: Polly would often come down for the day in her buggy, and Archie would take the train to Chelmsford and stop over at the Swan Hotel.

Sometimes they met up with Effie Mackay, who would shortly

begin training at the Chelmsford and Essex Hospital, and the three friends would go to suffragist meetings together and the Variety Playhouse. In the summer they would take the train to Maldon or Southend, or even Clacton, and Bartholomew Spratt would bring a picnic.

But the wagging tongues in Walthamstow didn't know about Effie or Bart.

'Gawd knows what they was up to all over Easter,' said Mrs Reeves, her rolling eyes and pursed lips speaking volumes.

'Laid up in bed with their injuries, weren't they?' the new Mrs Fitzell said, out shopping with her husband, one hand fondling her silver fox fur, the other resting protectively on her swelling belly.

'Laid up in bed with something,' said the other, looking up and down the street for eavesdroppers.

'Wouldn't have thought he was her type, Bertha. She seems a bit strait-laced to me.'

'Don't be fooled by them big eyes o' her'n,' said her friend. 'There's things she ain't telling us—'

When Archie asked Polly, for the sake of decency, to marry him, she declined.

Not that she wasn't very fond of him, she said, but she had worked hard all her life, and she was jiggered if she was going to hand over the reins to any husband, particularly one with such a poor head for business. So, until married women were enfranchised and could own property in their own right, she would remain a spinster. Despite her misty-edged photographs of angelic children, she had no illusions about the little monsters and no desire for a family.

Rebuffed and a little relieved, Archie did not press her. They continued to enjoy each other's company, and the neighbours could think what they liked.

But Mrs Reeves had to eat her words when the *Chronicle* did a three-page article about the Fitzell murder and its connection to the Little Nessing train crash, publishing Archie's drawings of the gang, mentioning clues such as scraps of paper and bent matchsticks, and including photographs taken by both Polly and Archie. (Tuddy may have destroyed plates in Polly's make-shift darkroom at the Giffords', but the negatives from the 'detective camera' were on a new sort of film that could be used to print out again and again.)

'Gawd 'elp us,' cried the publican's wife. 'See that!' Her stubby forefinger jabbed at the newspaper. ''Im and 'im? They was in 'ere, they was, drinkin' my best scotch, making out they was 'er brothers. Cheeky blighters. If I'd known they was train robbers and murderers I'da laced their drinks with rat poison. Gawd, what was I thinking, letting 'em in 'er shop, cleaning her out, poor little cow? *And* they 'alf-inched my candles!'

She read on. The gang, from London, had been under the protection of Lord Peregrine Beasley, a wealthy landowner out near Chelmsford. 'Whatja reckon, Perce? They coulda come back 'ere and murdered us in our beds, for being witnesses like?' She paused to read on, and Percy heard her sucking her teeth. 'Tch, tch! He weren't no angel, that Peregrine whatsit. 'Ad dirty pictures all over 'is bedroom walls. It's 'is wife I feel sorry for, poor cow.'

Though Lady Beasley was enjoying her widowhood, having sold all the 'dirty' pictures she could find, including some in a tin box that she found under the bed. It was surprising how eager the museums and galleries were to purchase them. And she soon learned to drive the Bremer.

Archie had two of his *Nightmare* paintings (oil on wood) accepted by the Royal Academy for their summer exhibition. 'The shape of things to come,' said the judges. On the strength of his success, George Whittaker, the high street framer, gave his shop over to Archie's summer output. Colourful gypsy pictures caught the visitor's eye, and scenes set in music halls, with various famous singers, comedians and hypnotists. 'Ain't that old Charlie Whatnot what we saw at the 'Orse and Groom last month? He's a caution, ain't he? He's married to that singer with the feathers, on the same bill. *You* know, she sang that song we like. *You* know…'

As for Marquis Guglielmo Marconi, he was not only a genius but an astute businessman, who employed lawyers to ensure that the land on which he mounted his wireless masts could never be contested. He opened the world's first 'wireless' factory under the name the Marconi Wireless Telegraph & Signal Company in Hall Street, employing around fifty people, and ensuring that Chelmsford would always be credited as the 'birthplace of radio'.

Thereafter the tenant farmers, the villagers and gypsies of Little Nessing were able to gather kindling in Membury Wood, plough the land and graze their animals in peace, for 'perpetuity', while the rest of the world was brought up to date.

Acknowledgements

I have to thank Wikipedia for providing answers to my queries about early photography, Victorian market towns and infrastructure, Senor Marconi, the suffragists, painting trends at the turn of the century and Lois Gibson for her book on Forensic Art – the bones of the story. As for the how, the structure, I must thank Janet Thomas, my editor, for her gentle and tactful nudges in the right direction. And thank you, Honno, for publishing another Archie Price story.

More from Honno

Short stories; Classics; Autobiography; Fiction

Founded in 1986 to publish the best of women's writing,
Honno publishes a wide range of titles from Welsh women.

A Time for Silence, *Thorne Moore*
A gripping dark family mystery
1933: Gwen is a loyal wife but her duty to her
husband John will have a terrible price for herself
and her children. Now: When Sarah finds her
grandparents' ruined farm she becomes obsessed
with restoring it and turning it back into a home.
Finalist in *The People's Book Prize 2012/13*
Runner up in the *Beryl Bainbridge Debut Novel
Award*

"A skilfully crafted novel in dual time…"
Alex Martin
"Haunting, gripping – I couldn't put it down."
Lindsay Ashford

Motherlove, *Thorne Moore*
One mother's need is another's nightmare…
Every day a woman goes to a park, still trying to
understand an event 22 years earlier that tore her
life apart.

**A gripping psychological thriller
from the author of *A Time for Silence***

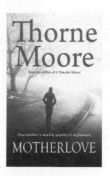

*"…a heart-wrenching tale of three mothers and their love for their
children… which kept me enthralled until the end."*
Rosie Amber

Someone Else's Conflict, *Alison Layland*

Jay has been home for a long time, but the ghosts of Yugoslavia are still with him as he busks his way round the country. Marilyn is fresh out of a controlling relationship and desperate to reassert her independence.

When the past catches up with the present and stories become reality, Jay and Marilyn must decide who to believe and who to betray.

"A highly original, contemporary thriller…Layland builds a plot that's cleverly layered, with plenty of twists to keep the tension up… an utterly engaging read."
Nicla Nira, Thriller Books Journal

The Mysterious Death of Miss Austen,
Lindsay Ashford

No-one has ever been able to provide a satisfactory explanation for the tragically early death of Jane Austen. A shocking new possibility emerges in this intriguing novel…

"An intriguing and compelling variation on the theory of the death of Jane Austen."
crimeficreader
"Ashford borrows the 'mischievous spirit' of Austen herself in this thoroughly entertaining mingling of fact and fiction."
Anna Scott, Guardian

All Honno titles can be ordered online at
www.honno.co.uk
twitter.com/honno
facebook.com/honnopress

ABOUT HONNO

Honno Welsh Women's Press was set up in 1986 by a group of women who felt strongly that women in Wales needed wider opportunities to see their writing in print and to become involved in the publishing process. Our aim is to develop the writing talents of women in Wales, give them new and exciting opportunities to see their work published and often to give them their first 'break' as a writer. Honno is registered as a community co-operative. Any profit that Honno makes is invested in the publishing programme. Women from Wales and around the world have expressed their support for Honno. Each supporter has a vote at the Annual General Meeting. For more information and to buy our publications, please write to Honno at the address below, or visit our website: www.honno.co.uk

Honno, 14 Creative Units, Aberystwyth Arts Centre
Aberystwyth, Ceredigion SY23 3GL

Honno Friends
We are very grateful for the support of the Honno Friends: Jane Aaron, Annette Ecuyere, Audrey Jones, Gwyneth Tyson Roberts, Beryl Roberts, Jenny Sabine.

For more information on how you can become a Honno Friend, see: http://www.honno.co.uk/friends.php